P9-DEN-926

THE DEAD DON'T LIE

BY STUART M. KAMINSKY

Abe Lieberman Mysteries

Lieberman's Folly
Lieberman's Choice
Lieberman's Day
Lieberman's Thief
Lieberman's Law
The Big Silence
Not Quite Kosher
The Last Dark Place
Terror Town
The Dead Don't Lie

Lew Fonesca Mysteries

Vengeance
Retribution
Midnight Pass
Denial
Always Say Goodbye

Toby Peters Mysteries

Bullet for a Star
Murder on the Yellow Brick Road
You Bet Your Life
The Howard Hughes Affair
Never Cross a Vampire
High Midnight
Catch a Falling Clown
He Done Her Wrong
The Fala Factor
Down for the Count
The Man Who Shot Lewis Vance
Smart Moves
Think Fast, Mr. Peters
Buried Caesars
Poor Butterfly
The Melting Clock
The Devil Met a Lady
Tomorrow Is Another Day
Dancing in the Dark
A Fatal Glass of Beer
A Few Minutes Past Midnight
To Catch a Spy
Mildred Pierced
Now You See It

Porfiry Rostnikov Novels

Death of a Dissident
Black Knight in Red Square
Red Chameleon
A Cold, Red Sunrise
A Fine Red Rain
Rostnikov's Vacation
The Man Who Walked Like a Bear
Death of a Russian Priest
Hard Currency
Blood and Rubles
Tarnished Icons
The Dog Who Bit a Policeman
Fall of a Cosmonaut
Murder on the Trans-Siberian Express

Nonseries Novels

When the Dark Man Calls
Exercise in Terror

Short Story Collections

Opening Shots
Hidden and Other Stories

Biographies

Don Siegel: Director
Clint Eastwood
John Huston, Maker of Magic
Coop: The Life and Legend of Gary Cooper

Other Nonfiction

American Film Genres
American Television Genres (with Jeffrey Mahan)
Basic Filmmaking (with Dana Hodgdon)
Writing for Television (with Mark Walker)

THE DEAD DON'T LIE

AN ABE LIEBERMAN MYSTERY

STUART M. KAMINSKY

A TOM DOHERTY ASSOCIATES BOOK
NEW YORK

This is a work of fiction. All of the characters, organizations, and events portrayed in this novel are either products of the author's imagination or are used fictitiously.

THE DEAD DON'T LIE

A Forge Book
Published by Tom Doherty Associates, LLC
175 Fifth Avenue
New York, NY 10010

www.tor-forge.com

Forge® is a registered trademark of Tom Doherty Associates, LLC.

Library of Congress Cataloging-in-Publication Data

Kaminsky, Stuart M.
The dead don't lie : an Abe Lieberman mystery / Stuart M. Kaminsky.—1st hardcover ed.
p. cm.
ISBN-13: 978-0-7653-1602-8
ISBN-10: 0-7653-1602-1
1. Lieberman, Abe (Fictitious character)—Fiction. 2. Police—Illinois—Chicago—Fiction. 3. Chicago (Ill.)—Fiction. I. Title.
PS3561.A43D42 2007
813'.54—dc22

2007009597

First Edition: August 2007

Printed in the United States of America

0 9 8 7 6 5 4 3 2 1

THIS ONE IS FOR

VALLIERE RICHARD AUZENNE

WITH LOVE FROM THE FAMILY KAMINSKY.

How dreadful knowledge of the truth can be
when there's no help in the truth.

—SOPHOCLES, *OEDIPUS REX*

All our mortal lives are set in danger and
perplexity: one day to prosper and the next—
who knows? When all is well, then look for
rocks ahead.

—SOPHOCLES, *PHILOCTETES*

THE DEAD DON'T LIE

1

Ankara, Turkey, 1915

Aziz Akan was deaf in his right ear and blind in his left eye.

Both the deafness and blindness were the result of a bomb dropped two years earlier on a cave just outside of Malik in Armenia. Aziz was in the cave with more than one hundred Armenians and two Greeks.

Twenty-two people, not the Greeks, emerged from the cave, including Aziz. When he emerged from the cave, dazed, screaming with pain, and soaked with his own blood and that of others, he had something in the pocket of his shredded jacket that he did not have when he had entered the cave.

Mistaken for an Armenian, as he wanted to be, he recovered slowly and not very well in a small ill-equipped Malik hospital. When they had taken his jacket, Aziz had ripped his prize from the pocket and clutched it to his chest where it stayed. He was released five days later.

When he made his way to Ankara, he found himself being called *horoz,* rooster, because he turned his head like a rooster.

If he wanted to hear the person in front of him, he cocked his head left to present his good ear. Similarly, when he wanted to see, he turned his head in the opposite direction. The Rooster.

He didn't mind. What he minded was that he might be dead on this night.

He was on a narrow street in the Old Quarter, a street of haphazardly placed white stone blocks on the hill on which Ankara had stood for more than two thousand years. The stones had been worn down by more than twenty generations of merchants, shoppers, soldiers, and thieves. Aziz had cowered in alleys wider than this street.

His back was against a rough brick wall. There were a few windows on the street glowing dimly from oil lamps, which was good for Aziz. What was bad for Aziz who, praise God, would live through the night, was the almost full moon.

Aziz was in the shadows, but the two men at the end of the street knew he was there. They were waiting for him.

The two men, who had been sent by the Three Pashas who now ruled Turkey, were patient, even amused.

The Three Pashas, members of the Young Turk revolution of 1908, Ahmet Cemal, Ismail Enver, and Mehmet Talat, were rumored to have ordered the murder of more than 500,000 Armenians and 100,000 Greeks. Aziz believed the rumors. He had been in that cave, had been other places where he had seen, heard, felt, and hid from the Chetas. The Chetas were bands of Turkish refugees from Thrace, violent criminals released from prison and warrior Kurds on horseback. The Chetas had been recruited by Enver Pasha's Ministry of War to do just what they had done, massacre Armenians and Greeks.

The night was cool, but not cold. It was better to be a bit cold than to step into the light and be dead.

The two men at the end of the street were armed. They were enjoying themselves, talking, even laughing. No, it was more like chuckling. That was why they hadn't come down the street to simply drag him away or shoot him. They wanted him quivering with fright when he finally emerged, quivering, wetting his pants afraid and ready to talk.

From time to time a single word from the men could be heard by Aziz, who cocked his head to listen. *Cinayet,* murder, and *Cehennem,* Hell, were two words that made the most impression.

Aziz was in this fix because he had made a mistake. He had divulged his secret to Gani Bey Thothsis. Gani Bey, fat, jowls jiggling when he nodded yes, had been a conduit for Aziz in the past. Gani Bey had rank, far lower than a Pasha, but rank nonetheless. Gani Bey had traded a gold jewelry box for a passport. The passport description perfectly matched Aziz and the name that had been created suited him. There had been other mutually beneficial transactions with Gani Bey until this night, when Aziz became a commodity Gani Bey could sell to the secret police of the Three Pashas' government.

Aziz had moved freely through Greece, Turkey, and Armenia, selling secrets he seldom really had. But business had been bad for quite some time.

Aziz had been Greek, Armenian, Turk, and once, not very productively, he had been a Kurd. He had moved easily from Christian to Sunni Muslim to Greek Orthodox when he crossed borders. But now it was getting so that Aziz didn't know who to betray anymore. He had been Armenian when the attack on the cave took place. Wrong place, wrong time, wrong nationality.

Thankfully, he had lied to Gani Bey about where he had hidden his treasure from that cave. Gani Bey should have and probably did know Aziz had lied. Gani Bey expressed indifference. They had both lied. It had been civil.

Aziz knew he would not be able to bargain with the two men at the end of the alley. They would torture him.

He would talk. They would kill him.

He decided to look at the other end of the street, the end away from the men of the Three Pashas. To do this he would have to step out of the shadow and cock his head. He decided to chance it.

He did it swiftly. There was no one he could see blocking the distant end of the street. He ducked back in the shadow breathing rapidly.

"*Ne ahmak esak,* you stupid ass," one of the men called out. "We see you. This is no longer enjoyable."

Aziz was frozen with fear and then a light came from the shuttered window directly across from where he hid, a distance not much more than the length of a man. The window swung slowly open and a thin woman, a candle in her hand, leaned out.

"Who shouts?" she said. "Fevzi?"

The candlelight, weak as it was, exposed Aziz. His good eye met those of the woman who saw something there she definitely did not like. She closed and locked the shuttered window as Aziz began to run. The bomb that had turned him into Horaz the Rooster had not damaged his legs.

The two men behind him wore uniforms and carried weapons. Aziz was unencumbered and driven by a fear like no other he had ever felt.

He ran. Two shots were fired. One screamed past him into a moonlit wall. The other tore off a finger on Aziz's left hand. He was slowly losing his body to Turkish attacks. He ran faster, wondering if the finger that was gone had a ring on it.

Except for some cash hidden with his treasure, Aziz had, since he was on his own at the age of fourteen, converted whatever cash or salable goods he had stolen into rings, which he wore at all times. Many of the Sunni looked with disfavor on the wearing of ornaments, but to punish all who did would require the condemnation of many thousand Effendim, Beys, and even some Pashas. Fortunately for Aziz, religion had taken a decided rest while the country fought ruthlessly for its existence and its expansion against Greeks, Armenians, Kurds, and Russians.

He could hear them behind him. It sounded to Aziz as if he had increased the distance between them. He had been too frightened to make any plan other than getting to a turn, hiding on another street in a doorway, or into a house where the door had been left unlocked.

But now, he could keep running. All he had to pray for was not being shot again, not leaving a bloody trail they could follow, and not passing out. He sent out a prayer using the words of two religions, Christian and Muslim, weaving them together and running.

His goal now was the left bank of Enguri Su, the tributary of the Sakarya River that ran alongside Ankara.

He knew a friendly storm drain, one that had supposedly been built by Alexander the Great when he paused in Ankara with his army. If he made it to the drain, Aziz vowed that he would also offer a prayer to Alexander. Deep down he knew he would offer no such prayer, but nearer the surface of thought, Aziz really meant it.

Two or three hundred yards farther, out of the partial protection of the darkness of the Old City streets, Aziz limped dizzily through a newer and only slightly better neighborhood than the one in which he had taken refuge.

The water was no more than another hundred yards away, but it looked like the distance to Mecca.

He stopped, took a chance, looked over his shoulder with his good eye. They weren't there. He turned his head the other way, straining to lull his panting, so he could hear. Echoing down the Old City street from which Aziz had emerged was a voice coming toward him. He held up his hand, the one with the missing finger. Blood, lots of blood, and a numbness, but he hadn't lost a ring. The ring on what had recently been his finger clung tightly to the stub of what remained.

He gulped, turned, and hobbled, tugging at the ring, but it didn't come off. The swelling had begun. That there was little pain did not surprise him. It would come, but he couldn't afford to have it come soon.

He passed no one on his way. It was sometime after midnight. He didn't know or care how much as long as the sun did not suddenly shine. At the bank, he didn't pause to catch his breath and look at the moonlight reflected in the still water.

He strode into the ankle-high water and moved sluggishly to his left. He knew where the stone drain was, how far he had to go. He knew there were still dangers. No more than three minutes later he faced the next danger and plunged into the cold water, dog-paddling across the water, fighting off the wish to simply close his eyes and float. When he did reach the other shore, one hand holding him steady on the rough stone, he looked back.

Two hundred paces back, the two uniformed men stood at the water's edge and argued about which way to go. Common sense would tell them to split up, common sense would eventually win because the two men had much to lose by failing to bring in Aziz Akan.

Aziz, water-soaked, in agony, pulled himself up slowly. As soon as his body cleared the lip of the narrow drain, he rolled himself into the darkness and began to crawl.

When he had rested at the far end of the drain, he would bind his finger and make his way, not back to the small room he had been renting, but to the shop on Necmi Caddesi, Necmi Street, where cheap furniture was sold, and where Aziz had hidden his cave treasure under a stone block against the wall. The owner of the shop, Habib, was a gentle soul, who would awaken in a few hours, go to his shop, find a window broken, and nothing missing.

That is, if Aziz had no further trouble on the way.

Then, having retrieved the package wrapped in waterproof leather, Aziz would be on his way out of Ankara, out of Turkey; perhaps if he could talk his way through it, he would be on his way to America.

What was certain, if he lived, tomorrow he would be celebrating his twenty-first birthday and on the way to somewhere.

2

Present-day Chicago

Someone knocked gently at the bathroom door and slowly began to push it open. Abe Lieberman, a slightly coffee-stained copy of the *Wilson Quarterly* in hand, lay naked in the bathtub. Warm water, which he replenished with a barrage of hot water about every ten minutes, surrounded him.

His grandson Barry pushed the door all the way open and entered. Barry was in his blue Jockey shorts and an oversized blue T-shirt with a Chicago Cubs logo.

"You want it closed?" Barry asked.

"That depends on whether or not you plan on attacking me with something heavy you're hiding behind your back. If you pull out a crowbar or a spatula of genuine chrome steel, I might make a mad leap out of the tub and run past you through the house screaming. If that should come to pass, what do you recommend I scream to get the attention of your sister and grandmother?"

"The British are coming," said Barry.

"No, the British no longer pose a threat. They'd be welcomed. I think I'll scream 'pancakes' or 'latkes.' What do you think?"

"I'm not a man," Barry said seriously.

Lieberman placed his magazine on the wooden stool next to the tub. The stool had been purchased almost twenty years ago in Cashiers, North Carolina, during one of Abe and Bess's infrequent attempts at a vacation. On the stool was also Abe's cell phone and his pocket watch. It was almost three in the morning.

Abe touched his white, almost pencil-line mustache, brushed back his full head of white hair, used the little finger of his right hand to remove a bubble of soap from his ear, and turned his spaniel-like face toward his grandson.

"You're not a man," Abe said. "Lots of possibilities here. Kafka. One day Barry woke up and discovered that he had been turned into a girl."

"No," Barry said patiently.

"All right," Lieberman said, "I'm a police officer. I should be able to deal with this. You've discovered your inner girl and you want to free her. You want a gender change. Well, I don't think the idea would sit well with your mother, your father, Grandma Bess peacefully sleeping in the other room, or your sister innocent of knowledge of this confession. And I'd refuse to let it happen till you were twenty-one. Remember, it's costly, painful, and takes a long time. And believe me, I've seen some poor souls who go through this and most of them come out looking like men in drag. There are exceptions. Antonia McIntyre, a lovely . . . but not as lovely as your grandmother . . ."

Abe nodded toward the closed door a few feet behind him, beyond which Bess lay sleeping.

"You look like Edward G. Robinson in *Key Largo,*" said Barry. "When he took a bath."

"The difference is he was round, had a big cigar, and a drink. I am lean with a glass of water over there on the sink in case I feel dehydrated."

"I'm a boy," Barry said, crossing his arms, his hands clutching his elbows.

Though he had little contact with his and Melissa's father, Barry had some gestures like this one that were purely Todd Cresswell, Ph.D. Fortunately, he had few signs of being the child of Abe's only child and only daughter, Lisa, who now lived in California, now the wife of Marvin Alexander, M.D., a successful pathologist who wrote books, spoke Hebrew, and was black.

"Where were we?" Abe asked.

He wanted to make the tub water hotter, but he controlled the urge so he could hear his grandson.

"You told me I couldn't get a sex change operation till I was twenty-one," Barry said.

"You really want one?"

"No," Barry said with exasperation. "Grandpa, no more games."

"Speak," said Abe.

"You told me I couldn't have a sex change operation till I was twenty-one because I'm a kid. I'm thirteen years old. If I were really a man, I could make a decision like that on my own. I worked on my bar mitzvah for a year, and Rabbi Wass says I'm a man. I know it means I can be part of a minyan, which I am not planning to be. Grandpa, I feel like a kid. I am a kid. I want to be a kid for a while."

"You are a kid," Abe said solemnly.

The water had grown tepid. He wanted to reach over, drain some of it out, and replace it with hot water, but he waited.

"When I am a man, which won't be for a long time," Barry said, "I want to be like you."

"Insomniac with high cholesterol?" asked Abe.

"A police officer, a detective."

"I'm not opposed," said Abe. "But don't expect a show of wild abandon and celebration from your grandmother or your mother when you make the announcement."

"I know," said Barry. "Mom will blame you."

"She'll say, 'Better a sex change than being a cop,'" said Lieberman. "If you still feel like you want to be a policeman when you get closer to being a man, we'll talk about it and what it means to be a cop."

"About murderers you've caught?" asked Barry.

"About hours of sitting in a car watching the doorway of a building out of which your suspect never emerges. About regulations, piles of them. Rules that contradict each other. Senior officers who don't want to make tough decisions. About thirteen-year-olds who, like you, are not men but have murdered more than one person and are ready to do it again. About . . . you get it."

"Yeah, but I still want to be a detective," Barry said.

Lieberman looked at him. His grandson was still short, but he would soon spurt, tower over Abe. Barry already had the golden look of his father. Blue eyes, lean body, smile. Lieberman thought it was time to have another eye check for the boy. He was doomed by genetics to need glasses.

"Well, if your grandmother and your mother don't talk you out of it, we'll see. You'll still have to go to college."

"Northwestern," said Barry.

Todd taught at Northwestern, which was a twelve-minute drive from Lieberman's house in West Rogers Park.

Abe nodded. Barry was, indeed, thirteen. He might change

his mind three or four times about being a cop and going to Northwestern by the time he graduated from high school. He might decide to become an anthropologist or a history teacher. He might decide he wanted to go to college in Hawaii or Texas. Money was being put away, invested, to cover both Barry and Melissa's education. Lieberman had inherited a few hundred thousand dollars when Ida Katzman died. Ida had been the foundation of Temple Mir Shavot. Lieberman had sat on many frustrating committees with Ida and they had become friends. The bequest had been as welcome a surprise as Ida Katzman's death at the age of eighty-eight had been an unwelcome one.

"It's a school night," Abe said. "I take adult responsibility in telling the boy in front of me, my much loved grandson, that he should get back in bed and get three more hours of sleep. You have time for sufficient REM cycles."

"You know a lot," Barry said.

"I owe it all to insomnia, which I do not recommend, and to the *Wilson Quarterly,* the *Smithsonian* magazine, *Entertainment Weekly,* and the Discovery and History channels."

"Are you going to get some REM cycles?" asked Barry, reaching for the handle of the door.

"I will make the water hotter, finish the article I was reading on worldwide consumption of soy products, and attempt to get a few hours of sleep without disturbing your—"

The phone on the stool buzzed. Abe reached for it, looked at the screen to see who was calling, and said, "Yes."

Lieberman listened. Barry hesitated at the door, wanting to know what was happening.

"Right," said Lieberman. "No, I'll call him. Tell the uniforms at the scene that I'll be there in half an hour."

Lieberman turned off the phone and climbed out of the

tub. He was a sight to behold. A slightly sunken chest covered in curly gray hairs, a gut threatening near-future expansion. Thin legs. His best feature was his arms, taut and lean.

"Somebody got killed?" asked Barry.

"Somebody got very killed," answered Abe, reaching for his underpants on the white plastic hook on the door to the bedroom.

No help for it. Abe would have to slip into the bedroom, get his clothes, and retrieve his gun from the locked drawer next to the bed. The odds on Bess waking up were about even.

"Bad?" asked Barry.

"Bad," confirmed Abe, as he finished drying himself with his faded Michael Jordan beach towel. "Bed."

"Good night," said Barry.

"Good morning," said Abe.

When Bill Hanrahan felt the cell phone in his pocket vibrating, he said to his wife, "I'll be right back."

He didn't think Iris heard him. Hanrahan left the room, pushed the door closed, and answered the phone.

"Father Murph," Lieberman said. "We've got a homicide on Catalpa just off Broadway. I'm on my way."

"Can't come," said Hanrahan, rubbing the sharp stubble on his face.

There was a long pause and then Bill Hanrahan figured out what his partner might be thinking.

"No, Abe. I'm sober and I'm tired. Iris is in labor, has been for ten hours. We're at Woodrow Wilson Hospital."

The Woodrow Wilson Hospital was a few blocks from Hanrahan's house. Abe wondered if they had walked to the emergency room.

"Can't leave her, Rabbi. You're on your own for a while. Maybe they can give it to McIntyre and Polk."

"That," said Abe, "would require me waking up Kearney and, as you know, that would be folly. Besides, McIntyre and Polk have a hit-and-run death with perp in tow. They're at District persuading her to confess."

"Sorry, Rabbi," said Hanrahan.

"Not needed, Father Murph. Catch up with me when you can. I'll be as close as your pocket."

"Will do," said Hanrahan.

"Hey, take care of Iris and tell her Uncle Abe promises the baby will be round and beautiful."

Abe and Bill clicked their cell phones closed at the same time. Bill pocketed the phone and looked at his reflection in the window of the room in which his wife lay in drugged agony. An hour ago, Dr. Benny Vargas had said he needed her off the drugs to help with the delivery. If she didn't dilate sufficiently in the next twenty minutes, he was going to give her an injection to induce labor.

Normally, Bill would not choose the brother of a very violent gang member to deliver his wife's baby. But Benito Vargas was not like his brother Carlos, an enforcer for Los Tentaculos. Benito was carrying some deep bruises and a sincerity Hanrahan didn't think could be faked. The bruises came from growing up on West Side ghetto streets. The sincerity came from learning about growing up on those streets.

He heard the rolling rubber wheels of a cart coming down the empty corridor. He recognized the ultrasound machine and pushed the door open so the woman in blue hospital garb could move past him into the room.

With the door slowly closing, he looked at Iris. Her eyes were closed, her mouth open, lips slightly swollen. Her long dark hair was tied back with a few stray strands clinging to her perspiring forehead. A sound, like the single echo of a small sigh, came from her as the woman with the cart moved to the side of the bed, leaned over to Iris, and said something Bill could not hear.

Iris was almost fifty. They had been warned of the danger, but Iris had insisted, had been happy, heavy, and without complaint throughout the pregnancy.

William Hanrahan's fifty-fourth birthday was coming up. He was a recovering alcoholic cop with an ever-aching leg from a college football injury. He had been on a possible path to the pros when the knee went during a routine Illini scrimmage. He became a cop by default, and only because his father had been a cop and had pushed the right buttons to have Bill's leg problem overlooked.

Bill hadn't had a drink for more than a year and he was fine with that, though he did still like the smell of a good or even mediocre whiskey.

Bill was tentatively returning to his Catholicism through Father Sam Parker—Whizzer—the black streak who had run for two hundred and forty yards in a single game at Illinois almost a decade after Bill had left the field for the last time. Bill Hanrahan had seen the game on television from ground level on a Saturday afternoon.

After one solid, if not superstar, season with the New York Giants, Sam Parker had quit and turned to the priesthood. He entered a seminary outside of Chicago and a few years later, his turned-around white collar in place, he had found himself at St. Bartholomew's Church in Edgewater.

The congregation was a very mixed bag of Vietnamese, Chinese, Southern whites, black families, the homeless, and strays like Bill who came more for the priest than the preaching.

The first time Hanrahan had confessed to the former running back, it had taken forty minutes. Bill had much to tell. His marriage to Maureen had failed miserably and it had all been Bill's fault, his drinking, his depression, his absolute neglect of his two sons who were now grown. Both sons had rejected him, moved out as soon as they could, didn't stay in touch, not until irony stepped in to keep them together. His older son, Michael, had come home to Bill to tough out the alcoholism, which seemed to run in their very DNA.

"I suspect a Jesus trick in this," Bill had told the priest when Michael had reluctantly turned to his father. "Son becomes an alcoholic and comes back to live with alcoholic dad before son loses his family."

"And dad helps him."

"I'm trying to help him."

"It seems all the saints have to start as sinners," the priest had said. "How can you help others stay away from the bottom unless you have seen the bottom? Read the lives of the saints."

"I'm no saint," Bill had said.

"Give yourself time."

"Too many sins," said Bill.

And then Bill, in the relative safety of the confessional, had told Sam about the young madman named Frankie Kraylaw. Bill had lured Frankie into his house. The determined, violent, religiously fanatic madman knew Hanrahan was sheltering his wife and little boy. Bill had lured Kraylaw into the house and killed him. He had seen no way around it. If he didn't kill Kraylaw the lunatic would eventually kill his own wife and son.

"And I can be forgiven for all of this?"

"You can."

"Then the system's broken," Bill had said.

"No, it's just incomprehensible."

"How many Hail Marys, Our Fathers, acts of contrition . . . ?"

"William," Whizzer had said, "you were a great defensive lineman, but you are one lousy liar. I can't give you absolution now. You lack a principal ingredient."

"Which is . . . ?"

"Contrition and full and certain belief in our Lord Jesus Christ."

That had been more than two years ago. Now, today, the former Iris Chen, now Iris Hanrahan, who would bear his child, lay in the room he entered as the ultrasound ended. When the baby came, Father Whizzer Parker would be called.

"What did you see?" Bill asked the woman in blue.

The technician looked young, very young. She wore no makeup, had the outdoor sunburnt face of a downhill skier.

"Dr. Vargas wanted to see this," the girl answered. "I'll tell him you want to talk to him."

And then she was gone.

Bill turned to the bed and touched Iris's hot cheek.

She turned to look at him. Her mouth was open, her tongue pushing up on her palate to hold back the contraction pains that seemed to be coming more quickly now.

"Iris," Hanrahan said. "How you holding up?"

She answered him in Chinese. Bill couldn't understand a word of Chinese.

3

Abe parked on Broadway in front of a red Toyota Corolla and next to a fire hydrant. He flipped down his visor to show his police identification card and stepped onto the sidewalk.

It was a nice April night, no less than fifty-five degrees. The sun was a few hours from rising and the city lights at this hour didn't completely obscure the stars, the moon, and Venus.

Abe paused at the corner where Catalpa met Broadway to look at the sky and finish the container of coffee in his left hand and the low-fat lemon poppy seed muffin he had picked up at the twenty-four-hour Dunkin' Donuts on Touhy.

There were no pedestrians and only a few cars moving a little above the speed limit, some of them going south toward the heart of the city, some north toward the fringes.

A light was blinking not far down Catalpa Street. He moved toward it, muffin and coffee now almost finished. There had been a trash container nearby right at the corner. He didn't even consider tossing his garbage. There might be something dropped in there by whomever had killed or been killed. Abe even knew an instance in which Detective Oren Polk had tossed a coffee container in a wastebasket at a crime scene. The crime scene team had found it, tested it for DNA, and Polk had a hell of a time convincing Kearney that he hadn't—as much as he would have liked to—murdered two drug dealers.

Abe wolfed down the last of the muffin and the coffee, crumpled the cup and put it in the pocket of his black windbreaker.

Bess would not have approved of the muffin or the caffeine-leaded coffee, but she would have understood.

A year ago, Abe's brother, Maish, who owned the T&L Restaurant on Devon off of California, had said, "Abe, we got ourselves a bitter irony. I'm older than you. I'm—let's face it—fat. I get no exercise and I eat anything that looks good. No cholesterol problems. No heart problems. And you? You're skinny. You run around a lot. You don't have the opportunity to violate the laws of common sense as often as I do, surrounded by pastrami, tongue, corned beef, chopped liver, chopped herring, and fresh-baked bread delivered daily to my door by Hyman's Kosher Bakery. And you, you are the one with the problem. If I was still on cordial relations with God, I'd thank him for my good fortune and ask him to continue to take care of my brother. Meanwhile, Bess and I have to do our best to save you. I have no great hope for your salvation."

Maish's son David had been murdered. Maish was waiting for an apology from God that he never really expected to come. David's death had not caused Maish to cease his belief in the deity. It had, however, been the start of an open war with God for what he had allowed to happen on earth.

Two days after his warning speech to Abe, Maish had suffered a heart attack. It had been a bad one, but not the worst possible. Two weeks later Maish had been back behind the counter of the T&L. He and God were no longer on speaking terms.

The light on top of a patrol car was flashing. The flood lamp on the driver's side of the car was directed at a dead man inside a red circle of barrier tape, which was imprinted with the legend DO NOT ENTER. This inner perimeter was where evidentiary material was likely to be collected. The inner perimeter was surrounded by a larger circle of yellow crime scene barrier tape. This was the area large enough to protect the scene and accommodate the personnel conducting the thorough investigation.

Inside the inner perimeter, a woman Abe recognized was taking tent-shaped markers from a plastic bag and carefully setting them down to cover blood drops or other bits and pieces that might be evidence or might be nothing. She looked like a game player setting up a tent city.

It was all by the book. A call had probably been made to someone authorized to bring in the Forensic Services Division. It might have been Kearney or the supervisor of the first officer at the crime scene. If Abe had been there, he was authorized as a detective to make the crime scene call.

There were no curious civilians watching on the street. There were a few houses and a three-story brick apartment building from whose windows people, awakened by sound and light, might be looking.

Two forensic investigators wearing white disposable gloves—one a man taking pictures, the other the woman who had been creating the tent city—were kneeling inside the red circle, searching with a flashlight.

In the center of the circle lay the dead man.

The crime scene duo stood up and nodded at each other,

indicating that they were finished with this one for now. They would be on their way on to another call in another district, a possible murder.

They walked carefully away from the dead man.

Lieberman moved next to a lone uniformed cop standing outside of the outer perimeter. The cop, arms folded, watched the forensic people move out. He recognized Abe and nodded. Abe tried to remember his name. The patrolman was young, in great shape, uniform pressed and a perfect fit. He looked a little like a young Lew Gossett. Then Abe remembered. A double suicide about a year ago.

"What have you got?" Lieberman asked the woman, who was removing her gloves.

Her name was Angela Flowers. She was about forty and had been in the forensic unit for almost ten years.

"Looks like six knife wounds, one to the neck, one aimed at the right eye hitting the bone above the eye, and four to the abdomen," she said. "ME's going to be busy with this one. My guess is that any of the wounds but the one above the eye could have killed him. He died where you see him. There's no blood trail."

"I'd say the same," said her partner, a beefy young man in need of a shave.

"Any sign he fought back?" asked Abe.

"Didn't see anything that says he did," said Flowers. "Knuckles, nails look clear, but we bagged the hands anyway. Assailant was facing him. *Wham-bang*, the first strike. Then . . . the rest was just for fun and to be sure."

"Thanks," said Abe as they walked toward their double-parked van about three car lengths down Catalpa.

"I'll call in, try to get help for a search," said the uniformed cop.

"You're Danton, Robert Danton, right?" said Lieberman.

"Richard, but you were close," the young cop said.

"Richard," said Lieberman, pulling the crushed cardboard cup from his pocket. "When you've got a secure place, I'd like to dispose of this."

"Evidence?" asked Danton.

"Only of my addiction to caffeine and lemon poppy seed muffins."

Danton took the cup from Lieberman and said, "I'll take care of it."

"You might start the search with the trash can on the corner."

"I will," said Danton who, cup in hand, unclipped the cell phone from his belt.

Lieberman pulled a pair of disposable white plastic gloves from his jacket pocket and moved across the yellow line and then over the red line. Inside the secure area, he stepped around the evidence tents.

Abe Lieberman knelt next to the body.

The dead man, maybe forty-five or fifty, was on his back, eyes closed, arms sprawled, white shirt bloody, a deep red liquid pool next to him, his hands encased in clear plastic bags. His suit was definitely expensive as were his blood-dappled shoes. The tie he wore was silk, also stained with blood. The tie was red and on it were small crescent moons to the left of tiny white stars. The man's hair was turning gray gracefully, probably touched up, in television-ready style. Clothes, hair, shoes tasteful. The man had style, class, and money. This was probably not his neighborhood. So what was he doing here at three o'clock on a weekday morning?

The dead man carried his wallet in the left inside pocket of his jacket. Abe gently pulled it out. This was almost certainly not a mugging. A mugger would take the cash and credit cards and wouldn't bother putting the wallet back in the pocket of the man he had just murdered.

Abe opened the wallet and was sure it was no mugging. He counted two hundred and seventy-one dollars in twenties, tens, and singles.

The driver's license, Illinois, identified the dead man, who looked pretty much the same dead as he looked under the surprise lights of the highway department. He was Lemi Oraz Sahin. The home address was in Lincolnwood, a few miles from where Abe lived.

A business card in the dead man's wallet told Abe that Lemi Sahin, M.D., was an oncologist, with an office in Lincolnwood not far from his home.

There were AAA cards, credit cards, an insurance and a library card, and, on the bottom, a membership card with a red flag in the left-hand corner and at the top the organization's name in gold. In the center of the small red flag was the same star and slice of moon that was on the dead man's tie.

The card said that Lemi Oraz Sahin was a member in good standing of the Turkish-American Society, Cook County Chapter.

The dead man was a Turk.

People just didn't understand.

That was Elsie Cuervo's first thought when she woke up. It had been her first thought upon waking for the past seven months.

She looked at the red digital numbers of the electric clock on the table next to the bed and reached over to turn off the alarm before it rang. All but once since they had begun their early morning forays she had been awake minutes before the alarm rang. The alarm was already off when she felt the button. The time was 3:15 A.M. Jamie was already up. The light under the bathroom door and the sound of running water let her know where he was, not that there was much choice. There was just this small bedroom and an equally small room that served as living room, kitchen, and dining room.

Windows in both rooms faced out on nothing, unless you wanted to call an alley and garages something.

People didn't understand.

She pushed the blanket back and sat up, fully awake.

She brushed her hands through her short auburn hair and reached over to turn on the lamp behind the clock.

"How you doing?" she said, not too loud, but loud enough as soon as the water stopped running.

The walls were reasonably thick, which was good and bad. Good because it tended to keep the neighbors' noise and their own confined. Bad because the insides of the walls provided plenty of space for the rats. As far as she knew, the rats had never come into the apartment. She didn't even mind them being behind the wall except for their night noise. It happens.

She could live with it. What she couldn't live with was not having money. Elsie didn't consider herself and Jamie poor. They just didn't have money. But they did have some minor celebrity.

They were both known by a few thousand people in Cook County and probably in DuPage and even into Indiana.

"Okay," said Jamie. "Coming out. It's all yours, babe."

Jamie was fully dressed, black slacks, black shoes, black polo. His hair was combed back and she could smell that he had shaved. He was a good-looking man, thirty, muscular, nose slightly crooked, big smile. Women sometimes came on to him. He always beamed them his toothy smile but he never bit. Elsie was as sure of her husband as he was sure of her.

She was nude, always slept nude. She looked her best with no clothes, trim, tight, small firm breasts.

And she was definitely a looker. That's what he called her, a "looker," maybe a little more on the tough than the tender side. They looked great together. On the dresser across the room was a framed two-year-old article of the two of them after a night at the Aragon Ballroom where they had both won their bouts.

Jamie was a middleweight, a hard-fighting, never-back-away middleweight who watched the scale and kept his weight between one hundred and fifty-four and one hundred and fifty-six pounds. People on the way up had to make it past him, which they sometimes did, or they had to consider ending their move up when he beat them.

Elsie weighed in at one hundred and eighteen pounds.

They worked out together at the Lions Park Gym on Hoyne just north of Montrose when they could afford it.

Jamie kissed Elsie on the cheek. She reached over and touched him between his legs. Let him think about that. Maybe when they got back. . . . He had shaved for her. He knew how much she liked his smooth skin.

Great together. Almost read each other's minds.

All they needed was money—money to pay Eddie "Chiclets" Gleason at Lions Park Gym—money for food, rent, bills, and clothes. They could get the money from Paddles Patalnowitz. He wouldn't even want it back, but Elsie and Jamie had decided that if they couldn't make it on their own, it wasn't worth making.

The problem, they both knew, was that there was little money in being a pair of undercard Chicago club fighters. The money was at the top. They were paid somewhat reasonably when they fought, but reality limited the number of times a year they could fight or anyone would want to see them in the ring. The few times they had ventured outside of Chicago they had done well, gotten some publicity, even fans, but the financial cost had been bad, really bad—transportation, motel, food, cut man, Richie Fein's percentage. They had sometimes come back to this apartment with two wins and a few hundred dollars in the hole.

Elsie washed her face, brushed back her clean auburn hair. She would shower later. Shower and go back to bed.

Elsie and Jamie didn't begrudge Richie his manager's cut. Richie had done a good job. When they had decided they needed a manager, Sosh Belknap, the trainer at the Lions, had said sagely, "Pick a Jew. You can't go wrong."

So they had and they weren't sorry.

Elsie looked at herself in the mirror once more, decided she looked fine, and went back in the bedroom where Jamie sat on the bed watching her as she crossed to the dresser and began to put her clothes on.

Jamie had won a six-rounder a little more than a week ago. He had won a unanimous decision over Manuel "The Furious Dominican" Rodriguez. The crowd, almost completely Hispanic, had booed not Jamie's performance, but that of Rodriguez, who had been less than furious. In fact, Jamie was sure that in the clinches he smelled alcohol on Rodriguez's breath, and it wasn't rubbing alcohol. Unlike the crowd, Jamie had been surprised that under the circumstances and probably somewhat under the influence, Rodriguez has made it through all six rounds.

Jamie had won, but he had a cut on his cheek that needed stitching. If they could have stopped the bleeding, Jamie would gladly have accepted the scar. The problem with going to the ER was that Elsie and Jamie had no health insurance and they were too embarrassed and proud to accept free service provided for the indigent. They had no health insurance because no one would provide it at anything near an affordable rate for two people who lived by getting and giving beatings.

She dressed quickly, also in black, her slacks and polo shirt almost identical to Jamie's.

She held up her arms for his response. He nodded in approval and rose up quickly, gracefully. Elsie loved the way he moved.

Lately she had wondered if she detected a slight slurring of his speech, very slight, probably her imagination. Jamie had a record of thirty-two wins, twenty-one losses, and two ties. He should have been a contender. Instead, he was a survivor. Elsie, realistically, at fourteen wins and two losses, was much more likely to move up the ladder. The problem was, among other things, that the purses for women, unless your father was Muhammad Ali, were far less than that for men.

And so one afternoon when they couldn't pay their gym fees, they had a conversation over Diet Cokes and a shared doughnut and considered what skills they had that could be turned into cash.

Neither had gone to college. Neither could use a computer. They had no sales skills. Minimum wage in a stockroom would mean the end of their training and the whole point of getting a job was to earn money so they could keep training and fighting.

What they could do was fight. They could punch. They could take a punch. There weren't many careers, other than the one they were in, that made use of these abilities.

"Bodyguard," Elsie had said, nursing her half doughnut with small bites. "People know you. You could do it."

"Bodyguards have guns," he said. "They don't need to punch anybody or take a punch. They can be fat and old. All they have to do is be willing to shoot people if they have to. I'm not willing to shoot people."

"I know," she had said, finishing her doughnut.

"What's that leave us?" he said.

"Not much. Jamie, face it, we're not getting any younger."

"Well, who is?"

"I don't know," she said, "but I'll let you know if I find him."

She smiled. So did he.

Then she got an idea. Over the noise of the Greek diner next to the Lions Park Gym, she had made the suggestion.

"I don't think so," he said.

"The hours are good. Doesn't take much work."

She could see it working on him. He was reluctant, but having his career go down the tubes was not an option he wanted to consider.

"We can try it," he said.

She hadn't smiled, hadn't felt like smiling, but she had nodded and it was settled.

They had decided to be muggers.

4

Jane Mei Hanrahan gave her first cry at 4:06 A.M. She weighed seven pounds and six ounces and was, according to the delivery room nurse, quite healthy.

Jane Mei had met the world after eleven hours of painful labor and a cesarean delivery.

Bill had been in the delivery room.

Iris had clutched his hand and smiled before the anesthesia took effect and then he had stood at the head of the delivery table, hands at his side. He had been warned by the masked and gowned Dr. Benny Vargas that even though he was masked and gloved, Bill was not to touch the table, Iris, or the baby.

When it had ended, Bill had looked at his exhausted, sleeping wife and said, "How is she?"

"She'll be fine," said Vargas.

After a nurse had cleaned her, the baby was handed to Bill.

Looking down at his daughter, Hanrahan thought that she was perfect.

Jane was the first name of Bill's grandmother on his mother's side. Mei means "beautiful" in Chinese. The name had been decided on when Iris was in her sixth month.

The baby was plump with open brown eyes. There didn't, thank the Lord, seem to be much Hanrahan in her, at least on the surface, which was a blessing. There was already a strong resemblance to Iris, if for no other reason, because the baby looked more Chinese than Irish. Another blessing.

His first daughter. His only daughter. In spite of her father, she would grow up smart and beautiful.

"I'll take her now," a nurse said softly.

"All right if I . . . ?" Bill began.

The masked nurse nodded yes and Bill leaned down and gently kissed the baby's forehead before the nurse took her saying, "You can come see her later."

Bill moved to his sleeping wife's side. He kissed her cheek and Benny Vargas motioned to follow him.

"She'll be out for a long time," Vargas said, mask down, cap off, removing his gloves, just like on *ER*. "She's been through one hell of a lot."

"But she's all right, right?"

"We'll observe her for possible infection or complications, but she looks . . ."

"Fine," said Bill.

"She looks fine," Vargas agreed. "You, on the other hand, look like dreck."

"Dreck?"

Ben sighed and said, "Medical terminology I picked up from Jewish doctors."

"Dreck means shit," said Hanrahan.

"Check the mirror. I've got to go. Another baby has decided to greet the fluorescent glare of a delivery room. Congratulations. Beautiful baby."

"Thanks, Benny."

Benny smiled and said, "You can call me Dr. Vargas. Go home and get some sleep."

And he was gone.

Bill moved to the mirror across the room.

His eyes were puffed, the lower lids red. His hair was uncombed and undecided. He needed a shave, a serious shave. The collar of his badly wrinkled blue shirt sagged and there were stains of sweat across his chest.

He needed sleep. The dog had to be walked and fed. He needed to get out of these clothes.

He took out his cell phone, went to his frequently called list, and punched the second name.

Three rings and an answer.

"Rabbi, it's a girl."

"Mazel tov, Father Murph."

"Iris and the baby are fine."

"What's her name?"

"Jane Mei. She looks like her mom. C-section."

"Wrest untimely from her mother's womb," said Abe.

"What's up?"

"I'm about to talk to a possible witness," said Abe. "Dead man's a Turkish doctor. Never had one of those before. Got to go. Get some rest."

"Don't want rest," said Bill. "Where are you?"

Abe told him and added, "I've got the dead man's widow to talk to."

"Okay, I'll catch up with you later, Rabbi. Looks like a long day."

"A long day indeed, Father Murph."

Finding the witness had not been difficult. This was not a Turkish neighborhood. In fact, there was no specific Turkish neighborhood that Abe knew of. He had sometimes encountered first, second, and even third-generation Turks in Old Town, New Town, Gold Coast high-rises, and Rogers Park.

There were Turkish restaurants in the city. One of them, Anatolia, was around the corner on Broadway about fifty feet from where Lemi Sahin lay dead.

The police ambulance pulled up behind Abe alongside the patrol car. The ambulance moved silently, no sirens, but top lights blinking. There was no hurry. The patrol car's top light was still flashing and the car's side floodlight continued to spotlight the corpse. The street was blocked now, flickering with a carnival of police car and ambulance lights. In death, Lemi Sahin had moved to the center ring.

Abe knew the Anatolia was there. He knew as did every detective, every officer, what business was on each block from Albany Park South to Howard Street at the edge of Rogers Park, and Halstead on the west to Lake Michigan on the east.

Abe had never eaten at the Anatolia. He had thought about it, discussed it with Bess, but they had never gone there or most of the restaurants they had discussed in and outside the district.

The outside lights of the Anatolia were out and the interior of the restaurant was hidden by thick, deep red drapes held up by gold-colored hoops on a seven-foot-high gold-colored bar that stretched across the restaurant window. There was a finger-thin strip where the drapes did not quite touch. The Anatolia was definitely closed, but Abe could see the reflection of a light on the ceiling through the narrow slip between the drapes. The light cast a shadow. The shadow moved slightly.

Lieberman knocked at the window, his eyes on the shadow.

The shadow moved.

He knocked again.

The shadow disappeared.

"Police," said Lieberman, moving to the front door, voice raised, now knocking more dramatically.

Something stirred inside the restaurant when he paused in his knocking.

"Open up," said Lieberman. "Police."

"What is it you want?" came a man's voice.

"To talk to you."

"About what at this hour?"

"Open the door and find out," said Lieberman.

The door opened slowly. The man was tall, thin, about thirty, dressed in a dark suit with no tie.

That was the moment at which the phone had rung and Bill Hanrahan told him about the baby. When he finished the call, Abe turned his attention to the man and said, "You are . . . ?"

"Erhan Turkalu."

"What are you doing here?"

"I am the proprietor, owner, headwaiter, cashier, and much put-upon focus of all complaints. Have I violated some law?"

"You always here this late?"

"I'm sometimes here this early," the man said with a smile that suggested Abe would understand all the many reasons a man might want to come to his work or away from his home at four in the morning. "But tonight I have been unable to get away."

"One of your customers may have been murdered around

the corner about an hour ago. I'd like your cooperation in helping to find the killer, Erhan, but you are free to stop talking whenever you wish."

It was what Lieberman had to say to every witness. It was a directive that could give him trouble if it were ignored.

"What makes you think this man was a customer of mine? Other people have been murdered in this neighborhood and they were not customers."

"Dead man is a Turk. His name is Lemi Sahin."

The name clearly shook the darkly handsome man who looked down and closed his eyes and muttered, "The doctor. The holy Koran says, 'He gives life and causes death, and to Him you shall be brought back.' "

"Dr. Sahin was here?"

The man nodded yes.

"What was he doing? Who was he with?"

"He was eating, drinking, engaged in some business with a fat little man. I don't know," Turkalu said. "When closing time came four hours ago, I couldn't bring myself to tell them to leave. That's why I'm here so late. Dr. Sahin is one of the best-known Turkish Americans in the city, a tireless laborer on behalf of all Turks."

"What did Dr. Sahin and the other person talk about?" asked Abe.

"I didn't listen. I went in the kitchen to clean up, record the cash and checks. I did see the fat man give Dr. Sahin something, a package of some sort wrapped in cheap old leather."

"The other man, what did he look like?"

"As I said, short, fat, dark, a large space between his front teeth. He was possibly Turkish, Syrian, Armenian, Bulgarian, who knows . . . I don't know."

"Did he leave with Dr. Sahin?"

"I think yes, yes, together."

"Would you be able to identify the man who was with Dr. Sahin?"

"Absolutely," said the man with a clipped, decisive nod of his head.

"Good. I'll need your phone number in case we need you."

"Certainly," said the man. "One moment."

He retreated into the amber darkness and returned a few seconds later holding a card out to Lieberman, who looked at it.

"Business number and cell phone," the man said.

"Fine," said Abe. "Any members of your staff see the man or possibly hear anything that passed between him and Dr. Sahin?"

"Only me and my wife," he said. "She was cooking in the kitchen, didn't come out or look out here, never. I sent her home just after midnight. If you'll excuse me, I would like to lock up now and go home for a few hours. I am quite upset as you can see."

"I'll be in touch if we need you," said Abe.

"I will be happy to help in any way I can," said the man.

He closed the door.

There were several things Abe could do to get the man to open the door and answer more questions. Some of the things he could do were even legal. He decided that there wasn't much more he could get from him and he wanted this witness cooperating if and when he was needed; so Abe decided to let it go, for now.

Lieberman had one more thing to do before he left.

He went back around the corner onto Catalpa as the body bag was being put in the back of the ambulance. Abe moved past the crime scene and looked down the street.

The dead man had an automobile insurance card in his wallet. On the card were the make, year, color, and license plate number of a Lexus. He moved down the street, looking at the parked cars, as the ambulance moved silently past him. A hand reached out of the driver's window, waved at him in slow motion, and passed.

Abe waved back.

Thoughts racing, racing, imagination in control or out of control. Placing orders, order after order, baking pastry, thin, soft, and crisp crepes, tortes, making up jokes, remembering the last, or was it the next-to-last, episode of *Monk* or *House* or *24* or . . . diseases, what diseases could Jonas remember, list? Alphabetical: anorexia, bulimia, carbon monoxide poisoning, death. Was death a disease? No, a truth, an inevitable. The body stopped functioning. Jonas Lindqvist, pastry chef at Le Sourire, felt no fear. His mind couldn't even slow down enough to contemplate its end. It was like the cartoon coyote with zip lines behind it, each line with different words bobbing inside it, going too fast to read, pages flipping by.

This was not the first time he had been in this state. Sometimes it was a nice place to visit, a place where he had once seen the vision of perfect orange perfumes, oranges with honey, orange flower water and cinnamon. Nice place to visit, but I wouldn't want to die here. He would say that to Jean-Baptiste Fualo, the chef, if he could remember it when he was back at the restaurant tomorrow. Not tomorrow, today. Yesterday had gone, a *pop*, very small, like the opening of a wine bottle. Jonas was a pastry chef, but he knew how to serve wine.

He lay on the bed in his son Peter's room. He had been lying, seldom sleeping, in his son's room to keep from disturbing his wife. Lydia was a light sleeper. She was a good person. She had her faults, a renewed level of sexual interest he could not and did not want to fulfill. The titles and images of books Lydia had read flowed through him. He couldn't remember any real ones, but that didn't stop titles and authors from coming. *Joy to Everest, The Last Tanglewood, Hovering in Space, The Old Neighborhood.* Justin Flanner, Anita Day Wilcox, Jean Rusthaven, Hugo Marx.

Jonas sat up in the darkness. The Ambien, to which he was sure that he was, after two months, addicted, was definitely not helping. The pain pills, which Dr. Lovesy had told him should be used for pain and not for sleep, did not help his sleep. The pain from his abdominal surgery had completely passed almost a year ago, but he still had pills and one refill remaining.

Jonas looked at his watch. Luminous dial. A little after three in the morning. Yesterday had become today when he wasn't looking. He felt like singing "Yesterday," started to and stopped. He could almost hear a medley of Beatles songs flying by against a sky of blue and into a *Yellow Submarine* sea of green.

Jonas reached over and turned on the light on the end table near the bed. He was soaked with sweat. No more this night. He would get up, shower, and watch television, anything, an infomercial would be fine, something about a gadget that sliced and diced and chopped up. He couldn't read, couldn't concentrate on the words.

Jonas was forty-seven years old. So was his wife. His son was nineteen and at the University of Wisconsin, where he was taking a political science class on the Middle East, and another class on . . . no, stop. He knew the next step was remembering all of his son's classes for this semester and then last semester and last year.

Jonas got up.

Dr. Lovesy looked as if he were twelve years old, while his predecessor, Dr. August Torvald, had looked as if he were one hundred and two when he retired . . . what was Dr. Torvald wearing when Jonas last saw him five, six years ago? A suit, dark, a vest, a pocket watch and gold chain? No, that was a doctor with a little doctor beard in some movie—*Spellbound,* that was it.

Jonas went into his son's bathroom and turned on the tap, cold. He filled the sink and plunged his face into cold water to freeze the thoughts. He lifted his head and sang, "I took one look at you . . ."

He looked at himself, a large, broad, somewhat pudgy man with thinning blond hair and tired blue eyes.

His voice was a croak. He scooped water from the tap to his mouth. He tried to sing again, ". . . And my heart stood still."

Not a croak, but off-key.

His T-shirt, one Peter had sent him from Wisconsin, was now wet at the neckline. He didn't need a shave, had done that before he had gone to bed, had followed the rituals. Shower, shave, shampoo, brush teeth for about thirty seconds, talk to Lydia about things in the news.

Lately he had been particularly irritated by the misuse of language on television news and sports coverage.

"Nothing is very unique," he had said to Lydia. "It is either unique or it's not."

"It can be nearly unique," she had said.

"But they never say that," Jonas had said. "And I don't know if it can be, nearly unique I mean."

"Is it important?" she had asked.

"No, just irritating."

He had to prepare food for people politely while they consumed it too quickly and assaulted the English language. Since he was the pastry chef at the Le Sourire, he could correct the staff if he wanted to, but that would create tension. One of his functions, he believed, was to reduce friction, not cover it with gravel.

The biggest offender of word and meaning, the mangler of syntax and garlic mashed potatoes à la Jean-Baptiste, was Chef Jean-Baptiste Fualo, a dark little man with no sense of humor who labored in the kitchen at the pace of Jonas's racing thoughts. Jean-Baptiste was born Tui Magsasaya on the island of Luzon in the Philippines. He had learned his skills in the kitchens of ocean liners on which he worked his way up from busboy to waiter to cook's helper to assistant chef to chef. The process had taken him twenty-seven years, but it had paid off when he transformed himself into a Frenchman and opened Le Sourire.

Jonas and Lydia had agreed not to watch television in bed. Dr. Lovesy had recommended that he watch nothing, not get stimulated for several hours before going to sleep. It hadn't helped. Thoughts of syntax, precise definitions, and kitchen protocol invaded.

Now he was up and almost fully awake.

"Anxiety, depression, bipolar disorder," he told his mirror image.

New thought. He would dress casually, jogging sweats that he seldom wore, and go out for a walk and a little jogging, maybe, hadn't done that for months. Dr. Lovesy had suggested he get out and jog if he couldn't sleep. Lydia, were she awake instead of gently snoring upstairs, would have told him not to go out in the middle of the night, in darkness.

She was right, but at the moment, he didn't care. The house

wasn't big enough right now. Television wasn't an interesting option. Music, reading, writing e-mails? Not good options. He had tried them. Peter had responded to one about a month ago saying his father's two A.M. message hadn't made sense. As Jonas remembered it, he had listed forty movies he liked and forty he hated, but he kept changing his mind about which ones belonged on which list. Jonas had stopped writing e-mails at night though the computer uttered a near-silent call.

When he had changed into his blue sweatpants and blue T-shirt with the words *Le Sourire Softball* in white script across the front, he got a small bottled water from the refrigerator, put his wallet in one pocket and his penlight flashlight in another pocket. His sweatpants didn't sag too much.

Into the night now. Good. Almost a full moon. He could head for Foster Avenue beach five blocks away or just move west, turning at corners, going down streets chosen for reasons he couldn't put into words.

He walked down the wooden steps and down the short cement path to the sidewalk. Then he turned left and began to walk quickly.

He was alone with his thoughts, a dangerous thing. He could have taken the Walkman his son had left at home because Peter had a new something or other.

Jonas had simply forgotten the possibility of music until he was almost two blocks away from his front door. Music seldom helped. Speed-of-sound thoughts gloated happily on top of any oboe, trumpet, or drum.

"Then I saw the Congo," he said, possibly aloud, as he moved down a street, houses on either side, older houses like his own and a few dirt-smudged three-story apartment buildings. There were very few trees and those that existed were either wrist-thin limbed, large, old, or lifeless or dying.

Lydia would have said the jog was a very bad idea.

Jonas was now sure that he had been right. His thoughts ran more slowly as he moved and he could smell grass on the lawns and gas from the cars parked tightly on the street.

Lydia would have said, "Jonas, there are muggers out there."

He would have nodded, determined, and gone anyway, but she would have been right.

At seven minutes after five A.M., Abraham Lieberman pressed the door chime button at the large two-story Lincolnwood house. The house, one among a dozen on the block with twenty feet of elbow room between them, was set back. A narrow brick path with knee-high shrubs on both sides led up to the door.

Across from the house was a green rolling football field expanse of park where birds were gathering in the predawn in search of food.

No answer. Abe pushed the button again. This time he heard something, padding feet moving closer.

"Who is it?" came a woman's voice.

"Police."

"I didn't call the police," she said. "But I will if you don't go away."

"I know you didn't call," said Abe. "I'd slip identification under the door, but I don't think there's enough space down there to get an identification card through."

"What is this about?" she said.

"Your husband."

"Then you should talk to him. He's sleeping. I'll get him."

"He's not sleeping, Mrs. Sahin. He's not at home."

"He is," she said. "And he has a gun."

"He's not home," said Abe.

"How do you know?" She paused.

"Mrs. Sahin?"

"Has something happened to Lemi?"

"Yes."

The door opened and Lieberman found himself looking at a blond woman wearing a purple and white silk robe. She wore no makeup, but her skin was perfect, clear, almost white. She couldn't have been more than twenty-five and probably not that. She was at least five-eleven and quite remarkably beautiful.

"What? What's happened to Lemi?"

The panic in her voice seemed genuine. Abe had heard the real and faked and he could almost always tell the difference. He looked past her shoulder to an entryway table, light walnut, with framed photographs on it.

"Your husband?" Abe asked.

She turned her head to look at the photograph.

"Yes."

"I'm sorry," said Abe. "He's dead."

"No," she said with a smile.

"I'm sorry," he said.

"How . . ." she began. "No. Lemi? No. You're . . . no."

"I'm sorry," Abe said.

Her eyes closed and she swayed slightly. Abe had seen this before too. He stepped quickly through the doorway and into the house to catch her as she began to collapse. She was solid, heavy, deadweight. Abe's back felt the sudden pull.

Abe knelt gently to lay her on the bronze carpeted floor. Don't go out now, Abe ordered his back. He imagined the comic scene of him collapsing under her weight, the two of them on the floor, a passing car or early-morning neighbor walking their dog, seeing the sight through the open door.

Abe got up and closed the door, his back twinging, teasing, and then quickly settling into a warning ache he could deal with. When he turned, the woman's eyes were open, looking at him. Her mouth was slightly open.

She tried to make sense of what she was seeing, what she had heard. A man who looked like a very sad spaniel with a white mustache knelt at her side. The man had told her Lemi was dead. The man was a policeman.

"Daddy, Loo-Loo?"

Abe looked up. At the top of the stairs stood a dark, round-cheeked boy about two years old. He was wearing Wallace and Gromit pajamas and clutching a small ornately stitched pillow.

"Oh, God," the young woman said, sitting up. "Max."

The boy's eyes met Lieberman's. The boy broke into a big, friendly grin. Abe smiled back.

5

Elsie and Jamie had gone at least two miles from their apartment. They were hiding behind some bushes next to a three-story apartment building on a street just north of Lunt. They knelt, not talking. The double-thick glass door of an apartment building opened and a man came out. The man was wearing a suit, about average height, build, maybe forty years old. He was carrying a briefcase.

He was their man. The man cinched it by pulling out a pocket watch and checking the time in the light from the lobby of the apartment building. The only person they knew who had a pocket watch was Paddles Patalnowitz, who always carried heavy money in his pocket.

They watched the man with the pocket watch and stood up.

"Let's go," Jamie said, ready.

They both wore black knit ski masks tucked over on their heads to look like watch caps. All they had to do was pull the masks down over their faces and get the job done.

Then they heard a voice.

"Looking for something?"

The voice, almost a whisper, came from behind them.

A flashlight beam hit their faces. They were caught.

The cop would bring them in, bring in the men they had mugged to look at them, bring them down, count them out. They might lie their way out with a good lawyer. They had always worn masks. But lawyers cost money. They could always turn to Paddles who might or might not cover them, but the newspapers would put them on page three and the television stations would put them on the six o'clock news, and that would end their careers.

"Let me give you a hand," the man behind the flashlight said.

A light in the window at their backs came on.

Whoever was inside could now see the man with the flashlight. So could Elsie and Jamie.

The man stood in the light from the window, holding a flashlight. No weapon. The man was big, blond, soft in the middle, not a cop in a jogging suit. He didn't carry himself like any kind of fighter.

Someone was in the window above them and at their backs. Jonas Lindqvist smiled up at whoever was there and shook his flashlight to indicate that everything was okay.

"What'd you lose? A ring, watch, money, medicine?" asked Jonas.

There was something a little crazy about his voice, hyper, manic. They had seen it with fighters who came into the ring on a natural or drug-aided high. They smiled, like this big one, unafraid, ready to go.

Jonas saw that the man and woman were wearing black gloves. It was too warm a night for gloves unless you had some kind of skin disease. The odds of both of them having the same skin disease, he decided, was possible, but remote. He considered making a list of all the skin diseases he could think of in alphabetical order starting with acne.

Jonas looked down the street. The man with the pocket watch was walking slowly toward a parked car almost directly in front of the apartment building he had come out of.

Both of them sprung forward. Jamie threw a solid right to Jonas's midsection. Elsie sent the doubled-over man to the grass with a left jab to his nose. She hadn't hit him hard, didn't want to risk harming her knuckles, but she heard his nose break. The man lay there, dazed, groaning. The light in the window behind them went out.

Odds were a coin flip that whoever was in that apartment would call 911 or decide to go back to bed and mind their own business.

They checked the fallen man's pockets quickly. He didn't resist. One of his hands cupped his nose. The other pressed against his stomach where Jamie had hit him.

A wallet, seven dollars. They took the money, left the wallet.

"Let's go home," said Jamie.

"No, let's do it," said Elsie, moving out to look at the man with the watch who seemed to have heard nothing.

"No," said Jamie. "Let's get outta here."

Jonas was on his back, mouth open, moaning. Now he was holding his stomach with both hands. The flashlight lay on the ground a few feet away, beaming into his face, turning it white.

"I'll do it myself," Elsie said.

Now she was feeling the rush. It took over. It had only been about a minute from the time the big man had first spoken. Elsie and Jamie knew how time could stretch, slow down. Three minutes of time in the ring could feel like an hour unless it was the last round and you were behind and you had to put whomever was beating you down if you had any chance. Then three minutes felt like ten seconds.

Elsie went past Jamie and jogged down the sidewalk, headed for the man with the pocket watch. The man, briefcase in hand, stood on the thin patch of grass along the street and took his keys out of his pocket.

Elsie pulled down the hooded ski mask to cover her face. Jamie looked at Jonas who was on his knees now, groaning, trying to stand, nose bleeding.

"Shit," Jamie said, shaking his head.

He didn't know why, but he patted the arm of the dazed man who cringed and held his arms against his belly.

Jamie followed his wife down the street. It wasn't till he had almost caught up to her that he realized he had lost his ski mask. It was too late to go back for it.

Jonas stood on wobbly knees. He picked up the flashlight and saw the ski mask. He picked it up and looked down the street. Two dark figures were jogging in the direction of a man with a briefcase who was opening the door of a car. They would catch up with him in seconds.

Jonas tried to shout, scream, warn the man with the briefcase. He could only croak. Flashlight still on, he trudged after them, a deep pain in his stomach, a trickle of blood from his nose. He knew the woman had broken his nose. He had heard it, but there was little blood.

He turned his flashlight beam down the street but he was still too far away for it to have an effect.

The man with the briefcase had his back turned to the man and woman in black who ran softly, lightly.

Even when he hadn't been beaten, there was nothing light about Jonas Lindqvist's tread. He was an elephant in pursuit of a pair of panthers with sharp teeth and claws. His thoughts continued to race. He wanted to speak them aloud.

Recently, he had begun talking aloud when no one was around. Not exactly talking to himself so much as to an unseen audience. He had taken to making faces at himself in the bathroom mirror, singing songs he had long forgotten. And the thoughts—the racing, raging thoughts.

It was very possible, Jonas had concluded, that he was going mad.

He decided, as he grimaced and continued to move after the two who had beaten him, that he would buy a very small tape recorder and talk to it, sing to it. Then he would play it back or play it to Dr. Lovesy to prove . . . something, provide some clue to stopping the rampage.

Elsie hit the man with the briefcase, hit him from behind, short right to the kidneys, no time to demand his wallet, no time to be nice, follow the rules. The man went down, briefcase and keys dropped in the grass.

The man, Robert E. Lee Chang, was on his knees now, facing away from them, trying to reach the agony where he had been punched, expecting to feel blood from a knife wound. Instead he felt a second blow, a solid punch to the back of his neck. His glasses flew toward the street. He went down on his face, felt his wallet being removed. Then the wallet landed a few inches from his face. Robert Chang knew that they had taken the nearly seven hundred dollars he had in it. They could have the money. It was something other than the contents of the wallet or even his own safety that concerned him.

"Don't move, don't turn around, don't look," said a man

whispering into his ear. Robert E. Lee Chang could smell a minty mouthwash on the man's breath. Chang thought he was going to vomit.

"You turn, look, move, we break some ribs," the whispered voice said, moving away.

Then silence, except the sound of his own panting, the taste of his own bile and of grass that dogs had urinated on.

"Look," said the whisperer, only now he was not whispering. He was excited. Robert Chang knew what must have caused the excitement.

"Get it," a woman's voice urged.

There was a gun, a very small one tucked into Chang's jacket pocket. He started to roll slightly to his left so that he could reach it. The gun was small, his vision questionable, and his aim certain to be poor, but his life depended on keeping them from getting the briefcase.

"Oh, shit," said the woman. "Someone's coming. Let's go. Now."

Chang plunged his hand inside his jacket pocket and felt the handle of the .380 pocket gun.

Something touched his shoulder. He fumbled for the gun, found it, and rolled onto his back to face what looked like a big man in a jogging suit.

Robert had one advantage, the gun. He had three disadvantages: he could see very little without his glasses, had never fired a gun before, and was in great pain.

Though he couldn't see much, Robert, still on his back, was close enough to see the man's face and to see the black ski mask in his hand.

"Are you—" Jonas began.

Jonas backed away as Robert Chang struggled to get to his feet, gun in hand. Both men were breathing heavily. Both had been beaten by Elsie and Jamie Cuervo. Technical knockouts in the first round. They were losers and they knew it.

Robert E. Lee Chang, chest and stomach aching, raised the gun, blinked at the hazy figure in front of him and said, "My money. Give me back the money."

"The money?"

Chang fired. A *pop* in the night. The sound of a champagne bottle opening.

Jonas turned and ran. Chang fired again.

Jonas let out an animal roar of agony. Jonas ran. At least he did something that resembled a painful run.

"Max calls me Loo-Loo because his mother's name was Lucille. I guess I'm Loo number two, Loo-Loo."

Mary-Catherine Sahin started to smile, but didn't. She held an oversized pink Fiestaware mug in two hands and looked down at the warm tea like a fortune-teller.

They were in a breakfast nook just off of the kitchen, which had three chairs, a small round table, and a view of the hedge-encircled garden lit by a garden lamp just outside the window.

Darkness was giving way to the light of a new day, but the night wasn't giving up easily.

"Thank you for making the tea," she said.

"You're welcome," said Abe, who held his own mug, a blue one.

He didn't look into it. He really didn't like tea, had difficulty understanding its appeal. Hot water with a hint of flavor, usually a flavor that did not appeal to him.

Mary-Catherine Sahin had gone up the stairs holding the rail with one hand, the child's hand in the other.

"I think Max is sleepy. What do you think?"

The boy shook his head up and down twice and said, "Max is sleepy and Loo-Loo is crying."

She had led him into his bedroom, saying, "Yes."

"Go to your room," the boy commanded dreamily, waving a finger at her.

"I will," she said.

No more than fifteen seconds later she had come back onto the second-floor landing, closing the door to the child's room behind her.

Standing in front of Lieberman, who was waiting at the bottom of the stairs, she felt her knees shaking.

"Someone you can call, someone to be with you?"

She shook her head no and said, "I don't want to talk to anyone."

"You've got coffee?"

"Yes, I can make some, but . . . I can . . . Lemi is dead?"

"You've got tea?"

"Yes."

Five minutes later, with the help of a microwave oven, they were sitting across from each other in the breakfast nook.

"I'm sorry about the coffee," she said. "Lemi usually makes a pot in the morning. Turkish coffee. Almost black."

"I'm not supposed to drink coffee," Abe said. "Or eat anything that tastes good. Easy diet to remember. You up to some questions?"

"You up to some answers?" she asked, putting her cup on the table and wiping her eyes with the back of her hand.

"Some," Abe said.

"What happened?"

"He was killed by someone."

"Not an accident?" she asked, her eyes fixed on Lieberman.

Not unless he stabbed himself repeatedly and then got rid of the weapon, Lieberman thought, but said, "Someone attacked him with a knife near a restaurant on Broadway. Do you know why your husband was at a Turkish restaurant at three o'clock in the morning?"

"No."

Her answer had come after a slight hesitation, a beat a cop would recognize.

"Did he go out a lot in the middle of the night?"

"He . . . sometimes," she said.

Abe nodded.

"It's not that. Not other women. Not Lemi," she said, touching the cup in front of her, unsure of whether she wanted to keep drinking, keep busy, or take a pill to put herself to sleep. But she couldn't go to sleep. Max would be getting up in a few hours. She lost touch with what the sad-looking old detective was saying. She forced herself to pay attention and heard, ". . . doing?"

"I'm sorry. Could you say that again?"

"What was he doing when he went out at night?"

"He's a doctor. Emergencies." She shifted in her chair and said, "Emily Fabrikant."

"Emily Fabrikant," Abe repeated. "He went to see Emily Fabrikant?"

"No, I mean her husband's a urologist. That's not relevant, is it? No, I mean her children are grown up. She might be able to come over. There's going to be so much . . ." Her voice trailed off and she gently bit her pouty lower lip. Her teeth were even and very white.

"Good idea," said Abe. "Just a few more things."

"Was it an addict? Kids? A crazy person, what?" the woman asked, trying to settle her hands on the table.

"No money or credit cards were taken," said Abe.

"Maybe the mugger . . . I don't know."

There was a tinge of confusion in her voice. She took a deep breath, sat even straighter than she had and said, "I'll save us both some time. I watch *Law and Order* so . . . I've been here all night with Max. Lemi and I have . . . I can't think of him in the past tense. I just can't. Not yet. We've been married for a year. We met at a grief-counseling meeting. His wife, Lucille, had died, ironically, from stomach cancer."

Abe believed everyone died ironically. Irony was the kishkes of life and death.

"And you were grieving over . . . ?" Abe prompted.

"At the time, nothing. I was the counselor. Shall I go on?"

"Sure."

"Lemi has no enemies that I know of. His friends, our friends, are other doctors and their wives, and members of the Turkish-American Society. Lemi is passionate about three things: defending Turkey and the Turkish people from, as he puts it, 'a century of misunderstanding'; Max; and then me."

"You're third?"

"I knew I would be when we got married. Lemi's been a good husband."

"Can I have the names of his friends and someone in the Turkish-American Society I could talk to?"

"Yes," she said. "You want to hear some more irony?"

"Sure."

"We're not rich, but we're far from poor. Funny, when I found out how much money Lemi had after we were married, I thought I had accidentally done exactly what my mother wanted me to do, marry a rich doctor."

"You're Jewish?" asked Lieberman.

"My father is a second-generation Danish-American," she

said. "A Lutheran. My mother is Jewish. Her maiden name was Shansky."

"Then you're officially Jewish," said Abe.

She shrugged. It clearly didn't matter to her.

"Your husband was religious?"

"His father was a Muslim," she said. "Lemi says he is a Muslim, but he doesn't pray or go to a mosque and he never talks about religion. Lemi's bible is newspaper and magazine articles and online news about Turkey."

"What's in the package?" Abe asked.

"Package?"

"The one your husband got from a fat man in the Anatolia restaurant. The one that's missing now."

Something Abe said had startled her. She stood up.

"He found it," she said. "My God. He found it and it got him killed."

"Found what?"

"The book, the diary, journal, whatever it is," she said. "He's been going out in the middle of the night, leaving the hospital early, having someone fill in for him on an emergency basis. For the last three or four months, he's been following leads about some book or diary being here. He was determined, obsessed. I think he carried a lot of cash to buy the book. He didn't explain it very clearly. He was very passionate about it."

"Passionate," Abe repeated.

"I suppose," she said, wrapping her arms around herself. "It's cold in here."

It wasn't cold in the house. In fact, it was a little warmer than Abe liked.

"Let's give Emily Fabrikant a call," he said.

"Oh, God," she said after a sigh. "Yes."

She went to the wall, took down the cordless phone, and brought it back to the table where she sat.

"It's funny," she said. "I'm a trained grief counselor. I know the stages. I know what I'm going through now. Denial. I know what the other stages will be, but knowing and feeling are not the same."

"I know," he said.

She looked at her cup of tea. She had drunk very little of it. Neither had Abe.

"Lemi liked coffee," she said. "I already told you Lemi liked coffee, didn't I?"

"Yes," Abe said as she punched buttons on the phone.

Abe noticed that, for the first time since he had arrived, Mary-Catherine Sahin had spoken of her husband in the past tense.

6

"You ever see anything like this?"

Dr. Geoffrey Aukland, gangly and in need of a shave, had asked Nurse Kim Ampour the question in the Woodrow Wilson Hospital Emergency Room. They were standing over the man on table two, which was surrounded by a curtain of blue cloth that almost matched Nurse Ampour's uniform.

"No," she said.

She had been a registered nurse for only three years, but in those years there was little she hadn't seen but this was, indeed, unusual.

The patient groaned slightly, eyes closed, and started to reach both hands toward his groin. Nurse Ampour took the two hands by the wrist and firmly but gently moved them back to his sides.

The man was sedated, but not enough to put him to sleep,

not yet. For the moment, Dr. Aukland wanted the patient alert enough to answer questions.

"His nose is broken," Nurse Ampour said.

"I doubt if he feels it," said Dr. Aukland. "He has other pain blocking it out."

Jonas squirmed at the doctor's words.

"We don't want to restrain you," Nurse Ampour said gently. "You understand?"

The man nodded yes and continued to groan.

The first bullet fired at Jonas Lindqvist had missed.

The second had hit the ground and ricocheted off of the sidewalk. The bullet had enough velocity to penetrate and lodge inside Jonas's right testicle. In pain, losing blood, Jonas had hobbled to Sheridan Road and stood there, sun inching slowly up over the horizon behind the houses. He had tried to remember where the nearest hospital was.

Cars passed, most with their lights on. No one stopped. He turned right. He would go home. Lydia would be frightened, but she would know what to do.

He reached Foster Avenue and waited for the light to change. His left arm clung to a lamppost.

The pain between his legs attacked, throbbing. He didn't want to think about it, about anything but getting to Lydia, a hospital.

The light changed. A pair of uniformed policemen stood in front of him.

"What happened?" one of them said.

Jonas looked to his right and left and to the sky and then said, "So much."

Now, less than an hour later, he lay in the emergency room, his mind focused on the pain and what he had heard the doctor say. He knew he had been shot, but until he heard the doctor say the bullet was in his testicle, he had been certain that the wound was in his right side just above the groin. He had never really touched it to find out.

"I'm a surgeon, Mr. Lindqvist. I'm going to get that bullet out. You'll be fine."

"I'll be fine," Jonas repeated. "Fine."

"Who shot you? Why?" Dr. Aukland asked. "How did your chest get bruised? Your nose broken?"

Nurse Ampour thought Aukland was asking the patient too many questions at the same time, but Jonas answered, "Blind Chinese man shot me. Woman in a ski mask beat me up. All I wanted was to walk, slow the thoughts down."

Aukland shook his head.

"He had a ski mask in his pocket," Kim Ampour said.

Doctor and nurse looked at each other to confirm that they were thinking the same thing.

"In the last few months," she said, "we treated three people who were robbed and beaten. They all said the two people who had beaten and robbed them had worn ski masks."

"Not me," said Jonas through a drugged fog. "The man with the flat nose."

"Call the police," said Dr. Aukland.

"We did," said the nurse.

"Let's get that bullet out," said Aukland. "Can you sign a consent form?"

"Anything," Jonas said. "I'll sign anything. Just get it out and stop the pain."

"Call the anesthesiologist and get him to surgery," said Aukland.

As if there were another choice, thought Kim Ampour.

Elsie and Jamie counted the money.

They were seated at the table in their apartment.

"Seven hundred and two dollars in his wallet," said Jamie, putting the money on the table.

"One hundred and fifty thousand in the briefcase," Elsie said, looking at the stacks of bills in the middle of the table.

Elsie reached her right hand across the table to Jamie who took it.

"Who was that Chinese guy?" Jamie said. "Carrying all that money?"

"Banker, business guy, criminal, I don't care," she said. "We've got enough to keep going for a couple, three years, maybe more if we're careful and we get some fights."

"We don't have to rob people anymore," he said.

"We don't have to rob people, leastways not for a couple of years and by then, who knows, we might not have to."

"Else, I lost my ski mask."

"I know. I don't think we're going to need it anymore, but if we do, we'll buy another one."

"The big guy in the sweats, he saw my face," he said. "Yours too."

Elsie touched his face, her elbow hovering over the money.

"We look like lots of people," she said. "You have no criminal record. Besides, he probably won't go to the police. He probably just went home."

"We're not bad people," Jamie said.

"We're not bad people," Elsie said. "We don't take drugs, gamble, drink, cheat."

"We're good people," he agreed.

She threw a sharp right jab across the table, making sure it would stop a few inches from his nose. Before the punch hit its mark, Jamie bobbed right so the punch would miss him and he could come across the table with a right cross to the body if she hadn't protected it with her left arm. He didn't throw the punch. He leaned over the table. So did Elsie.

"We just want to walk to that ring, go through the ropes, and fight," she said.

They kissed.

"Yeah?" he asked when they broke the kiss. "You want to?"

"Why not?" she answered.

They moved to the bed, undressed, and made love. It wasn't just sex. It was love.

"You still at the hospital?" asked Nestor Briggs.

"Still here," said Bill Hanrahan, who had moved into the hallway near Iris's room to take the call from the Clark Street Station.

Sergeant Nestor Briggs, who lived in an apartment near the station, had never married. He lived with his dog and dreaded the mandatory retirement that was only fourteen months away. Nestor was the dispatcher. Before that he had been on the front desk. Before that he had spent fifteen years in uniform on the streets. The very good old days of mayhem, bad guys, drugs, drunks, senseless murders. The good old days.

"How is she?" Nestor asked.

"Doing fine," said Hanrahan.

Nestor was easy to talk to. Bill knew the question had not simply been one Nestor was obliged to give. Nestor really cared.

"Baby?"

"Girl. She's fine too."

"Bill, we're tight here and we got a call from the Woodrow Wilson ER, which is where you are."

"Which is where I am," Bill agreed.

"Ski-mask mugger might be there. You know the one?"

"I know the one."

"He's in surgery now. Somebody shot him in the balls. Can you take it?"

"I'm on it," said Bill. "Iris and Jane Mei are asleep."

"Jane Mei," Nestor said. "Good name."

"I'm going down to the ER," Bill said, signing off of the cell phone and putting it back in his pocket.

Bill went back into his wife's room to be sure she was asleep. Iris's father, Chai Hang Chen, small and very thin, sat in a chair looking at his sleeping daughter.

Chai, who refused to Anglicize his name and resisted all, including customers at his Black Moon restaurant, who tried to give him nicknames. The resistance was futile.

The owner and cook at the Black Moon was often referred to as Chai the Guy, particularly by longtime customers. He suffered ignominy stoically.

Iris had worked as the only greeter and waitress at the Black Moon. Now her younger cousin, Xiang, held that job, though Iris sometimes came in to help. Bill had met Iris at the Black Moon one night when he was both drunk and on the job.

Bill didn't know what the beautiful Chinese woman saw in him, but he didn't question it. Iris had led him out of drunkenness and Abe had saved him from losing his job.

"I've gotta go downstairs," Bill told his father-in-law. "Police business."

Chai nodded. He didn't much care where Bill Hanrahan went. He had been opposed to the marriage. Hanrahan was a policeman, a recovering alcoholic who had recently divorced. He had two grown sons and two grandchildren. Worst of all, he was not Chinese. Old Mr. Woo would have been a better choice of husband. He had money, would not live long, and would have treated Chai and his daughter well. The fact that Mr. Woo was a criminal was of no consequence. There was a point at which a criminal made enough money, enough friends and enemies, to qualify as a respected person. Mr. Woo had achieved that. Chai's pink-faced bulk of a son-in-law had not.

But two years had passed since the marriage, and Chai had come to accept the big Irish policeman, a wary acceptance.

"I will watch out for my daughter and my granddaughter," he said.

It was Bill's turn to nod. He went to the bed, kissed his sleeping wife on the forehead, and went out the door heading for the emergency room.

Abe got to the T&L restaurant at 7:15 A.M. The T&L had been open for fifteen minutes. The stools were full as were the tables, including the one by the window where four old men, the *alter cockers,* gathered every morning to have breakfast and talk. The total complement of *alter cockers* was eight, but they didn't all show up for breakfast.

The short-order cook, Jerome Terrill, known simply as Terrill, was an ex-con Abe had gotten his brother to hire more than a dozen years ago. Terrill had learned to cook in prison but after Maish hired him the prison recipes were gone, and Terrill quickly developed a passion for Jewish cooking—brisket, matzoh ball soup, chopped liver, latkes, chicken, cabbage rolls. He even made his own lox. He cooked by taste and smell, never used measuring spoons or cups. He loved the smells, the taste, the lack of concern about what the ingredients might do to the human body. Abe shared these loves with him.

There was an empty booth across from the *alter cocker* table. It was known as the Cop Booth, because Maish reserved it for any policeman or policewoman who wanted to patronize the T&L. In this neighborhood, though not as bad as many, the presence of a policeman and the knowledge that the police were often present served as a warning to criminals and the gangs of Indians, Pakistanis, Mexicans, and tough Jews who demanded tribute from business owners on Devon. Maish had refused to give them a nickel and Abe had helped convince their leaders that the T&L should be stayed away from.

Thus, the Cop Booth.

Abe sat and his brother Maish, who had spotted him coming in, came over with a cup of coffee. When he sat it down in front of Abe, Maish wiped his hands on his starched white apron.

"Thanks," said Abe. "Busy today?"

"It's a morning," Maish said with a shrug.

"I'd like a slice of Terrill's apple pie," said Abe. "What kind of kugel you got today?"

"Raisin, brown sugar," said Maish.

"I'd like some of that too and I'd like to start with an omelet with grilled onions, an order of hash browns, and two onion bagels toasted with a schmear of cream cheese."

"You would like?" said Maish.

"I would. What am I going to get?"

"Egg white omelet with onions. One more cup of coffee, half decaf, and, let's live a little, a slice of Terrill's mashed sweet potato side."

Maish hurried off.

Abe drank his coffee, took in the kitchen smells, the sound of seven or eight conversations, none of them distinct except for that of the *alter cockers,* who normally spoke in a shout.

The *alter cockers* were all Jews except for Howie Chen, who had owned a Chinese restaurant one block away from where they now sat. Howie was retired, had been for seven years. The restaurant was now an Indian grocery that dabbled in Bollywood video sales and rentals.

Occasionally the *alter cockers* lapsed into Yiddish. When they did, Howie joined in.

"The Irish's baby. It came out last night I hear," said Herschel Rosen.

"Jane Mei Hanrahan came into this world healthy and vulnerable," said Abe. "How'd you find out?"

"Sources," said Herschel Rosen.

"Sources," Sy Weintraub agreed.

Sy Weintraub was the athlete of the group at the age of eighty-two. He walked five miles every day and spent an hour in the Jewish Community Center on Touhy working out on the machines.

Al Bloombach and Howie Chen both agreed and said, "Sources."

"You look worse than usual," said Rosen.

"I feel worse than usual," said Abe.

"You look tired," said Bloombach.

"It's the insomnia," said Sy. "I've got a friend who can get you some pills'll put you to sleep. Guaranteed."

"Will I wake up?"

"That," said Sy, "is another story."

"I'll give it some consideration," Abe answered.

Maish came to the booth with the omelet and a small scoop of mashed sweet potatoes. The omelet was soft, the way Abe liked it, and on top of the mashed sweet potatoes was a melting yellow square of something that looked like butter, but that Abe was certain was not.

"What's that?" asked Rosen, looking at the potatoes. "A new kind of tzimmes?"

"Terrill's famous New Orleans tzimmes," said Maish, sitting across from his brother.

Abe ate and drank his coffee. Maish had something to say. Abe thought he knew what it might be.

"More coffee?" called a man seated at the counter, cup in hand, looking at Maish.

The man was dark, wore a suit and tie and an apologetic smile.

"Singh, you see the coffeepot sitting there on the burner back there?" said Maish. "You see it every day. Take your cup, walk around the counter, fill your cup, sit back down, and drink while you think of the good old days in Bombay."

"I am from Calcutta," said Singh.

"I stand corrected," said Maish.

Two other people at the counter stood up with cups in hand.

"Ho," called Maish. "Singh'll get your coffee."

"And," called Singh, going behind the counter with his cup, "if I spill this coffee on me, I'll sue you for millions."

"Schmuck," said Maish. "In the first place, I don't have a million dollars. In the second place, you just told all these witnesses that you plan to burn yourself and blame it on me."

The other customers paid no attention to the banter. If you ate at the T&L you suffered or enjoyed the show.

"I'll testify," said Sy Weintraub.

"Me too," said Al Bloombach.

"Me too," joined Howie Chen.

"I'm Spartacus," said Hersh Cohen.

"Whose side you testifying for?" asked Maish.

"We haven't decided," said Hersh. "We can, however, be corrupted to join a worthy and just cause."

Maish shifted in the booth to face Abe and folded his hands on the table.

"Singh's my new lawyer," said Maish. "He knows more about the law than Alan Dershowitz."

"What about Irving Trammel?" asked Abe.

"Irving Trammel? I don't like him. Never did."

"He's good."

"I still don't like him."

"Neither do I, but he's good. Omelet's good, sweet potatoes great," said Abe.

"My thanks to my brother, the gourmet who will eat anything that has the slightest chance of blocking his arteries," said Maish, who then added softly, "Tonight."

"Tonight what?" asked Abe. "We robbing a bank?"

"You know what I'm talking about. Tonight I leave the congregation."

Since Maish's son, David, had been murdered in what his father still believed was the work of a random mugging, Morris Lieberman had been at war with God. He had not renounced his religion, his belief. In fact, Maish was probably the strongest believer in the Mir Shavot congregation. He was simply, painfully, constantly angry with God and took every opportunity to carry on the one-sided debate at Shabbat services and temple events, including the monthly singles meetings. He made it a point not to disrupt bat mitzvah and bar mitzvah services. Maish had been married to his wife Yetta for almost forty-five years, but that didn't keep Maish from attending the singles meetings where he chastised God for choosing to make lonely the ten people who normally attended. He had a cause and an argument suited for any gathering. Not even a heart attack six months ago had slowed his campaign and now he had announced that he was . . .

"Quitting," said Abe, putting down his fork.

"I'm announcing at the men's club dinner tonight," Maish said. "After you speak."

"Speak?"

"You're the speaker at the annual dinner, Avrum. Tonight. You losing your memory to old age?"

Abe remembered. He remembered being cajoled into speaking by Bess and Rabbi Wass. What he didn't remember was that this was the day he was to speak. Previous speakers had been politicians, writers, religious scholars, members of the Kneset, musicians. Everyone thought a policeman, a member of their own congregation, would be a welcome and illuminating change—everyone but Abe Lieberman.

"What are you going to talk about?" asked Maish.

"I don't know. Maybe God will inspire me."

"You're mocking me, Abraham," Maish said, pointing a finger at his brother.

"You'll embarrass Bess," said Abe.

Abe's wife was the president of the congregation.

"She'll survive," said Maish. "She's stronger than you or me or both of us put together."

"Yetta? What does she think?" asked Abe.

"I don't think she's been any too happy with God either," said Maish. "David, my heart attack. Jobian testing going on here, Avrum, and I don't like it and I'm not going to play God's game."

Abe sat silently, looking down at what coffee remained in his cup.

"What?" asked Maish. "What're you thinking?"

"I was just thinking what you and I put together would look like. It wouldn't be a pretty sight."

Maish slid out of the booth and leaned over inches from his brother's face to say, "You are hopeless."

"And I love you too," said Abe. "While you're up, can I get some more coffee or do you want me to ask your lawyer Mr. Singh?"

"I'll get it," said Maish. "I mean what I say about tonight."

"I believe you," said Abe.

Maish moved away.

"We heard," called Hersh Rosen. "Normally, I don't go to men's club events, but I'll be there tonight to watch you making up a speech and Maish making a scene."

"We'll all be there," said Sy. "Howie can come as my guest."

"Wouldn't miss it," said Howie Chen.

"I hear Noah Nathanson, the kvetch, is coming," said Hersch Rosen. "Count on long, loud complaints."

"Good," said Al Bloombach. "Sy, you can pick me up."

Abe wiped his mouth with a napkin and got up.

"You want more coffee? You don't want more coffee?" Maish, pot in hand, said from behind the counter.

"I changed my mind," said Abe. "People can change their minds."

"I'm not changing mine," said Maish.

"Suit yourself," said Abe, moving toward the door.

"We will see you tonight," called Rosen as Abe went through the door.

It had been a typical breakfast at the T&L. Later he would think about what he would say tonight. Now, however, reasonably full, he was ready to go find a Turk.

"He was Chinese, I think. Maybe Korean."

Jonas Lindqvist lay in the bed looking at neither his wife nor Bill Hanrahan. Lydia Lindqvist stood, arms folded, looking from her husband to Bill Hanrahan. Bill thought she looked like an ex-Olympic Nordic athlete. She was blond, hair tied at the back. She was solidly and powerfully built with clear skin and pure blue eyes.

It was a private room on the surgery floor. It would have been completely silent if the television suspended from the ceiling at the foot of the bed weren't blaring a six A.M. rerun of *All in the Family*.

"Okay if I turn the volume down?" Bill asked.

"I don't know where it is," said Jonas.

Lydia Lindqvist reached down to the bedside table to press a mute button.

"Thanks," said Bill, looking down at Jonas. "He wasn't Japanese?"

"Could have been. I don't think so. Lyd, when do I get another pain pill?"

"One hour and twenty minutes," she said, glancing down at her watch.

"Okay," Hanrahan said, writing in his notebook: Asian, probably Chinese. "Tell me what happened."

"I was out walking," he said with a definite grimace of pain. "Couldn't sleep. Mind racing. You ever feel that?"

"Yes," said Bill.

When he had been drinking, Bill never knew what would happen when he tried to sleep. Sometimes sleep would come instantly. Sometimes thoughts, fragments of thought, even images would fly by and refuse to stop or even slow down.

Sometimes when that happened, one more drink would do the trick. Sometimes.

"Well, I saw this man and woman sort of hiding next to a building. At first I thought they were looking for something in the grass. Then I got close. They punched me. You can see the marks on my stomach. I can't, but you can."

Lindqvist's wife pulled down the blanket over him and lifted her husband's hospital gown. The bruising was a large red, black, and blue splotch of color. Painful. But not as painful, Bill was sure, as what lay under the white padding and tape that covered Jonas Lindqvist's groin.

Bill nodded and Lydia Lindqvist pulled the blanket back up to her husband's chest.

"They punched you," Bill prompted.

"They punched me and ran down the street. I followed them."

"Why?"

"Why? They beat me up. Maybe they had a car and I could get their license plate number or maybe they were walking home and I could get their address. I lost them. I wasn't moving very fast. My stomach hurt like sin."

"But you caught up with them," said Bill.

"They were standing over this Chinese guy. He was on the ground. His briefcase just lay there open. I start moving as fast as I could. The man in the mask reached over and grabbed a pile of money, pushed it back into the briefcase."

"And?"

"They ran. The man and the woman. They were fast. I couldn't catch them even if they hadn't hit me in the stomach and if I caught them, they would just beat me up again and—"

"Would you recognize them if you saw them again?" asked Bill.

"Yes."

"Okay, what did you do then?"

"Then I go ask the Chinese guy if he needs any help. That's when he shot me. Pain or no pain, I ran. I knew I needed a hospital."

"And this was where?"

"I don't know. Three blocks north of Lawrence. I think it was Gunnison."

Hanrahan moved to the side of the bed, took out his phone, and punched a button that dialed the Clark Street Station.

"Hanrahan," he said. "Hey, did you get any mugging calls overnight?"

Hanrahan waited.

"Any out of the district, anything north of Foster?"

He could hear the tap of plastic keys while the computer searched. In less than a minute, he had an answer.

"Thanks," he said, and hung up.

"So?" asked Lydia.

No mugging reported, Bill thought. A man gets mugged, a briefcase full of money stolen. Then he shoots Lindqvist thinking he's the mugger and then doesn't report any of this to the police. Two conclusions: the gun isn't registered and the money is dirty. Maybe both.

"Mr. Lindqvist, can you pin down a bit better where the man shot you?"

"In the right testicle," his wife added.

"Yeah, thanks. I've got it here," said Bill, showing his notebook. "I mean the place, the street where the man shot you. The apartment building he was in front of, anything you can remember?"

Lindqvist tried to readjust himself on the bed. He let out a slow whine like the sound of air coming out of a balloon. His eyes were closed and he had an overbite grip on his lower lip. He turned his head toward his wife and said, "Lydia."

"I'll find a nurse," she said, meeting Bill's eyes as she left the room in search of a nurse.

"The place," Bill reminded him.

"Yes, I think I can find it. Maybe I shouldn't have gone out jogging."

"Looks that way," Bill agreed, putting his notebook away.

"But maybe if I had stayed home," Lindqvist went on through dry lips, "I would have had a worse thing happen. I mean maybe it was my time to have something happen, maybe God has a bookkeeper."

His words were slurred now and his voice was low. He was drifting off in spite of the pain.

"No more," Lindqvist whispered. *"Inte se langre an nasan racker."*

Then he was asleep.

"He said, 'Not for all the tea in China,'" Lindqvist's wife said. She was standing close to him and looking down at her husband.

"When he has a fever or drinks even a little, he says things in Swedish," she said. "I didn't get any pills. He has to wait."

"I'm going," said Bill. "But tell him I'll be back. If he can remember where he was when he got shot it would be helpful."

Lindqvist was snoring gently.

"You married?" she asked.

"Yes, my wife's in maternity upstairs. We just had a baby, a girl."

"Congratulations. So she'll be in the hospital tonight?"

"Yes," Bill said.

"And Jonas will be here at least another night," she said with a sigh. "He's a good man."

Her shoulder was almost brushing Bill's. She smelled as if she had just showered. He looked at her and she looked at him. Her skin was pink and clear and her teeth white and even.

"We'll both be on our own," she said.

Bill did not like where this was going.

"I'll be working," he said.

"Hardrock Hanrahan," she said with a smile.

Nobody but Whiz Parker, Father Sam "Whiz" Parker, called him Hardrock. No one else had called him that for almost twenty years.

"I know you?" he asked.

"My brother, Anders Persson, played with you at Vocational."

Her shoulder was touching his now.

"Andy Persson, offensive tackle, defensive guard," said Bill.

"I used to come to practices," she said. "Sit in the stands, watch. I was eleven, twelve. Came out mainly to watch two players, Anders and you. I talked to you a couple of times."

Bill nodded. He had no recollection of any girl.

"How's Andy?" he asked.

"Married, owns a construction company, three kids, all boys, all big like Andy, all strong like everyone in our family, and all of them played football at St. Andrews. Would you like to come to my house tonight?"

The temptation was there, but it passed before it was fully formed.

"Can't," he said, looking at the sleeping man in the bed.

"He may be a good man, but he doesn't like sex and when he does it, he's not very inventive."

This was more than Bill wanted to hear.

"Gotta go," he said.

She nodded in understanding.

"Since I married Jonas, I've never been with another man. Could have, many times. Jonas believes I have, but I haven't."

"I believe that," Bill said.

"I think I'll stay here tonight," she said with a sigh.

Bill went into the hall and headed slowly toward the elevators.

It wasn't the first time a woman had come on to him while he was on a case. It was the fourth time. He had given in to the temptation only once. That was while he was drinking. That was before he met Iris. That was when he and Maureen were always fighting, he shouting and crying, Maureen quiet, firm, enduring. One time. She was the daughter of man who had been murdered. She wasn't married. She wasn't pretty. It had been impulsive, unplanned during a routine interview in her studio apartment. She was grieving. An only child. It had happened only once. He couldn't remember her first name, but her last name was Prohanski. He hadn't thought of her for a long time. Now he wondered what had happened to her. He wondered, but not enough to try to find out.

There was a soft *ping* and the elevator doors opened. William Hanrahan pulled himself out of the memory of an almost forgotten woman and stepped into the present.

Now he had to find a Chinese man who had been beaten, had a briefcase full of money stolen, and didn't report it to the police.

7

"Tell me about the man," said Liao Woo.

Liao Woo could have been any age, but he was certainly very old. He carried a silver-handled cane and wore thick glasses. Liao Woo was always clean-shaven, imperially slim, and dressed in either traditional Chinese clothes or handmade suits from a favored tailor in Hong Kong.

He was, officially, an importer of Oriental goods and art. He was, unofficially, the most powerful man in Chinatown, the area south and west of the Loop between Canal Street and Lake Shore Drive on the east and west, and from the Stevenson Expressway to the Sante Fe railroad yards just north of Cermak Road. Chinatown contained a concentration of more than seven thousand Chinese, many of them like Woo himself, who had escaped when Mao and the Communists took over China. Passing tourists and Chicagoans came to Chinatown to buy and look, have lunch or a dinner of dim sum, and then depart Chinatown.

Woo had brought himself up on the streets and in the alleys of Shanghai, then lived briefly in San Francisco before coming to Chicago, where he reinvented himself. He spoke English with an accent, stood erect, and acted as if he were as entitled to power as a mandarin. Of course he had to back up his rise to respectability on a platform of intimidation and occasional murder.

Woo's shop was a modest one on Wentworth Avenue. Robert Chang had called to say he had to see Mr. Woo immediately.

He was told by one of Mr. Woo's assistants to come quickly and be brief. Robert, in suit and tie, had made his way through the shop being careful not to bump into a huge vase or knock over a small shiny snuffbox. He had been ushered into Mr. Woo's office by the assistant, a former martial arts teacher and bodybuilder.

"Speak," said Woo.

Seated across the large desk whose legs were intricately carved in the form of curled dragons, Robert contemplated how to answer Mr. Woo's order.

Doing his best to keep his voice steady, Robert E. Lee Chang adjusted his glasses and told his story.

"The man was big, blond hair cut short," he concluded. "He was wearing a sweatsuit. There was a woman with him. I heard her voice. When I got the gun and turned around, she wasn't there. He was. I know I shot him. I know he took the briefcase."

"In what part of his anatomy did the bullet lodge?"

"I don't know," said Chang. "He knocked my glasses off when he hit me. I didn't see him clearly."

"So you would not know his face or that of the woman if you saw either of them."

It wasn't a question. It was a statement.

"No," said Chang. "I only heard her. I never saw her and when I saw him, I didn't have my glasses, but I know I shot him."

"The nearest hospital?"

Chang recited the names of three hospitals where the thief might have gone if he went to a hospital.

Woo turned to his assistant and said something in Cantonese. Chang spoke neither Cantonese nor Mandarin and, though he didn't know it, Woo spoke a low-class street Shanghai Cantonese. He spoke it as little as possible. He spoke it at times to preserve his image and only in front of third parties, like Chang, who could not speak Chinese.

"You are responsible for the one hundred and fifty thousand dollars you lost," said Woo evenly. "You have two days, not including this one, to find the man and recover the money or pay the money from some other source."

Robert Chang had known this was coming from the moment he was certain the briefcase had been taken. He should have, but did not have, $150,000. He did have a little more than $30,000.

Two years ago, buoyed with confidence in himself, he had called himself Chang the Wily and began with games in Chinatown, sometimes with men and women who spoke only enough English to play the game. Chang had dreams of learning in Chinatown and moving on, buying in to poker tournaments. He imagined himself at a tournament final table in Reno, Las Vegas, Atlantic City, or an island in the Caribbean.

Chang imagined himself playing against poker greats for a bracelet and a payoff of more than a million dollars to the winner.

But Chang the Wily had never gone beyond the poker tables of Chinatown. He had won a little and lost a lot. Now he owed $150,000 to Mr. Woo. There was no one from whom he could borrow the money. He had to find the man he had shot, the man with his briefcase.

"Two days, Robert Chang," said Mr. Woo.

He was being dismissed.

Chang rose, almost imperceptibly bowed his head, and let himself be led out of the office and through the shop and out the door by the bodybuilder.

It was a little before eight o'clock, an hour too early for dim sum breakfast at Won Kow, which was less than twenty yards from where he stood, and two hours too early for most of the other restaurants.

There was a small grocery a block away, no tables no chairs, but they did serve early-morning black tea and fresh-that-morning chicken or pork steamed buns. He would settle for that, and then, fueled, he would head immediately to one of the three hospitals. He would start with Edgewater Hospital and work his way south to Woodrow Wilson Hospital.

When he found the man, he would get the money even if he had to kill him. Chang was prepared, if necessary, to do just that.

There were three Turkish-speaking officers in the Chicago Police Department. All three had been called. One had immediately volunteered.

Officer Turhan Kazmaka in full uniform was picked up by Detective Abraham Lieberman. Less than fifteen minutes later Turhan and Abe were parked in an almost empty parking lot in Lincoln Park. The car was a black Honda Abe had gotten out of the police motor pool.

"He'll be on that bench," said Kazmaka, white container of coffee in his hand.

Abe nodded. He had a container of hot coffee too.

Turhan Kazmaka was about thirty, well-muscled. He was movie-star dark, tall and handsome with curly black hair and a broad smile, nearly perfect white teeth.

Abraham Lieberman was more than sixty, short, thin, gray, far from handsome with a long-suffering smile. Thanks to Herby Kornpelt, DDS, Abe's teeth, while not perfect, were at least white and respectable.

Turhan had heard about the crazy little Jew detective who had faced down gang leaders, dope dealers, politicians, and millionaire bigwigs. There were few cops who hadn't. Turhan had heard that there was no chance Lieberman would ever be promoted, but also no chance the department would let him go.

Word was that Lieberman cut through the tape whether it was red, green, yellow, blue, or brown. He had, according to the "word," been warned, reprimanded, threatened, pleaded with, to stay inside the ever-constricting lines of the law laid out for the department. According to the "word," the very people who warned him secretly wanted him to go on doing what he was doing, what they would have liked to do themselves.

Now, seeing the myth, Turhan was not impressed. The Jew detective was small, old, and looked tired. He talked as if he were bored by life.

"You named after Turhan Bey the actor?" Lieberman asked.

"No. Turhan is a common Turkish name."

"Turhan Bey," said Lieberman. "Half-Turkish movie actor. Pretty good. I've seen all his movies, usually at two in the morning on television. *Ali Baba and the Forty Thieves, Arabian Nights, Amazing Mr. X.* Worked a lot with Maria Montez. Now that was a beautiful woman."

"That a fact?" said Kazmaka.

"A fact," said Lieberman. "You should see her in Technicolor."

"I'll try," said Kazmaka.

Both men were watching the bench about thirty yards in front of them on a curving park path.

"We'll give him an hour," Lieberman said. "Then we'll see if we can find him."

"He'll be here," said Kazmaka.

Lieberman had stopped at the Clark Street Station to find out if there was a Turk in the department. He had done a computer search of officers and come up with a single match, Turhan Kazmaka. He had called Kazmaka who said he spoke Turkish and was familiar with the Turkish community in Chicago.

After going through Lieutenant Alan Kearney to set it up, Lieberman had picked up Officer Kazmaka, and told him about the death of Lemi Sahin. Kazmaka had heard of him. Officer Kazmaka suggested that they contact a man named Kemal Mutlu.

"Kemal the Camel," said Kazmaka. "If you want the bright side of Turkish life in the city, I've got some names for you. If you want the dark side, Kemal's the one you want. He knows what's going on with Turks, Armenians, Greeks."

"What's he get from you?" asked Lieberman.

"Protection," said Kazmaka after another gulp of coffee. "Get-out-of-jail-free cards on misdemeanors. I don't have the clout to deal him for felony."

"Not yet," said Lieberman.

"Not yet," Kazmaka agreed.

"Ever hear of El Perro, the Dog?"

"The crazy Mex? Gang on North Avenue."

"Emiliano and I are good friends," said Lieberman. "Both

of us are Cub fans. You've got a talking camel. I've got a talking dog."

Kazmaka nodded.

Abe wished he had a cheese danish or, yes, a doughnut, a good, big, fat cop doughnut.

Lieberman knew Turhan Kazmaka was married and had one six-year-old daughter. Kazmaka's father, Martin, was a native-born citizen of the United States as was his mother, Helen. Martin Kazmaka had been a professional wrestler until he retired and opened a television sale and repair shop. Turhan's grandparents on both sides were Turkish-born. Turhan spoke fluent Turkish and had an unblemished record. In his five years in uniform, he had not missed a day on the job. He also had three commendation letters on file from his superiors including one about Turhan's superior skill on the firing range. There were only two other members of the Chicago Police Department who scored higher.

"You got a nickname?" asked Lieberman.

"Yeah, but I didn't choose it. I got it at the Police Academy. Turk."

"Turk," Abe repeated. "You like being called Turk?"

Abe had finished his coffee, the third cup of the day so far, and he needed to find a toilet or tall bushes. Neither seemed to be available.

"It's okay. Beats some of the names we give each other," said Kazmaka. "Paperweight, Little Dick, Big Dick, Eight Ball, the Stone, Hooch. My father, when he wrestled, was the Wild Turk. Bald head, big black mustache," said Kazmaka.

"I remember him."

"It was something," Kazmaka said with a smile. "This big, gentle guy, my dad, would go in there, growl at the crowd, fight dirty, put on an act, and make a good living doing it."

"You trying to tell me professional wrestling isn't real?" asked Lieberman.

Kazmaka looked at Abe. Was the man kidding? Everyone, except complete nuts, knew pro wrestling was a show. Dangerous, but not real.

"I've got your dad's autograph somewhere," said Abe. "I had an autograph book when I was a kid. My dad took me and my brother to wrestling matches at Marigold. Great hot dogs. Pete Shue, Chief Don Eagle, Verne Gagne. I've got them."

"Great," said Kazmaka, wondering how this old guy rushing toward dementia was still a cop.

"Somewhere in the garage or basement. Or maybe my brother's got them. I think I've even got a hair from your father's mustache next to his name. He sweated on me. That's how I got the hair. Scotch-taped it to the page."

Abe reached into his jacket pocket, took out his glasses, and put them on.

"I'll tell him," said Kazmaka.

"You do that," said Abe, looking down the path.

"No problem."

"However, I have two problems," said Abe. "First, I really have to pee. Second, is that your camel coming?"

Kazmaka turned in his seat to look down the path. Kemal the Camel was moving slowly in their direction. He was little more than a miniature in the distance.

"Yes."

"The three kids behind him," said Abe evenly. "You know them?"

"No."

Abe opened his door and started to get out.

"Let's go," he said, taking his glasses off and putting them back in his pocket. "You need a toilet?"

"No."

"I admire your bladder control. It won't endure. Let's go."

They got out of the car and closed the doors. Over the top of the car Abe said, "Go around and get behind them. They see your uniform and they'll keep walking."

"Walking instead of what?"

"Mugging your camel."

Kazmaka looked at the trio. They were talking to one another, laughing, poking. Kids in the park. He saw kids like this every day.

"They're just kids walking," Kazmaka said.

"One in the middle has something in his pocket, something heavy. It's pulling the pocket down. He keeps putting his hand in that pocket and when he does, his hand and arm tightens."

"Tightens?" said Kazmaka.

"Like he's holding onto something."

"He's playing with himself," said Kazmaka.

"No," said Abe. "The one on his right. What do you see?"

"A kid walking."

"He's wearing a long-sleeved shirt," said Lieberman. "His left hand is at his side. His right is bent at the elbow."

"Which means?"

"He's got something up his sleeve," said Abe. "Let's go and get it over. I really have to find a toilet soon."

"The third kid, what's his weapon of choice, an Uzi down his pants leg?" Kazmaka asked.

"No, his fists. They're clenched. Officer Turk, go."

Kazmaka moved to his left and was out of sight behind a row of bushes in a few seconds. Abe put his glasses back on, letting them rest at the end of his nose. He pulled the zipper of his jacket all the way up to his neck, hunched his shoulders, tilted his head slightly forward, plunged his hands into his pockets, and moved to the path. He walked slowly, mumbling to himself and nervously gripping his right wrist with his left hand.

Pinn Taibo laughed at nothing, looked around the park, gripped the cool gun in his pocket, and poked his brother José. José was tired of holding up his arm. The foot-long pipe in his sleeve kept getting heavier. José was beginning to lose feeling in the arm.

"Let's do it," said José. "Let's just do it."

"Yeah," said Herve.

Pinn had talked Herve into not carrying a weapon. Herve had gone too far when they robbed Skoll's Liquors on Diversey. Herve had a baseball bat. Herve used it, howling with delight as each swing brought a rain of flying glass and alcohol. Then he had used the bat on the guy behind the counter. The guy hadn't done anything. Herve was just enjoying himself.

He had been given the little man's name, told where to find him, and paid four hundred dollars. For four hundred dollars, all he had to do was kill the old man.

To pick up some legit money, from time to time he cleaned up the place where the guy who had paid him worked. The guy had approached Pinn. Pinn had accepted. No questions. They had shaken on it.

They had parked legally, money in the meter. They were out of their neighborhood.

They had followed the bent-over man who moved slowly with a slight limp.

Through the window of Banfield and Patrick's New York Deli, Pinn had watched the crooked man eat eat a big cinnamon roll and coffee at the counter and then pay his bill. When the man opened the wallet, Pinn could see that it was thick with bills. A bonus.

Pinn had prayed without speaking, "*Madre de Dio,* thank you for finding this man."

He uttered another prayer to the Virgin that he might be able to get the bills from the crooked man's wallet without his brother and Herve seeing it.

When the man came out of the deli, José, Herve, and Pinn had followed him into the park.

The little man moved slowly, as if he had a problem with his left leg. He definitely did have a posture problem. The man's right shoulder sagged, tilting him to the left. He was all fucked up.

The trio began to close the distance between them and the drooping little man in front of them. It was time.

That was when they saw another old man coming in their direction. This one wore a jacket zipped to his neck. His glasses looked as if they were about to fall off of the end of his nose. He was nervous, talking to himself as he neared them.

José and Herve didn't have to be told that they would have to wait till the old guy with glasses went by. But he didn't go by. He stepped in front of the trio.

They stopped. The Camel walked on.

"We don't have any spare change," said Pinn. "Move your ass out of the way, old man."

"I don't want spare change," Abe said, unzipping his jacket.

The man they were following, the little man with the lolling walk, was slowly getting away.

"José," Pinn said.

José took a few steps forward and stood eye to eye with the old man in their way. He started to drop his arm to let the pipe slide down his sleeve into his hand. As the pipe slipped down, Abe punched José's arm above the elbow. The pipe clattered onto the path.

Behind Lieberman, the Camel kept walking.

Herve stepped forward, towering over Lieberman, whose gun suddenly appeared in his right hand. Herve stopped. Pinn pulled his gun out of his pocket and aimed it at the crazy old man.

"You wanna die, you old piece of shit?" asked Pinn, aiming his gun at the old man's face.

"Look over your shoulder," said Lieberman.

"Fuck, no," said Pinn.

"Do it, *hermano,*" said José quietly.

Pinn looked over his shoulder at the uniformed cop a dozen yards behind them, a gun in his hand.

"You've got a lot of choices," Abe said. "First, you can shoot me and get yourself killed. The officer back there with a gun is the third best shot in the department. He will kill you."

"You're lying," said Pinn.

"About his being the third best? If I were lying, I'd say he was the best. Officer Kazmaka consistently scores thirty in the box on the range. Jeremy Cookson, who, by the way, wears glasses, is always thirty in the box, best score possible. Now I'm a decent shot, but I miss a lot. It's to be expected. I could, even at this distance, aim at your head or your chest and shoot you, by accident of course, in the neck or the groin."

"You're not gonna shoot," said Pinn, his fingers playing with the gun. "He's not gonna shot."

"Okay," said Lieberman. "More choices. You run. You get shot, maybe not killed. Maybe one of you gets away. I don't know which one. I haven't decided who I'll shoot. I'll let Officer Kazmaka shoot you."

Kazmaka took a few more steps toward the group.

"Hey, let's stop with the shooting shit," said José nervously.

"Let's," said Abe.

"Wait," said Herve. "I know you."

"You know me, Herve," Abe said.

"Viejo, right?"

Turhan Kazmaka had moved slowly, steadily until he was part of the gathering.

Lieberman nodded.

"Shit," said Herve to Pinn. "This is Viejo. You kill him and El Perro will rip out your liver, man. I mean really rip out your liver while you're still alive or worse."

"What's worse than having your liver ripped out when you're still alive?" asked José.

"I don' know, but if there's something worse, El Perro will think of it," said Herve. "He'll do it to all of us."

"You'll have to continue this discussion some other time," Abe said. "I've had a busy night and this looks like a busy day. Make your choice now," said Lieberman. "Or I start shooting."

"Pinn, he'll do it," said Herve.

Pinn looked at the man in front of him. In spite of the tired spaniel face and thin body, Pinn believed. He handed Abe the gun. Kazmaka moved in.

"I got no weapon," said Herve.

"Me too," said José. "I was takin' that pipe to my Uncle Hector. He fixes sinks and tubs and stuff."

Kazmaka put his weapon back in its holster and searched them for weapons or drugs. He came up with nothing but a total of fifty-seven dollars and change in their pockets.

"What have we got? Three young men out for a walk. One

is helping his uncle. Another is minding his own business and the third is carrying a gun that I'll bet is unregistered."

"I was going to turn it in after we went to our uncle's," said Pinn. "I found it on the street about half an hour ago."

"Conspiracy to commit robbery. Illegal weapon possession. Threatening the life of a police officer. Resisting arrest. I'll think of more. You're out of your neighborhood. Go home. If there's a next time we see each other and you are doing or about to do or have done something amiss, I'll shoot you."

"You can't do that," said Pinn.

"Of course I can," said Lieberman.

"Let's go, man," said Herve, pulling at Pinn's shirt.

"Jog," said Lieberman. "It'll do you good."

The three of them moved back down the path past Kazmaka.

"That is not a jog," said Lieberman.

Abe fired into the grass behind them. Then they ran.

Abe put his gun back in his pocket.

"Why didn't we take them in?" asked Kazmaka.

"It wouldn't be worth our time and the County's money. They'd all be back on the street in a few hours or days or locked up for a few months."

"I've got the one with the gun's license," said Kazmaka.

"Run it through the computer," said Lieberman. "Just for fun and frolic. Let's go talk to a camel."

"Le Sourire," said Jamie, sitting up in bed.

He pronounced it, "Luh-Sour-E."

The sun was up and he needed a shave. He looked at the briefcase on the table, the piles of money. It hadn't been a dream. Sometimes at night, particularly after a fight, Jamie had dreams. Mostly he dreamed about the fight, went through every round, every punch as if he were a television camera or something. Even in his sleep he could feel his shoulders move, his head bob, his fists tighten. Sometimes he would grunt with the memory of a solid jab to the other guy's stomach or to his own.

He didn't tell Elsie about his dreams. He didn't want her to worry. He wasn't sure she would worry and there wasn't anything to worry about, but something told him to keep his postfight dreams to himself.

"Le Sourire," he said again.

His mouth was dry. His tongue was a landscape of arid ridges. He slept nude as did Elsie and no matter how much he scrubbed in the shower the night before, he woke up with itches that demanded scratching. Each time he scratched the itches multiplied until there was no hope for it but to get up and shower.

"What?" asked Elsie, who in half sleep turned toward him and put a hand between his legs.

"The big guy, last night," Jamie said as she played with him, her eyes still closed. "It said that on his shirt."

"Jacket," she corrected.

"No, shirt. Sweatshirt."

"T-shirt," she said. "What's the . . . ?"

Elsie pulled back her hand, opened her eyes, and sat up. She brushed her short hair back with both hands and let out out a little puff of air.

"Yeah," she said. "He saw our faces."

"And I've been thinking you know. What if we get in the papers again or TV? He sees us, tells the cops. Next thing we know I'm fighting for nothing in Stateville and you're . . ."

"Yeah," she said again.

He looked at her. Her back was straight. Her arms taut, her breasts small. Jamie loved her. She looked at him.

"Le Sourire," he said. "That's the restaurant, fancy place on Belmont, you know? Looked it up in the phone book."

"We find him. Talk to him," she said.

"Just talk," Jamie agreed.

But they both knew that talk alone probably wouldn't do it. The big blond guy had come after them even after they had laid him out. He could take a punch. Could he take two punches? Three? The threat of more?

Iris was sitting up in bed, propped up with three pillows behind her. Bill stood a few feet away, looking down at the baby in the portable crib. Jane Mei Hanrahan was sleeping.

"She looks like you," Bill said.

"It's too soon to know," said Iris.

"No, she looks like you and that's good."

He had gone home, just a few blocks away, to take out the dog, shave, change clothes, and microwave the leftover Egg Foo Yung Iris's father had brought over the night before. It was Bill's favorite Chinese food. He had even, when in the kitchen alone, eaten it cold, right out of the refrigerator.

The dog, a hybrid of the streets and alleys, had no name. He was simply "the dog." Iris's father, Chai Huang Chen, had said once that, while dog meat was considered a delicacy in China, this dog would not be coveted for its meat. Too tough, lean. The dog and Iris's father were not friends.

The dog had been part of a murder investigation a little more than a year earlier. The stray had met a kindred spirit in Hanrahan and they had become friends. The dog was particularly protective of Iris and Bill and, having survived in the shadows and night of the city, he was particularly formidable.

"What?" asked Iris.

"She's so . . ."

"Vulnerable," said Iris.

"Yes, vulnerable," he agreed.

"We'll protect her," said Iris.

Bill nodded. His history of protecting witnesses, family, and friends was spotted with massive failures. There was and would be no room for failure with Jane Mei Hanrahan.

8

Abe didn't know what the breath of a camel smelled like, but he was sure it couldn't have been more offensive than that of the man he sat next to on the bench in Lincoln Park.

Everything about the man was offensive, from his food-stained pants to his wild mop of hair. Kemal the Camel needed a shave, a good toothbrush, a shower, a barber, and clean clothes.

"I was not always as you see me now," the man said, arching his bushy eyebrows.

"Let's hope not," said Abe.

Kemal turned to face Turhan Kazmaka.

"Your friend is blessed with a sardonic sense of humor," he said. "I like him."

"And I like you," said Abe. "How could anyone not like you?"

"It would be difficult," Kemal agreed.

"Detective Lieberman has some questions," said Kazmaka.

"Does Detective Lieberman also have forty dollars?"

"He has," said Lieberman.

"And is he willing to part with it?" asked Kemal, eyes suddenly wide.

"No," said Lieberman, "but he will part with it unwillingly for some good answers. Now, can we stop talking about me in the third person and start answering questions?"

Kemal shrugged and looked at Kazmaka for support. He got none.

"Tamam," he said. "Okay."

"The name Lemi Sahin mean anything to you?" asked Abe.

"Lemi Bey," said Kemal, with what Abe interpreted as a smile.

"He was murdered a few hours ago," said Abe.

"Insallah," said Kemal. "If God wills it. Lemi Bey was a very active member of the Turkish-American Society of Chicago. Very interested in removing whatever undeserved tarnish exists upon the image of Turkey, its history, its people."

"He had a package, something small, wrapped in leather," said Abe. "Someone took it, probably killed him for it."

Kemal shook his head and said, "The journal of Aziz. Unfortunately, well-meaning zealous people like Lemi Bey, educated though they may be, are often taken in by mountebanks and charlatans. Doctors, engineers, lawyers, businessmen, and they are so anxious to find the journal that they are taken in by crooks and sold false documents that are soon discredited."

"The journal of Aziz?" said Lieberman, looking at Kazmaka.

"Supposedly some guy named Aziz got his hands on a diary written by an Armenian back around 1913," said Kazmaka.

Kemal nodded in agreement.

"It's supposed to prove that the Turks didn't commit many of the atrocities they were accused of, particularly massacres of Armenians. It's a Turkish urban myth."

"No," said Kemal with a patronizing smile reserved for nonbelievers. "It exists. And it is in Chicago. Aziz came here and passed the document in question to his son and his son passed it to his son."

An automobile horn wailed out of sight. A screech of brakes and then a metallic collision. Kazmaka looked in the direction of the sound. Kemal looked at Abe.

"Why didn't this Aziz just show this journal to the Turkish embassy or the newspapers?" asked Abe.

"Ah, it was his legacy, his treasure, his gift, a secular relic like your Torah," said Kemal. "Meant to be passed down from generation to generation till the time when its value had increased to great proportions. This appears to be such a time."

"Because," said Lieberman, "Turkey wants to get into the European Union and they're being asked to make a public apology for their crimes against Armenians."

"Exactly," said Kemal with a smile. "You know our history."

"I've read," said Lieberman.

Three young mothers, all pushing their babies in streamlined walkers, jogged down the path. The young women wore designer workout clothes and running shoes. They were next to one another, saying nothing.

The women, one of whom might have been an Indian or a Pakistani, barely glanced at the three men on the bench. The three men had all halted their conversation to watch the young women run past them.

"Does a creature exist more able to stir the loins than a young mother?" asked Kemal.

"Aziz," Abe reminded him.

"Aziz," Kemal repeated. "Rumors, stories, lies. They come, go, grow, are embellished. One story is that the journal of Aziz was recently in the hands of a wealthy physician."

"Lemi Sahin?" said Lieberman.

Kemal confirmed with a nod.

"Another man is reported to be seeking the journal," said Kemal the Camel. "He is reported to be very determined to obtain it."

"Man have a name?" asked Abe.

"We all have his name," said Kemal. "However, when my friend Turhan called me this morning, I made a call and discovered that this man has acquired the journal and is rumored to now be offering it to a very wealthy personage."

"Eighty dollars for a name," said Abe.

Kemal grinned. It was not a pretty sight.

"Omar Mehem," he said.

Kazmaka was shaking his head.

"Omar Mehem uses the name Oliver Martin, has a Turkish radio show, talk, call-ins, music," said Kazmaka. "He likes hinting that he has connections."

"Does he?" asked Abe.

"Probably not," said Kazmaka.

Abe took out his wallet and counted out four twenty-dollar bills. He would, he hoped, get it back from department funds. That left him with eleven dollars.

"Where do I find Omar?" asked Lieberman.

"Station WTUR at eight tonight," said Kazmaka.

Abe handed the four twenties to Kemal who took them with surprisingly clean hands. Kemal was aware of the detective's taking in his hands.

"Disease," said Kemal. "Rampant. Major source for infection comes from one's own hands. Tie your shoes, touch the wall of a rest room, the handle of a door. Then you make a sandwich or eat a piece of sausage. Filth, disease. Clean, scrubbed hands are the key to good health. I'm never sick."

"I'll remember that," said Abe.

"Free information now," said Kemal, pocketing the cash. "Because you saved me from having to hurt those three who were following me. If I had hurt them, I might have to explain my actions and with no one of character, such as you or Officer Kazmaka, it might be difficult having my explanation accepted."

"I won't ask how you planned to hurt them," said Abe.

"It's best not to," Kemal said. "Free information now. Those three who you frightened away. They were not simple muggers. They were paid to hurt me sufficiently to ensure me from talking."

"Talking?" asked Abe.

"Talking to you even though I know very little. But now I'm safe. I've spoken to you, told you all I know that might help you," he lied.

Kemal got up and said, "*Allahaismarladik,* good day."

"*Güle güle,* goodbye," said Kazmaka as the hunched-over Kemal walked across the path and onto the grass heading for the street.

A siren sounded, probably a police car heading for the crash they had heard a few minutes earlier. A breeze kicked up a quintet of leaves, danced them in the air, and dropped them.

"What's he carrying?" asked Abe.

"Two pocket pepper spray guns," said Kazmaka.

Abe knew the pellets from the guns probably wouldn't kill, but they could destroy one or both eyes, tear up skin, and make life miserable for a few hours.

"Kemal the Camel's seen too many Peter Lorre movies," said Abe.

"Yeah," Kazmaka agreed. "He plays the role but his information is usually solid."

"Usually?"

"He's got a Turkish imagination."

"The Aziz business?" said Abe.

"Like I said, Turkish urban myth," said Kazmaka, shaking his head.

They stood.

"Where is this radio station where Omar works?"

"On Peterson Avenue," said Kazmaka.

Kazmaka pulled out a leather-bound pocket notebook and wrote an address. He tore it out and handed it to Abe, whose phone started playing "Take Me Out to the Ballgame." He took it from his pocket and flipped it open.

"Guy you talked to a few hours back," said Nestor Briggs. "Erhan Turkalu has the Turk restaurant on Broadway?"

"Right," said Abe.

"Morning cleanup guy found him and his wife dead about fifteen minutes ago," said Briggs. "Officers are at the scene."

The man at the restaurant had seemed nervous. No doubt, but he had reason to be. A patron had been murdered right outside his . . . Turkalu had said his wife had gone home. Was she being held hostage when Abe talked to Turkalu? Was she dead when Abe had knocked at the restaurant door? He should have smelled something was wrong.

"I'm on my way," said Abe to Nestor, closing the phone and putting it back in his pocket. Then to Turhan Kazmaka he added, "You know a man named Erhan Turkalu? Owns the Anatolia Restaurant on Broadway?"

"Buyuk Erhan," said Kazmaka. "Don't know him well. Why?"

"He's dead," said Abe. "And his wife."

Kazmaka took a deep breath.

"I'll drop you at home," said Abe.

Jonas Lindqvist lay in his bed at the hospital in a dreamy delirium. His eyes were closed and he thought he was smiling as he sang "On Wisconsin" inside the concert hall within his skull. A full marching band played in there—drums booming, cymbals crashing, trumpets and trombones just slightly off-key.

Oh, yes. The guy high-stepping, baton in his hand, whistle in his mouth, flashy uniform with a lamb chop hat, was the Chinese guy who had shot him. The Chinese guy's glasses were missing. Blindly he led the marching band—instruments swaying in unison from side to side—in a painful, patternless, aimless march. They were coming dangerously close to a pulsing soft white bulb attached to his brain. The bulb was not to be touched, but Jonas couldn't control the lost marching band.

On Wisconsin.

They were supposed to step into a formation that would tell Jonas something, but Jonas didn't know what it was. Maybe they would spell it out.

His son Peter was sitting alone in the stands. Thousands of empty seats. Peter was waving a pennant, wearing a porkpie hat and a raccoon coat. He was eighty or ninety years late for the game.

A drummer and a trombone player stepped out and serenaded the pulsing bulb. The band kept playing. Jonas kept humming and singing. He didn't remember all of the words. Most, but not all.

"'On Wisconsin, On Wisconsin, On Wisconsin, doh-de-dom-do-deh.'"

The drummer was the man who had punched him, the man who had taken the Chinese drum major's briefcase. The trombonist was the woman. Her face wasn't clear, but it was the woman.

She sent a blast directly at the pulsing bulb as the drummer dropped his drumstick and began to pummel the bulb. A left jab. A right cross. Jonas liked boxing. The man could box. He had seen him throw that combination somewhere, not at Jonas who had gone down with a single right to the chest.

No time to think about it. He stopped singing, stopped humming. The bulb being pounded like a punching bag started a steel pinball rolling down a spiral plastic tunnel though his neck, chest, and stomach. It exploded between his legs and his groin screamed with pain.

Sounds around him. His own loud moan, a voice, a woman, not Lydia. He had heard Lydia coming on to the detective. That had not been a dream. He knew. It was not the first time. The detective—O'Malley, Riley, Shaunessy? He didn't take the hook. He had a wife, a baby, a mission.

What was Lydia's success average picking up men? He wasn't sure. He didn't know about all of it.

His eyes opened. A nurse in white. Thin. Tired. Hair tied back but strands over her face. She had a syringe with an incredibly long needle in her hand.

"This will knock you out, Jonas," she said.

The room was blue. The light was blue.

"Knockout," he said. "The man who hit me."

"The Chinese man you told Dr. Huerengin about?" the

nurse said, easing the needle into the IV hanging next to the bed.

"No, the other one," said Jonas. "He's Rocky. Rocky Balboa. I saw him on television."

"Me too," the nurse said with a weary patronizing smile.

"No," said Jonas. "Rocky Balboa isn't real, is he?"

"No," said the nurse.

"Rocky Graziano?"

"He was real," she said. "How's it feel?"

"Better," Jonas said. "On Wisconsin."

"On Wisconsin," the nurse repeated.

Le Sourire didn't open till five in the afternoon. That's what the sign on the door said, but Jamie kept knocking and Elsie kept watching.

There was a car in the restaurant's parking lot, a Buick minivan with a bumper sticker that read, BUY AMERICAN. BE THE FIRST ON YOUR BLOCK.

"Nobody," Jamie said, looking around.

People were passing on the sidewalk. No one seemed to be paying any attention to them, but you never know.

"Somebody's in there," she said.

A small white truck bounced into the parking lot past the minivan and Jamie and Elsie's car. On the side of the white truck were painted serious-looking fish and the words, TOP OF THE WORLD FISHERIES, FRESH FROM THE SEAS, FRESH FROM ALASKAN STREAMS.

"Come on," Elsie said, moving onto the asphalt parking lot, following the minivan, watching it park.

A muscular little man got out of the minivan, moved to the back of the vehicle, and opened the hatchback. He took out a large box and struggled with it to a door at the rear of the restaurant.

The man was talking to himself. "Pick it up. Move it out. Get the check. Rawhide."

He knocked four times, hard. The door opened. A man, maybe Japanese, opened the door. The man wore jeans and a T-shirt. The T-shirt said *Le Sourire* on the pocket.

The delivery man had stopped talking to himself. He didn't talk to the man who opened the door either and the man didn't say anything. He opened the lid of the box. His hand disappeared. Elsie and Jamie could hear the chinkling of ice. She could smell the first waft of fish.

Jamie didn't smell anything. His nose had been broken four times. He needed surgery to correct his deviated septum. He would probably never get it done even though he had the money now to do it. No point to it. Sometimes if a fight went more than six rounds he could hear himself snort like a cartoon bull. But his nose didn't break anymore. There wasn't enough bone left to break.

The delivery man took a check from the man at the door, who easily hefted the box of fish and disappeared into the restaurant. The delivery man started to mutter. "Get in the truck. Head for Fullerton. Keep those fishes moving. Rawhide."

Elsie and Jamie moved quickly to the back door of Le Sourire. Elsie banged four times, just the way the delivery man had done. The door opened. The man who had taken in the box of fish stood there, hands in rubber gloves, a very sharp boning knife in his right hand.

"What?" the man asked.

"We're with the Cook County Sanitation Commission," Elsie said.

"Yeah, so?" said the man, looking at both of them.

"We have a report that one of your people may be carrying a disease," she said.

"Disease?"

"Bird flu," she said.

"Bullshit," said the man, starting to close the door.

"Big man, blond," said Elsie.

"Jonas?"

"Jonas who?" asked Elsie.

"Lindqvist," said Jean-Baptiste Fualo.

"We need to find him," said Jamie.

It suddenly struck Jamie that as cool as Elsie seemed to be, there was something they had forgotten. Now this man with the knife knew that a man and woman were looking for—what was his name?—Lindqvist. The man with the knife could identify them.

"He's in the hospital," said Fualo.

"For what?" asked Elsie.

"He had an accident," said Fualo.

"What hospital?" Elsie asked.

"I don't remember," said Fualo. "Goodbye."

"We have the power to close your restaurant," Elsie said as the chef started to close the door.

"Exercise your power," said Fualo. "For what I contribute to my alderman, I think it likely I'll beat whatever rap you dream up."

Jamie reached for the door as the chef started to close it.

"Grab the door, you lose some fingers," said Fualo.

Jamie pulled his hands back quickly. Without his fingers, he couldn't fight. The door slammed shut with a deep metallic ring.

"Name's Lindqvist," Elsie said. "He's in a hospital."

"We didn't hit him hard enough to send him to the hospital," said Jamie as they walked back to their car.

"Maybe you broke a rib," she said, getting into the driver's seat. "Maybe a broken rip cracked off, jagged, and stabbed him in the heart or liver."

"We didn't hit him that hard," Jamie repeated.

"Doesn't matter," Elsie said backing out of the space and turning the car toward the entrance-exit of Le Sourire. "We've got to find him and . . . you know."

"Yeah," agreed Jamie.

"Scare him enough so he won't talk," she said. "Give him a few thousand maybe. He takes it then he can't tell the cops, right?"

"Right," said Jamie. "We scare him."

What they really meant and knew and understood was that if they planned to keep out of jail and keep fighting the big blond guy was probably going to have to die.

How do you dress when you may have to shoot a man?

Until he shot the man who beat him and took Mr. Woo's money, Robert E. Lee Chang had never shot anyone. Now he might have to shoot the same man again. He hoped it wouldn't be so, but desperation might overcome his hope.

He had a list of four hospitals in the area.

"I'm searching for a large blond white male," he said when he reached someone at the first hospital.

"Aren't we all," said the decidedly gay voice on the other end.

"He was shot a few hours ago," Chang had persisted.

"I don't know about people being shot," the man said. "I'm

just delivering flowers. No one's around. The phone rang. I picked it up and there you are."

"I'd like to talk to a nurse or a doctor or someone who works there," Chang had said.

"Look . . . oh, here comes a dark maiden in white," the man had said.

"Give me that. Emergency room," came a woman's weary voice.

"I'm trying to find out if a friend of mine was brought in about two or three hours ago," he said.

"Name?"

"I'm Robert Duvall."

"His name."

"I don't know."

"You don't know your friend's name?" the woman said.

"We just met last night," said Chang.

This was proving far more difficult than he imagined and this was only the first hospital.

"He was shot," Chang went on.

"You saw him get shot?" she said.

"No, a neighbor saw and . . . is he there?"

"No one like that during the night," she said.

"You sure?"

"Sure as I am that I've got asthma. If you—"

He hung up.

The second call to the Woodrow Wilson Hospital Emergency Room went far better.

"Emergency room."

It was a man. He sounded as tired as the woman at the first hospital.

"My name's Fredericks," said Chang. "President of the

Neighborhood Watch of East Rogers Park. I've been informed that a man was shot on Balmoral Street, a big, blond man in a sweatsuit. Did he come to your ER?"

"Yes," said the man. "He's in pain, but he should be fine."

"Good," said Chang. "Have the police been there?"

"Police brought him in," said the man.

"I would like to send him something or come and see him," said Chang.

"He's out of emergency and in a room. No visitors except his wife for a few days. He's heavily sedated."

"I'm sorry to hear that," said Chang. "Can you tell me his name so we can send him fresh flowers?"

"Let me see," said the man. A long silence and then "Lindqvist, Jonas Lindqvist."

And did he have my briefcase, my money? That was the question Chang could not find a way to ask, so he simply said "Thank you" and hung up the phone.

He should consider himself lucky. He had found the man in the second hospital. He knew the man's name.

All of which led to the question: How does one dress when he goes to a hospital where he may have to shoot a man a second time?

He settled on a navy blue suit and a somber tie. The pockets of the pants were deep and heavily lined. The gun slid into it easily although it was uncomfortably heavy.

He looked around his living room. It was a room with a southern view between two high-rises of Lake Shore Drive and a narrow slice of downtown. The sun was up now, morning traffic heavy going toward downtown.

Until he had been assaulted and robbed, he had been comfortable in his apartment. His furniture was plush, immaculate white as was the carpeting. He had no children, no wife, no dogs. When in the apartment he took off his shoes as did the infrequent visitor. There were paintings on the wall, erotic copies of originals by Gustav Klimt. One wall was completely filled, floor-to-ceiling, by a golden copy of *The Kiss*.

There was no television in this room. The living room was not for living or dying but for existing, passing through, an easing space when he entered through the front door and a restful memory when he came out of his bedroom. The bedroom had dark ebony furniture and an ebony bookcase filled with neatly lined up illustrated erotic literature in Chinese, Dutch, and French—none of which he could read. Somehow erotica was acceptable if it wasn't in English. A massive flat television screen covered much of the wall across from the foot of the bed.

With a last look and a sigh, gun heavy in his pocket, Robert E. Lee Chang adjusted his glasses and went through the door in search of the man he had shot and the money he had lost.

"I'll be fine," Iris said, touching Bill's cheek.

He had slept for almost two hours in the chrome-armed pink imitation leather chair next to her bed.

"You sure?" he said.

She looked tired, happy. He brushed a strand of hair from her face.

"I'm sure," she said. "I'm tired. I'll sleep. Go on."

"I won't be long," he said.

"You'll be as long as it takes," she said. "Go."

He stopped at the maternity room window to look at his daughter. Jane Mei was sleeping. Others around her were moving, crying. He watched for several minutes till the baby turned her head and clasped her hands together. It looked as if she were praying.

He felt reasonably rested. He also felt that he had to get to the scene of the shooting of Jonas Lindqvist while it was still reasonably fresh.

No crime scene unit had been called in for two reasons. First, unless Lindqvist died, and it didn't look as if he would, there was little chance of getting a team to the site. With the workload the crime scene people had, it would take more more than a robbery and shooting to get them on the case. Second, Bill wasn't even sure of where the site was. He had gone back to talk to Lindqvist.

Lindqvist had said something about being a punching bag for Rocky Graziano in a marching band. He had followed this with, "On Wisconsin." Lindqvist had also said, almost sung, "Entwined by winding arms on Balmoral."

Bill drove to Balmoral Street and, starting at Sheridan Road, began cruising slowly, looking at the names of sixties and seventies apartment buildings—yellow blocks streaked by years of rain, snow, and sleet that carried filth from street and sky.

Michigan Shores, Lake View Apartments, Sheridan Arms, King's Crown Apartments, and then, on the left side of the street two blocks in, East Wind Arms. Lots of parking spaces. People were at work, out shopping, exercising, having coffee, committing a crime.

Bill parked, got out of the car, and crossed the street. Standing on the sidewalk in front of the East Wind Arms, he looked around and looked down at the sidewalk. The bloodstains were clear, trailing off toward the lake. The first one was a splatter, large as a pie plate, and still not fully dry. He followed the trail. The stains got smaller and were morning sun dry and more brown than red, but unmistakable.

Jonas Lindqvist had lost a fair amount of blood. Bill followed the stains for half a block, then walked back to the first splatter in front of the apartment building. There was no bloodstain trail from the west. Lindqvist had been shot right here.

Bill checked the grass. Bending at the knees was almost impossible. His knees had long ago surrendered the last of their cartilage and given in to injury and rupture from which he would never recover. So, he leaned over, which wasn't good for a man his size with a chronic back problem.

How was he going to play with his daughter? When the boys had been small, he had played with them, picked them up, threw them in the air. They had played Baron Von Stufuss. First one to throw the other one off the sofa won. The boys always won. They also always laughed when he said Baron Von Shhhhhtufuss. They, particularly Michael, had loved to repeat "Baron Von Shhhhhhtufuss."

He hadn't played the game or any other with them very often, nor with his grandchildren. The job, the drinking had begun. The memories of tackles and possibilities lost had haunted him. He had been one lousy father. He wouldn't be with Jane Mei.

He found nothing in the grass. He hadn't really expected to find anything, but then again, he hadn't expected the thick glass door of the East Wind Arms to open and a Chinese man to step out, which is just what happened. Bill had been about to enter the building, check the list of tenants for Chinese names. The man who was coming out of the building might not be the one he was looking for, but he fit the bill.

The man was well dressed, looked nervous, and, judging from the sag of his right pocket, he was carrying something heavy in his pants.

Could be a coincidence. Maybe the apartment building was filled with well-dressed Chinese men carrying weapons.

Not likely.

For an instant, the man, lost in thought, did not see Hanrahan. Then their eyes met. No doubt in Chang's mind. This was a policeman. He looked like a policeman—big, burly, dark, rumpled suit, and very loose tie. Most of all it was the man's eyes.

A choice had to be made now. Chang could lie, bluff. He was good at it. It might work, but he had a clock ticking. Mr. Woo had set the clock and it was running. Chang did not want to deal with the police. They would find that he was carrying a weapon. They would want to know why. Maybe they would test it, discover that it had been used to shoot the big blond man whose name, he now knew, was Lindqvist.

Robert E. Lee Chang made a decision. It was, decidedly, the wrong one. He reached into his pocket and gripped the gun.

Later, he thought, I'll tell them I thought the man was about to mug me. Later, he thought, I'll tell them it was a mistake. I had not taken a gun from my pocket. I had taken a cell phone. I was going to punch in 911.

"Sir, I'm a police officer," Bill said.

That removed Chang's plan. No, he could say he didn't believe the man.

"Yes?"

"I'd like to ask you a few questions," the big policeman said, moving toward Chang.

"Me? About what?"

"Early this morning," said Bill, still advancing. "Man was shot right out here."

"Shot?" Chang said.

"You all right?"

"Yes. Why?"

"Your hand was on your stomach. I thought you might be in pain," said Bill, now close enough to reach out and touch Robert E. Lee.

"No," said Chang.

"Nobody hit you?" asked Bill.

"Hit me? No."

"Can you give me just a few minutes of your time here," said Bill. "A man's been shot. You might be able to help. Your cooperation would be greatly appreciated."

"I'm late," Chang said.

"I could arrest you," said Bill.

"For what?"

"Concealed weapon in your pocket."

Bill's hand went out and grabbed Chang's wrist. He slowly pulled the hand from the man's pocket.

"It's registered," said Chang.

"We'll check on that," Bill said. "And we'll see if it's been fired and if it matches the bullet we took from the man who was shot right here in front of your apartment building."

"I want a lawyer," Chang said.

"And you'll have one."

Bill loosened his grip on Chang's wrist. A mistake.

Chang grabbed the gun, turned, and ran. No chance Hanrahan could chase him and he certainly wasn't going to shoot him or even fire his weapon.

Chang ran, jamming the gun into his pocket. He was fast

even with the gun weighing him down, even with whatever pain had been inflicted on him during the night.

Bill didn't have his name, didn't know why he had shot Lindqvist, didn't know why he was running, but he would soon have answers. All he had to do was go through the door of the East Wind Arms, look at the names on the mailboxes, and start ringing bells.

9

The black man looked up as Abe and Officer Richard Danton came through the front door of the Anatolia. The man wore sagging work pants and an orange shirt that had the word *Illinois* written in block blue letters across the front. The man started to rise from the chair he sat in but Abe said, "I'll be right back."

The man sat again on the edge of the chair. He looked neither frightened nor interested. His mouth was tight-lipped, his face resigned.

Abe moved through a swing door. The chalk outlines of a man and a woman were cramped together on the floor of the small kitchen of the Anatolia Restaurant. The smells of blood, meat, and olive oil hung in the air.

There were two windows in the kitchen, both opaque, both closed and locked. A large refrigerator taking up most of the room hummed and rattled. Open shelves held spices and neatly stacked cream-colored plates rimmed with a blue line.

Blood spattered the wooden floor, the sink, the shelves, and the refrigerator.

There was barely enough room for Abe and Danton to stand without violating the outlines and little tents on the floor or stepping in brown patches and lines of blood, which were slowly coagulating and drying.

"Crime scene crew?" asked Abe, hands at his sides, thumbs twitching.

"Same as earlier," said Danton. "Flowers will call you when they have something."

Abe imagined the two outlines rising, dancing crazily, trying to tell him something, but unable to make contact.

"Tell me a story," said Abe, looking around the room.

Danton, who looked as if he had changed uniforms in the few hours since he had last seen Abe, flipped open his notebook and read: "Eight forty-seven. Dispatched to scene. Call came from Clark Jackson, sixty-two—"

"The man sitting out there," said Abe.

"The man out there," Danton confirmed.

"He says he arrived at approximately eight twenty to do his regular morning cleaning. He found the bodies, called 911."

"He have a key?" asked Abe.

"Yes, but he said he didn't have to use it. The door was unlocked. Officer Drybeck and I found the bodies. Both were dead. Death confirmed at nine eleven by dispatched paramedics. Crime scene unit arrived nine forty-one. Officer Angela Flowers was the lead. Both victims, man and woman, were stabbed twice, man in the chest and neck, woman in the face and chest. Both fully clothed. No weapon found yet."

Both Abe and Danton were reasonably sure that when one was found, if it was found, it would match the weapon used to kill Lemi Sahin a few hours ago, just forty yards from the door of the Anatolia.

"Witnesses?" asked Abe.

"No," said Danton.

"None but God," said Abe, "and try as we might we've never been able to get him to testify."

"Not so far," said Danton, putting his notebook back in his pocket.

Abe looked at him.

"A sense of humor can sustain a man at times like this," said Abe.

"I wasn't trying to be funny," said Danton.

"Neither was I," said Abe.

Clark Jackson looked up when Abe came back to where he sat. Danton was still in the kitchen searching for a bloody knife neither he nor Abe expected to find.

"You have breakfast this morning?" asked Abe sitting next to the man.

"Yeah, rye toast, a couple of eggs mixed up in the frying pan, a cup of yesterday's coffee," said the man evenly. "Greasy frying pan and two-day-old coffee grounds'll be waiting for me when I get home."

"You okay?" asked Abe.

Jackson shrugged.

"As okay as any day," he said.

"You just found two dead people."

Jackson looked up.

"My war I found lots of dead people," said Jackson. "Nam. Mostly North Vietnamese. Some South. Lots of civilians. Some of our own. I've seen the dead. They don't surprise me. Living surprise me all the time. I try to avoid them."

"Your war was a long time ago," said Abe.

"To some," Jackson agreed. "To some."

"The dead man and woman . . . ," Abe said.

"Turkalus," said Jackson. "I'll give it to you fast and easy. Then I've got this place and other places to clean up. The Turkalus were decent people, at least to me. Paid in cash and always on time without having to be reminded. They didn't ask me questions, didn't try to get me to talk."

"You get to know any of the customers?"

"Never been here when the place was open, only in the morning like now. I never heard either of them talk about troubles, enemies, grudges, just worried about deliveries and argued all the time about bringing her mother here to live."

"Mind holding out your hands?" asked Abe.

Jackson held out his hands. They looked clean.

"You didn't touch anything since you came in?"

"Nothing but the phone," said Jackson. "Didn't have to touch the dead. I knew they were dead. Then I just sat here and waited."

Silence.

"They fought back," Jackson finally said. "I could see it. They didn't go gentle. I could see the signs."

"The signs?"

"I was a medic in Nam," said Jackson. "Planning to go to med school, working at the University of Illinois hospitals in the Center. I could have stayed out of the war. Should have. Then . . . I never went to med school. I grabbed a mop, a broom, and hot water and held on. Still holding. Not sure what I'm holding for. Anything else?"

Abe got Clark Jackson's phone number and let him go.

The restaurant was silent. Through the windows, Abe looked at the traffic going by, listened to the sound.

Questions. Why had Turkalu and his wife been killed? It

had to be tied to Sahin's death, but how? Common sense dictated that murders in the kitchen had taken place between the time Abe had talked to the restaurant owner and the time Clark Jackson had discovered their bodies. Why had they been killed? Why had the killer gone back to the restaurant after killing Sahin? What should Abe have noticed that he had missed?

The phone in his pocket began to play. He took it out, opened it, and said, "Hello."

"Abe, this a bad time?" Bess asked.

"There have been better."

"I could have left you a message."

"Have we ever had Turkish food?" he asked.

"You have a gift for non sequiturs," said Bess.

"Or a curse."

"Remember tonight," she said.

"I can't remember it till I've experienced it," he said. "When it's passed, I'll have the luxury or trauma of remembrance."

"Abe, stop."

"I'm stopped. Tonight I give a speech."

"That's right," she said. "You know what you're going to say?"

"That we live in perilous times."

"Be specific," she said.

"We live in perilous times and Joel Becker broke his leg last month falling down from his front porch."

"Barry told me this morning that he's still a kid," she said. "I agreed. The evidence stood before me."

"That's progress," said Abe. "He told me he wasn't a man. A negative has been replaced by a positive.

"We'll take him and Melissa out for a pizza tomorrow night," Lieberman said.

"Or for Turkish food."

"Or for Turkish food," Abe agreed.

"They'd rather have pizza."

"So would I."

"Settled," said Bess. "Pizza. You and I can go for Turkish some time on our own. What is Turkish food?"

"I'll find out," he said.

"Abe, I just called the hospital. Iris and the baby are fine. We're sending flowers to their house. She should be going home tomorrow. Abe . . ."

The pause was too long. Such pauses, Abe had learned, were a prelude to disastrous news.

"Yes."

"Lisa is pregnant."

"It's pandemic," he said. "You'll be next."

"This isn't a joke."

"I'll stop laughing."

The subtext was there without being stated. Their daughter Lisa had, essentially, left her children to be raised by Bess and Abe. Lisa was thirty-six, a biochemist, and the wife of Marvin Alexander, M.D., a black pathologist. She lived in California and had a lifelong love-hate relationship with Abe, the origin and fuel of which were beyond Abe's comprehension and Lisa's willingness or ability to articulate. The odds of her successfully bringing up a new baby were slim.

"They'll have a little brown baby," Abe said. "That's what Ingrid Bergman said in *Murder on the Orient Express,* that she took care of little brown babies."

"This isn't a movie, Abe."

"Unfortunately it is not. It is the chaos of mingled purposes," he said. "What do Barry and Melissa think about it?"

"I haven't told them," Bess said.

"Lisa can tell them."

"She wants us to do it."

"And you want me to do it," he said.

"I'm usually the bearer of domestic bombs," she said. "It's your turn."

"When I get home," he said. "What else?"

"I love you. Hard as that may be to imagine."

"Fortunately, I have an active imagination," he said. "I've got to go."

Abe closed the phone and returned it to his pocket. It started to play almost immediately.

"Rabbi," said Bill Hanrahan.

"Good morning, Father Murphy."

"Not so good," said Bill.

"Iris, the baby?"

Abe looked around the restaurant, the walls with photographs of villas on the Bosphorus, hills covered with small houses overlooked by jutting mosques, a girl kneeling next to a goat.

"No, they're fine. I caught a weird case this morning."

"You want to hear weird?" asked Abe, now sure he could smell blood through the odor of grease.

"We'll compare," said Bill. "Loser pays for lunch."

"Early for lunch," said Abe. "You hungry?"

"Yeah."

"I'll force myself. Red hots at Sammy's?"

"Half an hour."

"Half an hour, Father Murph."

Abe didn't even get the phone to his pocket this time.

"Yes," he said.

"Viejo, killed any bad guys yet this morning?"

"Not yet," Abe said.

"But you came close in the park, right?"

"You talked to Herve," Abe said.

"He talked to me," said Emiliano "El Perro" Del Sol. "Now I wanna talk to you."

The section of the Hispanic community in which El Perro reigned spread out north, west, and south from North Avenue. In that territory and even beyond, El Perro was legend. It was conceded by all, including El Perro himself, that he was probably quite mad. He liked it that way. The twenty-five or so Tentaculos—Puerto Ricans, Mexicans, Panamanians, and Guatemalans—who followed his orders, brandished their leader's reputation and did their best to keep from drawing his considerable wrath.

El Perro had once crushed a man's face and skull in with a lamp for looking away from him when he entered a bar. It mattered little that the man had not even noticed the gang leader's entrance. El Perro was convinced that the man had been repulsed by the gang leader's scars.

El Perro was fast approaching the age of twenty-five. The scars on his face, earned in knife fights and in the boxing ring, had not all blended into his cocoa skin. Several had gone a contrasting white. Emiliano had been a successful Golden Gloves lightweight fighter, and was a fearsome pro for three fights when he was thrown out of the boxing game for almost biting off the lower lip of an opponent and following it up by pummeling the referee.

El Perro was known to have a symbiotic and friendly relationship with Abe Lieberman, who had a reputation for meting out instant justice. The Lieberman justice was dispensed not with the frenzy of El Perro but with a quiet deliberation that would have been the envy of Clint Eastwood when he was making all those ketchup movies. Twice El

Viejo had come to El Perro to bypass the law to exact punishment. El Perro had been happy to oblige. No, he had been joyous.

To the degree that he could, Lieberman provided protection for all but the worst of the crimes of El Perro and the Tentaculos. In turn, El Perro provided information and, on occasion, provided favors for Lieberman that walked around the edges of the law.

The two men also shared a passion for the Cubs, though El Perro's extended only to the Hispanic players on the team.

"I'm kind of busy today, Emiliano," said Abe.

"Dead fuckin' Turkeys, right?"

"You are well-informed."

"Have to be, Viejo. Can you believe there are crazy people out there don't like me? Can you imagine that?"

El Perro laughed. Abe could hear the voices of others laughing nervously in the background.

"No," said Abe. "You are humble and lovable."

"Fuckin' right. You'll wanna hear what I've got and it's not coming over the phone."

"Where can I hear it?" asked Abe.

"I'm sittin' in El Marketa on Clybourne. Know this place?"

"I do."

"Sure. El Viejo knows this city like the hairs on his face."

"I'll be there in half an hour."

"You hungry?"

"No, but my partner is."

"Hey, okay, bring the Irish. My doctor cousin over there in the hospital tells me Irish's Chink wife had a baby. I'm sending him a gift basket, toys, stuff like that. Nice, huh?"

"Thoughtful," said Abe.

"Half an hour," said El Perro. "I've got a present for you."

Emiliano hung up. Abe punched the buttons on his phone before another call could come through.

"Father Murph, you in the mood for Mexican food?"

They had a name: Jonas Lindqvist.

They had a place: Woodrow Wilson Hospital.

What Elsie and Jamie Cuervo did not have was a plan.

They didn't even know why Lindqvist was in the hospital. They were both sure that they had not hit him hard enough to send him to an emergency room. He was a big man. What if he had a heart attack? If they caused him to have a heart attack and he died? Murder?

Jamie sat in the waiting room facing the reception desk and the woman behind it. The woman's glasses were thick, her white frizzy hair curly. She wore a look of bewilderment as she looked up at Elsie, who had put on a dress and a sad smile.

There were four people waiting besides Jamie. A young Hispanic woman, pretty, sat with a little girl about two years old who waddled away and was brought back by the yellow rope around her waist. The child would feel the tug, plop into a sitting position on the floor, get up, go to her mother for a hug, and start the whole process again. The third person waiting was a bald man with a paunch in a White Sox shirt whose lower lip pouted out as he leaned forward to read the copy of *Newsweek* in his hands. Finally a man with wild black and gray hair and a matching beard slouched over asleep. The man was wearing at least two sweaters.

"I'm sorry, Mr. Lindqvist isn't receiving visitors, only immediate family," the woman behind the desk said to Elsie.

"I'm his cousin," said Elsie.

"Not close enough unless he has no immediate family, wife, children, parents, brothers, sisters, all of which he does have."

"What happened to him?" Elsie asked.

"Trauma," said the woman, looking over Elsie's shoulder at the paunchy man in the White Sox T-shirt. He had a Marine insignia above his right wrist and a cartoon bug on his left arm. The bug was carrying a gun twice his size with the word *Awesome* under it.

The paunchy man was growing impatient, fidgeting, putting his *Newsweek* aside, standing, starting a slow waddle from right foot to left.

"Trauma?" asked Elsie.

"Gunshot wound," said the woman behind the counter, pulling her attention from the paunchy man. "He's resting comfortably."

Elsie got it now. The sound they had heard—the cracking sound she and Jamie heard when they were running away with the briefcase. The Chinese guy must have had a gun, shot the jogger. It could have been them.

"He's not going to die or anything, is he?"

"We all die, dear. It's not my place to speculate on the mortality of individuals."

"Thank you," said Elsie.

The paunchy man muscled past her and said to the woman behind the desk, "Teresa Mangoliani. I'm her brother."

The man was twice Elsie's size, but Elsie could have laid him out with two quick punches. At the moment, she didn't really feel like laying anyone out.

"You lookin' for somethin'?" the paunchy man asked Elsie.

Elsie didn't answer. She went over to Jamie who stood up.

"He's here. They won't let us see him," Elsie said.

"What's wrong with him?"

"Chinese guy shot him."

"Why?"

"He was handy. We weren't."

"So," said Jamie, "we just hope he doesn't some day recognize us or do we get out of town? Kansas City?"

"No," said Elsie looking back at the paunchy man who was still at the reception desk. "We get to him."

It was at this point that Robert E. Lee Chang stepped into the waiting room. Elsie saw him and said, "Shit."

Jamie followed her eyes, turned his head, and saw Chang who looked around nervously.

"How did he find us?" Jamie asked.

"I don't know," said Elsie.

Chang looked around the room, saw Elsie and Jamie, and kept on looking around.

"He doesn't recognize us," said Jamie.

"Or he's being slick," Elsie said.

Jamie nodded. D. D. Page in the *Sun-Times* had once called Elsie a slick fighter. Elsie hadn't forgotten. She tried to live up to the adjective and she thought she could detect someone who shared her title.

"I don't think so," said Jamie. "He doesn't recognize us."

The Chinese man walked directly toward them, brushed past them, and went to the reception desk where he stood behind the paunchy man who was still arguing with the reception lady.

Elsie imagined decking the paunchy loudmouth, the Chinese guy acting as referee, counting out the downed man.

The Chinese guy looked at his watch, adjusted his glasses, and looked around at Jamie and Elsie, who were watching him. His eyes met Elsie's. Elsie touched Jamie's arm and said, "Sit down. Talk. Say whatever. Look at me, not at him."

"Let's go," said Jamie. "That's talking. We can take the chance he didn't get a good look at us or maybe we find him when he gets out of the hospital."

The Chinese guy moved to the reception desk as the paunchy man finally moved away with a visitor's pass in hand. He had bullied and worn down the frazzled receptionist.

"I'm going to do it," she said.

"Do what?"

"Wait here," she said, following the paunchy man down a hall.

Jamie waited. The Chinese guy was saying something to the receptionist. He was being very quiet. Jamie couldn't hear anything but ". . . Mr. Lindqvist's attorney." Then ". . . his signature in my presence."

The reception lady blinked in apparent bewilderment and handed the Chinese guy a pass. The Chinese guy walked quickly down the same corridor where the paunchy man and Elsie had gone.

The worst, absolute worst part of being a boxer was waiting in the locker room before a fight. Something always itched, always. He would start scratching with the thumb of his gloves. Then there would be more places to scratch, more thinking to do. He couldn't sit before a match. He danced around the locker room, scratching, thinking about the fight, thinking about what he was supposed to remember. Ninety percent plus was not thinking, just letting the body take over, knowing, hoping it would retain the training. No time to think during the fight. Thinking took too long.

Jamie couldn't stand it. He couldn't get up to dance around the waiting room and he was feeling the first itch. He got up and followed the Chinese guy down the corridor, hoping no one would stop him.

Elsie got into the elevator with the paunchy man in the White Sox shirt who glared at her and pressed the circle with the number four in it. Elsie pressed number six. The doors started to close. The Chinese guy stepped in, looked at the illuminated buttons, pressed three, and turned to face the closing doors.

Good news: she knew the floor where Lindqvist was a patient.

Bad news: with the Chinese guy in the elevator, she couldn't lay out the fat man and take his pass.

The elevator doors started to close. Elsie looked past the Chinese guy and saw Jamie in a near jog heading toward her. Too late. The doors closed. The elevator started to move up.

Elsie looked at the paunchy man who glared at her. He needed a shave, a shower, and a really strong mouthwash. Good, thought Elsie, make me hate you, make it easier. When Elsie fought, she always wanted to hate her opponent. She would find something to hate. Once it had been the fact that Crystal Amendorn was married to a con who was locked away for armored car robbery. Elsie had imagined Crystal and her husband robbing the bank where Elsie and Jamie had an account. Belinda Crawford had said she would knock Elsie out by the third round. Easy to hate her. Others had attitude or bad tattoos or taunting smiles. Elsie had to hate to fight. Hating the paunchy man was easy.

The Chinese guy got off at three. When the door was almost closed, Elsie stepped forward and pressed the Stop button.

"What the fuck are you—" the paunchy man began, reaching forward to grab Elsie's shoulder.

Elsie spun and threw a right to the man's stomach. The man staggered backward against the wall. Elsie stepped in and threw a left to the man's jaw, not a hard left that might break the bones in her hands, more like a hard close-fisted slap that dropped the man to the floor in a sitting position. The elevator rocked when he hit the floor.

The man was having trouble catching his breath. There was no fight left in him, just an openmouthed hyperventilating.

Elsie had to shove him first to one side and then the other to search his pockets. The pass was next to a wallet crammed with singles. Elsie took the money and the man's keys and shoved them in the pocket of her dress. Elsie wanted the man to crawl out of the elevator when it went up to six and sob for help.

She wanted the man to think about his lost money and keys and forget about the pass. Maybe his description of her wouldn't be so good. He would have to tell the police that the robber was an unarmed one-hundred-and-eighteen-pound woman.

Elsie pushed the Open button and, as the doors opened, she reached back to click the Stop button and send the elevator and the moaning man up to the sixth floor.

There was one long hallway. A woman in white was pushing a cart toward the nursing station at the far end of the corridor. At the nursing station, a man in white with a stethoscope around his neck was talking to a woman in white. In this world of white, neither of the people at the nursing station looked down the hall toward the Chinese man who entered a room on the left.

Elsie, pass in hand, stood still, considering what she was going to do. Chances were more than good that the Chinese guy was after the money Elsie and Jamie had stolen. Lindqvist might be telling the Chinese guy right now that he didn't have the man's money, that it had been taken by a man and a woman, that he had a good look at them.

The elevator was on the sixth floor by now. The paunchy man would be crawling out, shouting. Whatever Elsie was going to do, she had to do now.

Elsie strode down the hallway, hoping that Lindqvist's room was a single and not a double. Another patient would mean another problem. She had enough problems. Elsie paused outside the door through which the Chinese guy had gone. After a heartbeat, she stepped into the room.

10

Killing gave him no pleasure. Neither did it disturb him. In fact, very little in the world, including life and death, moved him. People he dealt with called him Effendi because he had presence, wore good clothes, always appeared calm. They confused cold indifference with deep thought.

He sat in the dull white cubbyhole of a room at a chipped Formica table. A bottle of Coca-Cola, pieces of ice floating inside it just the way he liked it, sat before him.

The sound of Turkish music turned down low dreamily filled the room. He was transported to the streets of Istanbul and Ankara, the sounds of voices in Turkish, the smells of food, the faces of people who looked ancient and familiar.

What transported him was the packet in his jacket pocket. It was almost too large to fit, but he managed. Before doing so he had smelled the ancient and worn leather wrapping and had even put his tongue to it to taste the past.

Killing Dr. Lemi Oraz Sahin and taking the packet had

been easy. Sahin had not even struggled. He hadn't believed that his life was about to end, not at the hand of the familiar man from whom he had just bought the journal of Aziz. Sahin at the moment of the first thrust could still envision a tomorrow he would never see. With the next thrust, hope was gone and a dreaded, bewildered realization had replaced it. It was not that death was upon him, but that he could not comprehend the nonexistence of tomorrow.

After he had killed Sahin, he had gone back to kill the only witnesses. At first, Turkalu and his wife had suspected nothing. They were lulled by his tranquility, his reassuring patter when he entered the kitchen. They were tired. It was very late and they had had a long day. Besides they knew him, wanted to hear what he was saying, watched him casually pick up a slice of lamb from a platter and throw it into his mouth. They did not see the bloody knife behind his back.

And then when he had thrust the knife firmly into Turkalu's neck, the restaurant owner had reached out to grab him. It was too late. The second thrust sent the blade in with a satisfying thunking sound. The wife stood in stunned horror. He stabbed her as deeply as he could, between her ribs, into her heart. Turkalu had sagged to the floor. His wife, mouth open, one hand futilely trying to stop the blood, fell to her knees and then on her back. When he was sure they were dead, he had returned to the restaurant. Through the drapes on the window he could see the flashing of lights. The police had gotten there quickly, much too quickly. The body of Lemi Sahin had been discovered. There was nothing to do but remain in the darkness till the police had left.

And then the little dog-faced Jew policeman had knocked at the door and wouldn't leave. He had been forced to play the role of Turkalu. He had done it successfully.

Now he had another buyer, a far better and more wealthy buyer.

The journal, he was sure, was worth at least $25,000 solely as an important historical document alone. He was sure it was worth far more, perhaps as much as half a million dollars, to those who would want to present it to the world, to change history.

He had made the call two nights earlier and told the man in Turkey simply, "I have the Aziz document. I have read it. It is all you want it to be. Let's meet. You make a generous offer and you get the document. You fail to please me and I offer it to those who would like it destroyed."

The man had agreed. A time and place had been set when his emissaries would take the document and examine it.

With most others he had dealt with, he would not have taken the chance of turning the journal over for examination, but this was one of the wealthiest men in the world. Even half a million dollars would not be sufficient reason for betrayal. He had known about this potential buyer for years, had done his research. The wealthy Turk was as honest as the killer was not.

It was only after the time and location of the examination of the journal was arranged that the killer had decided to go ahead with his original plan to sell it to Sahin. He had set it up, put work into it, only now the sale to Sahin would be a bonus. The doctor would have the journal in his hands for only minutes before the killer took it from him.

The money was paramount. He had plans, but it wasn't just the money. Power, intrigue, a small thrill penetrating his lack of emotion. It was the same with women. He could rise, penetrate, release, and feel only the teasing instant of satisfaction, never the full response he sought and saw in the prostitutes he paid for and the women he seduced.

He lived alone. He was known. He was a respected voice of the Turkish community, a man who was selected for committees, asked to speak, even honored.

He was also a murderer.

The door to the room opened letting in more of the music and a young woman tucked her head in and said, "It's time, Effendi."

"Thank you."

He rose. It was time to work.

The door closed behind Elsie Cuervo, who found herself looking across the room at the big blond man who lay asleep in the bed, his mouth open. Next to the bed stood the Chinese man, who blinked, pushed his slipping glasses back up his nose, and ran his tongue nervously across his lower lip.

"I'm his lawyer," the man said.

Elsie knew that he was most certainly not the lawyer of the man in the bed. He was the one whose briefcase Jamie and Elsie had taken. It was clear from his declaration that he either had no memory of Elsie or he was bluffing.

"I'm his sister," Elsie said. "I don't remember Artie saying anything about a lawyer."

"I thought his name was Jonas," said Chang, his hand moving toward his pocket.

"It is," said Elsie. "We call him Artie. It's a family thing. He's not supposed to have visitors outside the family."

"But," said Chang, "I have very important business with him. It can't wait. A matter almost of life and death."

Elsie knew what the man wanted and she knew there was no way she could let the man talk to the man in the bed. The sleeping man might talk, tell the Chinese guy that a man and woman had taken his money, tell him what Jamie looked like.

He might even sit up, point a finger at Elsie and say, "She did it."

No way she could let that happen.

Then it struck her. What the hell was he doing here? His money had been stolen. Why hadn't he just gone to the police? Answer: he didn't want the police to know he had the money. Question: why? Answer: because the money was hot, maybe stolen or otherwise illegal.

The door behind Elsie opened suddenly and hit the wall with a crack. Jamie came in. Jonas Lindqvist woke up dreamily and looked around at the nightmare. There was the Chinese guy who had shot him. There was the woman and the man who had beaten Jonas and taken the Chinese guy's money. They couldn't be here. But they were. Why?

Jamie closed the door.

Now the Chinese guy had a gun in his hand.

"I remember," said Chang, looking at Elsie. "You are all working together. Someone told you I was carrying the delivery money. I must have that money back."

Chang was aiming the gun at the one defenseless person in the room, Jonas Lindqvist.

"You won't tell the police," said Elsie.

"I'll tell someone far more dangerous for you than the police," said Chang, looking now at Elsie and Jamie. "I'll tell the man whose money you stole. His name is Mr. Woo. Do you know that name?"

"No," said Elsie. "Tell him. We're keeping the money."

"The fighters," said Jonas dreamily, suddenly remembering their faces from a television interview.

Chang looked at him.

"Television, saw them," said Jonas, turning his eyes toward Chang. "You shot me in the balls."

"Where is the money?" Chang demanded, looking at Elsie, his lower lip quivering.

"Search me," said Jonas. "No, don't. Pain. This is just a nightmare, isn't it?"

The door started to open. Chang quickly pocketed his gun. Two nurses came into the room and looked at the trio around the room.

"One visitor at a time," said the older of the two nurses, a tired-looking, thin woman with no-nonsense eyes. "Family members only."

None of the three looked like they belonged to the family Lindqvist.

"Let me see your passes."

Chang fumbled for his and presented it. Elsie held hers up. Jamie said, "I can't find it."

"You didn't look," said the nurse.

"I tried to find it before I came in the room to see . . ."

"Jonas," Elsie supplied.

"Rina," said the older nurse. "Call Security."

The younger nurse, buxom, clear skinned, wide-eyed, who looked more like a relative of the man in bed than anyone in the room, moved to the phone.

"A man was mugged in the elevator a few minutes ago."

"We've been here for half an hour," said Elsie.

"At least," Chang agreed.

"No," said Jonas. "A few minutes. Nightmare. He shot me. They took his money. I hurt like shit. I really do. Put me out again, please."

"We're leaving," said Elsie.

The young nurse was on the phone.

"I'm late for an appointment," said Chang.

"Wait here," the older nurse ordered in a voice that

made it clear that she was accustomed to being obeyed.

"Put me out," murmured Jonas, closing his eyes.

Chang sighed, shook his head, and showed his gun. The older nurse saw it and said calmly, "Maybe you should all leave."

The young nurse had not seen the gun. She never did. She turned from the phone in time to see the three visitors leave the room.

The older nurse moved to the phone, picked it up, and punched in two numbers.

"Three people," she said. "One is Chinese. He has a gun. The others are a man and woman. Young. Man is Hispanic. They're in the corridor on the third floor."

"Are they gone?" asked Jonas.

"They're gone," said the nurse. "Would you like us to call your wife?"

"Not especially."

"All right."

"I'm not a violent man," he said.

"I know, Mr. Lindqvist," said the older nurse.

"How long before I feel like a human being?"

"A few weeks," she said as the young nurse opened the door a crack to look down the corridor.

"I'm a chef, mostly pastry," Jonas said.

"I know."

"I've got strong hands."

"I can see that."

"If that man with the gun who shot me comes back, I will strangle him."

There was an exit door halfway down the corridor. Elsie and Jamie went through it and Robert E. Lee Chang hurried past them toward the elevators praying to gods of all ilk that when the doors opened he would not be facing security guards.

The door opened. There was a security guard inside. He was dressed in navy slacks and a blue shirt with an identification tag on his shirt pocket. The man was big, about sixty, carrying extra weight, an extra chin, and a holstered gun at his hip.

Chang's gun was out before the man could react.

Lindqvist had thought he was in a nightmare. Robert E. Lee Chang was sure that he was living one. The security guard took his hand away from his weapon and Chang got into the elevator. He said nothing, kept the gun on the guard, motioned him against the wall, and pushed the button for the second floor. When the door opened, Chang motioned with his gun for the guard to get off. The man was happy to do so.

The elevator doors closed and Chang felt himself going down. He put the gun back in his pocket. It had been a disaster, a horrible disaster, a complete failure. No, almost a failure. What was it Lindqvist had said? Fighters? Television? Did he know what he was talking about?

The door opened. Three people let him come out. One of them was in a wheelchair. Chang bumped his knee on the chair as the trio moved past him.

Then Chang began a trot, trying to make it look as if he were in a hurry and not in a panic. He passed doctors, nurses, patients, visitors. They were a blur. He went through the door to the parking lot.

Now he ran to his car, aiming at the door with the remote on his key chain. He opened the door and looked around. Six cars down Elsie and Jamie stood beside a car. They had, miraculously, not seen Chang.

He sat behind the wheel, willing himself to be calm, to

meditate. Meditation had never worked for him in the past and it didn't work now.

He should flee the parking lot before the police arrived, blocked the exits, but he didn't. He waited till the couple had backed out of their parking space, the man behind the wheel. Then he backed out slowly.

He would follow them. They would lead him to Mr. Woo's money. They had to. He had some hope now and a great deal of fear.

Mr. Woo would not find his tale interesting. Mr. Woo would almost certainly not listen to Robert E. Lee Chang's excuses. Mr. Woo would do something quite painful if Chang did not return the money. Mr. Woo would probably do something painful even if he did return the money.

The Cuervos drove east on Wilson Avenue. Chang followed.

"Piedras is not perfect," said Emiliano "El Perro" Del Sol.

"I'm aware of his shortcomings," said Abe, looking at the big, almost feeble-minded, enforcer of the Tentaculos.

Piedras, the stone. Ironically Piedras was really the Enforcer's last name. He simply lived up to it. Lieberman knew for a fact that the somber-faced Piedras was responsible for three deaths and numerous efficient beatings. One of the deaths was the result of Piedras throwing a rival gang member out of a third-floor hospital window.

They were in a small private dining room at the rear of Le Marketa Restaurant on Clybourne Avenue. One solid wooden table, ten chairs, two windows covered with white lace curtains with little balls of material dangling at the fringes, on the walls a fresco of dancing girls with white toothy smiles in billowing white dresses. A festive room.

El Perro sat at the far end of the table. Piedras stood next to him on the right. Along the walls under the dancing girls stood the Viera brothers, Herve, Contraras, and Raymondo, the latest Tentaculo, also known as Chuculito. Chuculito was fourteen years old, his face that of a child. His goal was to be as good with a knife as James Coburn in *The Magnificent Seven*. Chuculito, El Perro had told Lieberman with pride, could outdraw any gun with his knife.

Raymondo was the replacement for Chuculo Fernandez, who had died protecting Iris Hanrahan from a man even more mad than El Perro. The sacrifice of Chuculo was a card El Perro held but never needed to play for Bill Hanrahan. Hanrahan owed El Perro and he knew it and was more than just a little uncomfortable with the understanding between him and the scarred and murderous rooster across the room.

"Try that tapas stuff," said El Perro, pointing to the plate in front of Abe and Bill, who stood across the table from El Perro. "*Callos a Madrilena*, beef gut and pig snout, Spanish stuff."

Abe picked up one of the small servings and took a bite.

"Delicious," said Abe.

El Perro laughed and said, "I told you. Viejo will eat anything. Irish?"

"I'll pass," said Bill.

"How's your Chink wife? The baby?"

El Perro, Bill knew, was not being intentionally insulting. Besides, he owed the lunatic.

"They're fine," said Bill.

"I sent her . . . what did I send her?" El Perro asked.

One of the Viera brothers, Bill didn't know which was which, said, "Toys and *frutas*."

"Toys and a basket of fruit," said El Perro. "Big one from Alesandro's bodega."

"Thanks," said Bill.

"*De nada,* Irish." He turned to Abe and got serious. "It's nice to have cop friends. Piedras has a problem, Viejo."

"Incomprehensible," said Abe. "*Dificile à créer.*"

Abe finished the tapas serving, rubbed his fingers together, considered reaching for another and did.

"You really like that stuff, huh?" asked El Perro.

"I'd ask for the recipe but my wife wouldn't make it," he said. "Not kosher. Tell me about Piedras's problem."

"Oh, yeah. He sort of, you know, played a little too hard with a guy owns a computer store. Guy named Solazano. Arm sort of got broken. I think a few teeth."

El Perro looked at Piedras, who nodded in confirmation.

"Yeah, a few teeth. Solazano told a cop. Now the cops out of North are looking for Piedras."

"Cop have a name?" asked Abe, unable to resist another tapas.

"Bingham. Bing-ham," said El Perro.

"I know him," said Hanrahan.

"You talk to him, make him see that it was all very innocent. Piedras just got carried away and the other guy started to get rough."

"With Piedras that would be a mistake," said Abe. "We'll talk to Bingham."

"He's a reasonable man," added Bill.

"Give Viejo and Irish flyers," said El Perro.

Piedras picked off two yellow sheets from a pile on the table and brought them to the policemen. In the upper left-hand corner of the flyer was a photograph of El Perro with his arms out and a smile on his face. It was a picture that would make anyone who knew him or knew of him feel a shiver of dread.

The words on the sheet were in Spanish and English. Their essence was that El Perro was going to preach on Sunday morning in the Neuva Iglesia de Esperanza, The New Church of Hope, on North Avenue.

"No more bingo parlor," said El Perro, showing a smile not unlike the one he wore in the flyer Abe held in his hand. "It's a church now."

"I thought you were a Catholic," said Abe.

"I am," El Perro said, crossing himself, "but there's big money in the church business, you know? I just get up there and talk and stuff about God and Heaven and Hell and shit like that."

Abe looked at Bill, who did his best not to respond.

"You come on Sunday," El Perro said. "Place will be full. We're rounding up people, but I'll save a seat."

"Thanks," said Abe.

"Okay," said El Perro. "Business. Here's the prize. This morning, Viejo, you ran Herve Rodriguez out of Lincoln Park."

"I did."

"They were following this guy," said El Perro. "You figured a mugging. Viejo, you were wrong. They were going to put that guy down forever. You didn't stop a mugging. You stopped a hit."

"I'm listening."

El Perro nodded and said, "I'm thinking of becoming a partner in this place. What you think?"

"You are an entrepreneur," said Abe.

"And that's a good thing, right?"

"Generally," said Abe. "The hit in the park."

"Yeah. Guy who paid for it was a Turkey, an A-rab something, you know? Not too old. Full of shit, full of himself, you know? Thinks he's hot shit like the A-rab with the sword in *The Mummy*. Herve didn't see him. Pinn Taibo just told me, he told him Gimpy in the park has a big mouth. Anyways, this Turkey with big white teeth, which I can have knocked out if you want, Viejo, this Turkey doesn't want Gimpy's mouth working anymore forever. Herve's out of the job, but the other two, Pinn and José Taibo, they still want to collect. They ain't Tentaculos, but you want me to stop them, they are stopped. You want them dead, they're dead. Gimpy and the Turkey too."

"I would appreciate your just stopping the Taibo brothers," said Abe.

"Then they are stopped," said El Perro, raising both hands.

"Does Herve know why the man with remarkably good teeth wants Gimpy killed?"

El Perro cocked his head to the right to look at Herve who nodded no.

"I guess you'll have to ask Pinn Taibo," said El Perro. "What about Piedras and his problem?"

"I think we can take care of his problem," said Abe.

"Piedras wouldn't hurt nobody just for nothin'," said El Perro.

"I'll try to sort out that triple negative later," said Abe, "but experience has taught me how gentle Piedras is."

"Question," said Hanrahan, looking at El Perro.

Abe looked at his partner.

"You know a boxer, has a tough wife, might also be a boxer. He's probably a middleweight," said Bill.

"Hey, before the *maricones* took away my license, I fought a guy named Jamie Cuervo. Just coming up then. Good fighter. Jab. Jab. Jab. Hook down low. Cross up high. Then *wham, wham* to the chest."

El Perro stood up and demonstrated on Herve, just missing him till the last shot, which landed solidly against Herve's chest. Herve gritted his teeth and closed his eyes, but he didn't go down or bend forward.

"Same thing. Over and over," said El Perro, turning to face Abe and Bill. "I knew what this Cuervo was going to do. Could have beaten him, you know, but I was disqualified by the fuckin' wop referee for head butting. I think I broke Cuervo's nose. Third round. I think I was ahead on points. Maybe he was. His wife was a fighter too. I don't remember her name."

"Thanks," said Bill.

"What did Cuervo do?" asked El Perro.

"I just want to talk to him," said Bill.

"Por cierto," said El Perro. "Okay, what else?"

"Nada," said Abe.

"Viejo, I got a starting lineup for the Cubs. All Latino."

The Viera brothers were nodding in support of El Perro's plan. Contraras blinked. Chuculito smiled, his unblinking eyes on Abe. Piedras stood like a stone and Herve stood in pain, trying not to be sick.

"This is the year of the Cubs. How long since they won a World Series, Viejo?"

"Ninety-eight years," said Abe. "October 14, 1908, almost 40,000 days ago. Eighteen years longer than the White Sox or Red Sox when they finally won. Almost 16,000 regular season games. They've had 1,500 players, forty-nine managers since 1908."

El Perro suddenly punched the nearest man on his left, one of the Viera brothers, who winced in pain but didn't put his hand on the arm that was hit. El Perro was smiling, the punch an expression of joy.

"See," said El Perro, looking around at his men and boys. "This is our fuckin' year. We got to win. Statistics on our side. Hispanics on our side. Everybody's gonna be happy. We'll have a big party."

"Some people, fans, like having the record," said Abe.

"Crazy people," said El Perro, running a finger along the white scar on his face. "What do you think, Irish?"

"He's a White Sox fan," said Lieberman.

"And you are partners?"

"I'm trying make him see the light," said Lieberman. "We've got to go now."

El Perro shook his head. "See you soon, Viejo. *Y tu tambien,* Irish. May your White Sox swim in shit inside a sick cow."

"I love you too," said Bill.

"Hasta luego," said Abe.

"Hey," called El Perro. "Don' forget Sunday. Church."

When they were back on Clybourne outside the restaurant, Bill said, "That was fun."

He reached into his pocket and took out his phone.

"Had it on vibrate," he explained, looking at the screen. "Hospital."

He punched in redial as Abe waited.

"Hanrahan," Bill said and then listened. "Thanks. I'll be right there."

He flipped his phone closed and said, "Hell is breaking loose at the hospital."

"Iris?" asked Abe.

"Nothing to do with her. Guy had his testicle shot off. Now it looks like a bunch of people want the other one."

"Cuervo, the boxer?" said Abe.

"Looks like. And his lady. And a Chinese guy. It's nuts, Rabbi."

"The world as we know it is nuts, Father Murph. You get the hospital crazies and I'll go talk to a Turk on someone's hit list."

"Promises to be an interesting day, Rabbi."

"That it does, Father Murph."

11

There were too many choices. Robert E. Lee Chang did not want too many choices. He wanted this all to be simple and done quickly.

He stood in front of the door of the second-floor apartment in a building in Edgewater. The building was no more than a mile from his own apartment.

When this was over, he would have to come up with a story about why he ran from the big policeman in front of his apartment building. That would not be a major problem. He would come up with something. He would simply go directly to the police and tell a lie, say that he had shot the Lindqvist man because he had mugged him, that he had run from the policeman because he thought the man was a mugger. He would even pretend that he had trouble understanding English even though he had been born in Chicago as had his parents and grandparents.

"Why did you have a gun?" the police would ask.

"To protect myself. I had read about muggers in the neighborhood. My gun is registered."

"Why didn't you go to the police after you shot the Lindqvist man?"

"I was afraid, confused, embarrassed."

Ah, he could pull another Chinese ploy.

"I was ashamed of being beaten, ashamed of what my family and friends would think and say."

"And the money Lindqvist says was stolen from you?"

"Money? There was no money. He was mistaken. Or he was lying. Why would I not tell you if someone stole money from me?"

Why indeed?

That would all be easy if he could retrieve Mr. Woo's money.

Robert adjusted his glasses, looked around the empty landing, put his right hand around the gun in his pocket, and knocked.

"Yeah?" came a man's voice, the voice of the man in the hospital.

Robert didn't answer. He knocked again. Harder.

"Answer it, Jamie," a woman said, almost too softly for Robert to hear.

The door opened. Robert Chang, gun now pointed at Jamie Cuervo's face, stepped forward as Jamie backed into the room.

Beyond Jamie, Robert could see the woman sitting at a table, a slice of rye toast in her hand, a cup of coffee in front of her.

Both the man and the woman looked surprised. Good.

Robert kicked the door shut. He wanted them afraid. He wanted the damned money. He wanted to deliver it to

Mr. Woo and then make one of his very rare visits to his mother who had an apartment with his sister in Albany Park. He wanted to be with people who cared about him. He wanted to stop trembling with fear.

"My money," he said.

The man and woman looked at each other and the woman said, "We need it."

"It is not yours," said Robert, his voice vibrating.

Jamie had backed away till he was almost at the table.

"We were talking about that, Jamie and me, and we wondered about whose money it was."

"Mine," said Robert, raising his voice, looking around the room for his briefcase.

"How'd you get it," Elsie said. "Why didn't you tell the police about it?"

"I didn't have time," said Robert. "I don't have time now. I have a gun."

"We have a sticky situation here," Elsie said, taking a bite of her toast.

Both of them were so calm.

"I will count to twenty," Robert said. "You give me back my money or I shoot him. Then I start to count to ten and if you don't give me my money, I shoot you."

"Then," said Elsie, "you'd have counted to thirty, shot two people, have the neighbors at the door, and still not have the money and no time to look for it. Delicate situation."

This was not working as Robert E. Lee had planned. He waited for her to speak again. Jamie still stood next to the table.

There was something seriously wrong with these people. Robert was now certain of that. They were not afraid. He could not shoot them. He wanted to scream, to cry, to rage, to destroy, to at least make them pay for the destruction of his life, to stop them from enjoying the money they had stolen—Mr. Woo's money. But, at that moment, Robert E. Lee Chang realized that it was not in him to do any of these things.

Jamie moved so fast that Robert did not have time to react. It was a painful repeat of what the same man had done to him only hours before. The punch to his already pained ribs was an electric shock. The sound of his own ribs breaking was a nauseating jolt. The gun fell from his hand. He fell forward knowing he was falling, putting his hands out to lessen the impact of his face against the floor. His head hit something, something hard, something . . .

. . . and Robert E. Lee Chang was . . .

"Oh, God, he's—" Jamie began.

. . . dead.

The mask of quiet confidence they had worn, the same one they took into the ring, had worked when they faced the Chinese guy with a gun in his hand. But now the mask was gone, stripped away by the sight of the man on the floor.

Elsie dropped her toast on the table and knelt next to the Chinese guy and turned him over with Jamie's help. The man's eyes were closed, his mouth open, his face, which had hit the edge of the dresser, had a deep open wound burbling dark red blood over the man's face and onto the floor. He was dead. No doubt. Count him out.

"What do we do?" Jamie asked.

Elsie stood. She wanted to say, "I don't know." She wanted him to take over, but she knew he wouldn't, that he would look to her for an answer. That's the way it had been since the first time they went out together to Dominica Dallas, the Jamaican restaurant over on Howard Street. She had picked the restaurant, done the ordering. She was comfortable with that. So was Jamie. They had never had an argument.

"Okay," she said. "We wrap him in something, get him out of here."

"Wrap him in what?" asked Jamie.

It was a good question.

"The rug," she said.

"Your aunt gave us the rug," he reminded her.

"We'll bring it back," she said.

"We'll never get the blood out," Jamie said. "Remember when my nose wouldn't stop bleeding after the Johnny Farris fight? The pillow, towel?"

"We'll do the best we can," she said, looking down at Chang. "Let's roll him up, drive the car to the side back by the garbage cans, get him in, and take him somewhere."

"Where?"

"It's a big city," she said.

Officer Turhan Kazmaka was still in uniform when Lieberman picked him up at the Old Town station. He looked good, professional, big, impressive, even more of all of these things when he stood next to Abe.

"Tell me more about Kemal the Camel," said Abe.

He was driving. Kazmaka was navigating. He knew the address, the building, the neighborhood.

"I know he won't like having the police come to his apartment. I've known where it is, but I've never been there. He's always said, 'The walls have ears and the streets have eyes.' Whenever we meet, it's some place he chooses."

"Known him long?"

"All my life," said Kazmaka.

Abe looked at Kazmaka, who was looking out the window.

Compromising an informant was not a good idea. It broke a covenant, created reasonable distrust.

"Someone wants to kill him," said Abe.

"More than one person probably," said Kazmaka. "Kemal the Camel has made some enemies."

"Someone wants to kill him now, today," said Abe. "Those three in the park. They weren't there to mug him for a few dollars."

"You know something more about it than what Kemal told us in the park?" asked Kazmaka.

"A nameless informant."

"Kemal is my only informant and it looks like he's not going to be nameless anymore," said Kazmaka. "Turn left up a block past the light."

They crossed Wells and turned onto Orleans.

"Tell me about him," said Abe.

"He's probably an Armenian," said Kazmaka. "Tells me he's a Turk. I think he's whatever gives him something he can sell. He's a member of everything, social clubs, soccer team backers, political campaigns and organizations. . . . He cleans up when he has to."

"Like the Turkish-American Society, Cook County Chapter?" said Lieberman.

"That's one of them," Kazmaka confirmed. "Impressive name, not much behind it. Cook County Chapter's the only chapter. It's a dozen maybe, business guys and hangers-on. Turkish Counsel politely avoids them. They piss off other Turkish organizations."

"Because . . . ?"

"They're loose cannons. They drain resources. They get attention by claiming they represent the Turkish community. The truth is that no group, no individual speaks for the Turks in Chicago," said Kazmaka. "That's the building."

Abe pulled in next to a fire plug and pulled down his visor to display his official business police card. Abe looked at Kazmaka, who was eyeing at the identification card. He shook his head once. Within an hour everyone in the neighborhood would know about the visit from the cops. It couldn't be helped.

"The Turkish-American Society?" Abe reminded him.

"Right, the Turkish-American Society—"

"Cook County Chapter," said Abe.

"Cook County Chapter," Kazmaka repeated with a smile, "has only one issue on its agenda, changing history, proving that the Turks back at the beginning of the last century didn't massacre people—Armenians, Greeks, Kurds, Bulgarians, you name it."

"Did they?" asked Abe.

"We've been apologizing for almost a century. Most of us want to forget it and concentrate on having Turkey regarded as a modern, progressive economic country."

"We?" said Abe.

"Yeah, I'm an American and I'm a Turk," said Kazmaka. "And you're an American and a Jew. And how do you want the world to think about Israel?"

"Good point," said Abe. "If there's a division pool on who's gonna make detective first, I'll put five dollars on you."

This time Kazmaka laughed.

"Let's go talk to the Camel," said Abe.

There was no one on the street. It was a cool, pleasant afternoon. People at work. Kids at school. The building was an old six-flat once-yellow brick. The bricks were faded and stained by dark tear streaks from decades of weeping skies. The single concrete stoop at the entrance was chipped at one corner and cracked zigzag right up the middle.

When they opened the door to the cramped hallway, they were greeted by the distinct smell of urine.

The hallway floor was covered by alternating black-and-white hexagon tiles, the kind that used to be found in public rest rooms. Some tiles were missing. Some were cracked. All were stained.

Flyers from Chinese, Italian, and Greek restaurants cluttered the floor.

"*Architectural Digest* must be informed about this charming abode," said Abe.

"Wait till you see the Camel's apartment," said Kazmaka, "you'll pick up the phone and tell them to hurry before *House Beautiful* beats them to it."

Abe definitely liked this kid.

There were six rusting mailboxes on the wall. Names had long since fretted and worn away. One mailbox was overstuffed with junk mail. Two were open, their locks broken, probably had been for a long time.

Kazmaka opened the inner door. It may have been a lock at one point. It was long past caring who abused it.

The smell wasn't quite so bad on the trip up the shredding carpeted stairs. Kazmaka led the way. There were no voices. There was no music. The stairs sighed as they went up to the second floor where Kazmaka stopped in front of an apartment door.

Abe knew. He knew even before Kazmaka knocked and got no answer. He knew even before Kazmaka tried the door and found it open. If someone had asked him how he knew, Abe would have no answer. It was something that cops who had been on the job for a while just felt. Maybe the sound of the silence had changed or the air, something.

Kazmaka pushed the door open and Abe got the sense that the young cop felt it too.

They both had their weapons in their hands, but neither

thought there would be any reason to use them. They were too late. Abe knew it. Simple as that.

The door opened into a high-ceilinged massive living room filled with dark, plush sofas and chairs barely visible in the light coming through the closed drapes. Kazmaka moved across the room to the windows and pushed back one of the drapes to let the light in.

Abe could now see that the furniture was all faded, everything facing the center of the room as if guests were expected for a party or a meeting. The walls were empty but there were lamps, seven of them, ornately shaded lamps in the corners and along the walls. And in the center of the room was a low, round table at least six feet in diameter covered with mosaic tiles that formed an intricate picture of a man.

Abe looked at the table and Kazmaka said, "Atatürk."

Abe needed no more. He had read a biography of Mustafa Kemal Atatürk, the general who had led Turkey out of chaos, into the modern world, protected his nation's borders, and brought a secular unity and pride to his people after World War I.

"Still want to call *Architectural Digest?*" asked Kazmaka.

"More than ever, Turhan," said Abe. "More than ever."

They moved down a hallway to their left. At the end of the hallway was light. They followed it, weapons at the ready, into a bedroom as sparse as the living room was ornate. A monk could be contentedly miserable in the almost closet-sized room with a single bed made up military-style with a raw khaki blanket and an almost flat pillow. The only other thing in the room was a small wooden dresser, nothing on top, drawers closed.

The bathroom was off the little room. It was where they found the body of Kemal the Camel on the floor.

He was grotesquely misshapen and nude, curled up in fetal terror, hands over his face. There was little blood in spite of the clear one-inch wounds on the dead man's chest and neck.

"Aw, shit," said Kazmaka.

"He was in a dangerous business," said Abe.

"And he's paid for it," said Kazmaka. "With his life."

"'I am sleeping,'" said Abe, "'but my heart is awake.'"

"What?"

"Song of Songs," said Abe.

"'When a man dies, those who survive him ask what property he has left behind. The angel who bends over him asks what good deed he has sent before him,'" said Kazmaka.

"The Koran?" asked Abe.

"The Koran," agreed Kazmaka. "What now?"

"We find a Gila monster named Pinn," said Abe.

"Events that took place almost a century ago are haunting the Turkish government which desperately wants to join the European Union," said Demetrios Hocking, professor emeritus of modern history at the University of Chicago. "A major barrier to this entry is the opposition—unified Armenians who insist on Turkey issuing an apology for the Armenian Holocaust before, during, and following World War I. Let's begin by addressing a single and singularly profound example. In 1915 and 1916 thousands of Armenian civilians were rounded up in Anatolia by the Ottoman Turkish government and marched across the mountains to the desert in Syria."

Hocking, a spindly little man known on campus for his large, colorful bow ties, leaned toward his opponent and delivered his comments in a staccato tenor voice that cried for the moribund telegram word *stop* at the end of each sentence. He had a habit of removing and putting on his glasses when he talked, but there seemed to be no rhyme or reason for when the switch occurred.

"Not thousands," said Omar Mehem calmly. "Possibly hundreds of thousands. There are no authoritative figures."

Mehem, tall, handsome, smiling serenely, had two names. He could be Oliver Martin when the situation called for it and Omar Mehem when it was more advantageous. Today, at this debate on the University of Chicago campus, he was Omar Mehem to emphasize his Turkish roots for both the audience of professors and students in the small auditorium and those who were listening on the WTUR radio hookup.

Mehem had decided with little thought needed that he had no serious interest in convincing the people in the room with him or the old liberal bumblebee of a professor in a silly bow tie who tried to provoke him. Mehem's audience was the several thousand regular listeners to his voice over the radio.

"So," said Hocking. "We begin with agreement."

"About the events," said Mehem, "and about the death of most of those Armenians from disease, starvation, and murder, yes."

"I'm perplexed," said Hocking with a smile, sensing a trap, taking off his glasses. "If you don't deny the genocide by the Turkish forces, we have nothing to debate."

"We have much to debate," said Mehem. "Most centrally, your assertion that the genocide was carried out by Turks."

There was a murmur among those in the room. Hocking's glasses went back on.

"Revisionist nonsense. The Young Turk regime in Constantinople," said Hocking, "the three men who ruled the empire ordered the massacre. Even Turkish military courts later concluded this. It brought down their regime and put Atatürk in power."

"We agree on two of your points," said Mehem. "The conclusions of the Turkish military courts and the rise of Atatürk. We still disagree on who was responsible for the massacre."

"I anticipate your argument but I will ask the question in any case," said Hocking. "How do you address the findings of the Turkish military courts, and if the Turkish military was not responsible, who was?"

"You are an historian," said Mehem. "I am a patriot. Turkey was under siege. It's very existence in jeopardy. Armed conflict with Greece, Armenia, Russia, Bulgaria. All fronts. Turkey sided with Germany and its allies to protect its integrity and borders. The Allies—the Americans, British, French—promised no such protection. When the war ended, the Allies insisted on a trial and the Turkish military put on the show to keep them from destroying the last vestige of the Ottoman Empire."

"Absurd," said Hocking, glasses off again. "Do you contend that the commanding general of the Turkish Third Army was lying when he testified that he had been commanded by the Turkish Central Committee—"

"Ittihad ve Terakki," said Mehem.

"Ordered," Hocking went on, moving his glasses back toward his eyes, changing his mind and using them to punctuate, "to commit the massacres."

"The general was under great pressure," said Mehem. "He was never cross-examined. In fact, all testimony was given by deposition and not cross-examined. It was part of the agreement to ensure the existence of Turkey. None of the original documents survived the inquisition. Even the British openly labeled the trials a travesty."

"The Turkish Special Organization—"

"The Teskilat-i Mahsusa," said Mehem.

"Yes, their mission was to go to areas within Turkey's borders to ambush and murder Armenian deportees, Christian Armenians in the main."

"There is no evidence of that," said Mehem. "And many scholars, American and British, have so concluded."

"Then," said Hocking, "who did commit this and other massacres if not the Turkish army?"

"Kurdish tribes working with corrupt Turkish police who slaughtered for the clothes, money, jewelry, and even the shoes of fleeing Armenians," said Mehem, reaching for the glass of water on a small table before him.

"You are familiar with the *Memoirs of Naim Bey* by Aram Anadonian?" said Hocking, glasses on again.

"Published in 1920," said Mehem. "In which Anadonian presents documents—letters, telegrams—given to him by Naim Bey, an alcoholic gambler, which purport to chronicle the organization of the massacres by the interior minister Talat Pasha. The documents are fakes, fed into a gullible market eager for a scapegoat."

"And your evidence for these assertions of Turkish innocence?" asked Hocking.

"There does exist a diary from 1915 by an Armenian who survived the massacre," said Mehem. "It completely vindicates the Young Turks and their government and verifies the statements I have made. This diary can and will be authenticated by scholars."

"You are talking about the Aziz papers?" said Hocking.

"I am."

"They don't exist," said Hocking.

"Oh, but they do," countered Mehem. "They most definitely do."

The murmur in the room had turned into a chair-moving rumble. Hocking had no choice.

"Let's have questions from the audience," said Hocking after a shake of his head.

More than half the people in the auditorium raised their hands.

Mehem preempted Hocking and pointed to a particularly pretty and very serious-looking young woman in the first row. Whatever the question she had, he was certain he would find it easy enough to pursue it in greater depth when the session ended.

Abe's shift was nearly over. Kazmaka had found WTUR on the car radio and they had listened to the discussion between Hocking and Mehem.

The station's signal was weak, kept going in and out, but they caught most of the debate till they turned it off when the questions from the audience began to mirror one another and became hobbyhorse mini-speeches rather than questions.

Abe and Kazmaka had left Kemal's apartment after a crime scene unit arrived and promised to give the detective a report as soon as they had one, which, given the volume of work they had today, would not be particularly soon.

Abe and Kazmaka had searched the apartment. It turned out to be easier than they had imagined. There was a file cabinet in the corner of a second bedroom off of the living room. The tiny room had been converted into a kind of den in which there was pile of large pillows against the wall across from a large-screen television and the file cabinet.

One drawer held newspaper clippings in various languages filed alphabetically by the last name of the subject of each clipping.

There was a file on Lemi Oraz Sahin. It contained no surprises.

There was no file on Omar Mehem or anyone who might be Omar Mehem under a different name.

In the second, the bottom, drawer were personal documents including income tax forms in which Kemal listed himself as a communications consultant.

"His name was Kemal Ataturk Peltola," said Abe.

"I know," said Kazmaka.

"Born in Erie, Pennsylvania, December 1, 1934."

"Didn't know that," said Kazmaka.

There was a lot Abe could still do today, but the change in departmental policy was clear, no overtime. He would either have to go back to the station and turn the case over to someone else or he could shelve it till the next day or he could, on his own time, track it. Four people murdered, all Turks. The story was *Sun-Times* and television network gold. Abe knew he could get an override and be on the case with pay if someone told a few media sources about the murders and the media sources started making calls. The problem was that while such calls might get Abe back on the case, they would also bring the cameras and questions and lots of pressure on his back, and that he did not wish. He was going home.

"Tomorrow?" asked Kazmaka when Abe dropped him in front of his house.

"Probably," said Abe. "I'll call the people who need to be called."

On the way home, the phone started playing "Secret Agent Man." Barry had programmed it in. Abe didn't care. When he picked it up, he noted that the battery was low.

"You off the clock?" asked Angela Flowers, the crime scene officer. She sounded tired.

"Close," said Abe.

"Conundrum for you," she said. "Turkalu and his wife were killed with the same knife that killed the first guy, Sahin."

"Figures," said Abe. "So what's the discrepancy?"

"Knife was found," she said. "Back in the rack of the restaurant kitchen."

"And?" Abe prompted, waiting in rush hour traffic for the light to change at Devon and Sheridan.

"The Turkalus were killed after Sahin, not long after. His blood is under theirs on the knife."

Abe tapped the heel of his left hand on the steering wheel and said, "Describe Turkalu."

"Five six, two hundred and twenty pounds, no visible scars, age sixty-two, hair—"

"Stop," said Abe.

Traffic was moving. Abe wasn't. A chorus of horns blared at him to move before the light changed.

The man he had talked to after he examined Sahin's body—the man who said he was Erhan Turkalu—was the murderer of Lemi Sahin.

Abe stepped on the gas, thanked Flowers, and closed the phone.

The son-of-a-bitch had just murdered three people, and with two of the bodies in the kitchen a few feet away from them, he had calmly conned Detective Sergeant Abraham Lieberman. Such contumacy, thought Lieberman, was not to be endured.

When Bill got back to the hospital, Father Sam "Whizzer" Parker, mufti-clad, was at Iris's bedside. Parker wore a black turtleneck shirt, black slacks, and a black zipper jacket.

Parker had been a running back at the University of Illinois and could, unlike Bill who had bad knees, have been drafted by the NFL in the third round or sooner. With his better-than-movie-star looks, great grades, and gift of patter, Sam Parker had before he graduated been the subject of articles in *Sports Illustrated* and *Vanity Fair* and had made the cover of *Ebony*. He could have been as big a black star as the pretrial O.J. or Jerry Rice or Jim Brown.

Instead, after one NFL season, Samuel Parker had received the calling and became a priest. Now he was at St. Bartholomew's Church in Edgewater. St. Bart's parishioners were primarily Vietnamese, Korean, poor whites, a few Chinese, and Bill Hanrahan. Iris was a Buddhist.

Parker looked like he was thirty years old. He was forty-two. Hanrahan didn't know what Bill Hanrahan looked like, so Sam Parker told him.

"William, you look terrible. Iris looks great. You look like the one who had the baby, which, if true, would rank right up there with immaculate conception."

Hanrahan moved to the bed and leaned over to kiss his wife's cheek. She touched his face.

"Go home and get some sleep," she said. "I'm fine. I can go home tomorrow."

"Beautiful baby," said Parker.

Bill took Iris's hand and turned to face the priest.

"Thank you."

"Fortunately, she looks like her mother," said Parker.

"I've been thanking the Lord for that," said Bill.

None of Bill's children—his two sons, the baby—looked like their father. The boys looked like Maureen, and for that Bill was forever grateful.

Bill nodded, thinking about Lindqvist two floors below and the story he had told Hanrahan a few minutes ago.

According to Jonas Lindqvist, he had been awakened to find the Chinese man who had shot him at his bedside apparently determined to finish the job.

"The money," Chang had said. "Where is it?"

Chang had a gun in his hand now.

"You shot my testicle," was Jonas Lindqvist's answer.

Then the door had opened and the woman came in. She started to argue with Chang. Jonas was lying in the bed between them. Then someone else came into the room and Jonas recognized him. He was the one who had punched him, the one who had taken the Chinese guy's briefcase and money.

"I remembered then. I saw them on television, the man and the woman. ESPN or WGN."

The Cuervos. El Perro was right. Bill was sure now, but it didn't come together.

"Oh," Lindqvist said. "I forgot this. He said—the Chinese guy said—that the money belonged to some scary other guy he called Woo."

That was a name Bill recognized. Woo, the man with whom he had clashed more than once, the old man who had wanted to marry Iris, the man with whom he had a fragile truce. Bill Hanrahan didn't want to be the one who broke that truce.

"You're sure?" Bill had asked. "He said 'Woo'?"

"He said 'Woo' I'm sure. Many things have happened to me in the past day, which by the way now feels like a week. Time drags when you're not having fun, you know?"

". . . thinking of converting," said Sam Parker.

"What?" asked Bill coming out of his reverie.

"Iris asked me what she had to do to convert to Catholicism."

"Convert to . . . we've been through this." He looked at Iris. "She'd have to give up her father, sisters, cousins, and friends."

"I should have discussed this with you first," said Iris. "I didn't plan it."

"You're not a believer," Bill said. "You just want to do it for me, for the baby."

"No," said Iris.

Bill ran a hand through his hair. He wasn't thinking straight and even when he was, Father "Whizzer" Parker could talk circles around him.

"It takes planning," said Bill. "Lots of planning. I don't know if it's a good idea, Sam."

"No hurry," said Parker. "Iris, I don't want you to go ahead with this if you're doing it because your husband is a Catholic, if you're doing it and don't really believe."

"William wants our baby to be baptized," said Iris. "I want to be a Catholic."

"Can Jane be a baptized Catholic?" asked Bill frantically. "I mean Jane and not Iris?"

"You two better do a lot more talking," said Sam. "There's no hurry. I'll take a look at Jane Mei Hanrahan on my way out."

Sam Parker moved lightly to the door.

"Don't sneak in a baptism on the way out," said Bill.

Sam Parker smiled.

"I hadn't considered that. Thanks for the idea."

It wasn't until the priest was gone that Hanrahan saw the flowers. The array was colorful, huge, dozens of flowers in a display against the wall.

"Who sent those?" asked Bill.

Iris's mouth went dry.

"Mr. Woo," she said.

Jesus is playing tricks with me this day, Bill thought, looking at the flowers.

12

Four dead Turks and one tired Jew.

Abe went through the front door as quietly as he could, knowing the mystery click when he got it almost half open might give him away. His plan was to remove his shoes and hope the silence of the house was an indication that no one would corner him with problems domestic till he had time to lie down for half an hour.

Such a hope was not to be realized.

He made it through the living room, shoes in hand, and turned into the dining room. The blessed bathroom, where he spent much of his nights reading, was just beyond. And just beyond the bathroom was his and Bess's bedroom.

His plan, which would not be realized, was to get out of his jacket, shirt, pants, and socks and lie down in darkness after he locked his gun in the night table drawer.

"Abraham," Bess said.

She was sitting alone at the dining room table, a magazine in front of her, a cup of steaming coffee nearby.

She was wearing a black dress, simple, his favorite, silver hair back, earrings glittering. She was, Abe thought, quite beautiful. She looked young enough to be his daughter.

"How was your day?" she said calmly.

"Four people were murdered," he said.

"They're yours, the four people?"

"Yes," he said.

"No children?"

"No," he said.

"Good. You want to hear today's issues now or after you shave and change clothes?"

"The Mens Club dinner," he said. "I haven't forgotten."

"You know what you're going to say?"

"No."

Bess nodded, drank some coffee.

"It will be interesting," she said.

"The kids?"

"Upstairs."

"Who's going to sit with them?"

"No one. Melissa has agreed to defer to Barry, who has agreed to behave responsibly. We won't be gone that long and if you don't know what you are going to say, we will barely be gone at all."

"What else?" he asked.

"Wear your blue suit."

"I was thinking of being more casual," he said.

"Abe, blue suit. Even if you have nothing to say, you can look as if you do."

"Blue suit," Abe agreed. "That's not all, is it?"

"Lisa is going to call the children later to discuss the news about her being pregnant," said Bess.

"You didn't tell them," Abe said.

"I consider that within the purview of their grandfather."

Bess had compartments for domestic responsibility. Abe was never sure why some responsibilities went in his compartment, some in hers, and some shared. She had decided who was to handle this one and there was no point in his arguing. Abe could not remember ever winning an argument with his wife. He could not remember ever believing in the long run that he was right and she was wrong. His conclusion, many years ago, was that Bess, the present president of Temple Mir Shavot and go-to person for instant solutions to problems both simple and difficult, was smarter than he was.

"When?" he asked.

"You can shower, shave, get dressed, and look like a modern Solomon or I can call them down and you can do it standing there in your socks, shoes in hand, stubble on your face."

"Now," he said.

"Abe, please. The bathroom. And don't start reading anything in there."

"She Who Must Be Obeyed," he said.

"You are no Rumpole," she said.

"But I'm lovable."

"Very lovable," she said with a smile.

He was, as always, charmed.

"I'll take a shower," he said. "Conduct all my ablutions and emerge again—a façade of confidence exuding judicial certitude I do not feel."

"Good," she said, standing as he moved around the table past her and toward the bathroom door.

When he was alongside her, Bess stopped him with her hand on his sleeve and gave him a hug, cheek to cheek. He felt her breasts, her breath, her perfume.

"I am a lucky man," he said.

"Don't I keep telling you?" said Bess, stepping back.

"I don't think it's a good idea," said Jamie.

"Honey, we haven't come up with a better one," said Elsie.

She was driving. The body of Robert E. Lee Chang, wrapped in the rug that had been given to the Cuervos by Elsie's aunt when they were married, bounced in the trunk.

"Fibers," Jamie said.

"Fibers?"

"You know," he said. "Those crime scene shows. They find the fibers from rugs and car trunk mats and wigs and I don't know what. And the worms."

"What worms?" Else asked, beginning to worry about her husband, who stared out the window, brow furrowed in thought under scar tissue.

"You know," he said. "Maggots. White, crawling. They can tell things from maggots."

"What things?"

"Who killed someone is what," he said.

"They can't do that," she said.

"Then why do they put it on television?"

"Maybe you heard it wrong."

"I don't know. Maybe."

This was the third time they had driven around the block. It looked good. There was a space open right where they needed one. They wouldn't have to double-park. Not much traffic. People weren't out walking. It was worth a try.

"This time," she said.

Jamie nodded.

"I pop the trunk. You get out, get him, roll him out of the rug, throw the rug back in the trunk, and we go," she said.

"They're gonna catch us, aren't they?"

"No," said Elsie, and she meant it.

"We should leave town," he said. "Kansas City. We've got money."

"Doesn't matter how much money we've got. This is where we do it. We fight. We make it. We don't know anything else. We don't want anything else."

"What about the big guy in the hospital? The cook? He knows what we look like. He'll see us in the papers or on TV or in the street or who knows where."

Jamie shook his head and kept shaking it till Elsie put her hand on his neck and rubbed gently.

"We'll have to kill him," she said. "His balls are shot off and he's half nuts. It'll be an act of mercy."

"No, it won't," Jamie said.

"No, it won't," Elsie agreed with a sigh, pulling into the open space at the curb and popping the trunk. "But we're gonna do it."

Jamie opened his door, jumped out, took in the street, the sidewalks, the buildings, the windows. He went to the trunk and pulled out the rug and the body of Robert E. Lee Chang. There wasn't much to the dead Chinese guy. He wouldn't have had trouble making scale as a bantamweight.

Jamie took five steps to the curb, put down the rug, and tugged. The rug came up in his hands and the body rolled out. A magician doing a trick. Behold the dead Chinese guy. Now watch me disappear. Jamie threw the gun on the ground next to the body.

Crazy thought. Crazy thought.

Jamie jammed the rug into the trunk. He wanted to slam the trunk closed, but he didn't. He quietly but quickly lowered it till the latch caught. Later he would check the trunk for blood. Later he would throw out the mat, scrub the rusting interior metal. Later, they would wash the rug and kill the guy whose balls had been shot off by the dead Chink in the grass.

He got back in the car, closed the door as Elsie pulled out of the space quickly but with no squealing of brakes, no revving of engine.

"Maggots," said Jamie.

"What about them?"

She was now seriously worried about him.

"Where do they come from?" he asked.

Iris had insisted, after they had a hospital meal in her room, that he go home, get some rest.

"About the Catholic business . . ." he began.

"I'll do some more thinking about it," she said.

"Talk to your father," Bill said.

"I will," Iris said, touching his hand.

She smiled.

"What?" he asked.

"You are trying to persuade me not to be part of your religion, the religion in which you believe, the Christ you believe in. That's why I'm smiling."

"I don't think you really believe," he said.

"You're sure, policeman?"

"A lot of the time I'm not sure I believe," he said.

"I know."

"Why do you love me?" he asked.

"Change of subject," she said.

"Yeah, sort of."

"I loved you the first time I saw you come into my father's restaurant."

"I was drunk," he said.

"You were sad. A big, sad-eyed man with eyes searching for his lost soul."

"And you loved that?"

"Yes."

"There is no accounting for the loves of women nor the drinking habits of men. My father used to say that. I don't know if he made it up or it was an old Irish saying."

"Go home, William Hanrahan, husband of Iris, father of Jane Mei, caretaker of a nameless dog."

"You're poetic tonight," he said, kissing her hand.

"I have reasons to be."

When he got home, he walked the dog for the second time that day. There was a park two blocks from the house. Sometimes, when there was no one around, Bill broke the law and let the dog run free, the way he had for the feral years he had lived in alleys and places kept secret from humans.

Bill had not picked the dog. The dog had picked Abe and then, much to the relief of Abraham Lieberman, the dog had picked both Bill and Iris, and Bill was sure the dog would also pick Jane Mei.

"You deserve a name," Bill said as the dog sniffed around the park bench where Bill sat, plastic pickup bag in his pocket, gun at his hip.

The sun was just going down and the park was empty. The streets of this neighborhood were relatively safe, but the park was a sanctuary for a few homeless men who wandered like zombies when the sun went down.

The truth was that the homeless were more likely to be mugged and beaten and even killed than the people who lived in the nearby homes. Bill knew this truth. He also knew that dangers did exist. It was the way of life in the city. Accept it, as he did, with a gun and a dog, or move to safety. With a new baby, Bill thought, the main issue on the table for him and Iris was not whose holy book to follow and how to do it, but whether they would sell the house he had lived in all of his life and move to someplace safer.

The cell phone in Bill's pocket hummed. The dog stopped sniffing and looked up at him. Bill pulled out the phone and flipped it open.

"Detective Hanrahan," said Nestor Briggs.

"Nestor, I'm off the clock. So are you. My wife had a baby. I'm walking the dog. I'm tired. Go home."

"How do you know this isn't a social call?"

"Nestor, you have a dog. What's a good name for a dog?"

"Boris."

"Thanks. What's on your mind."

"You were looking for a Robert E. Lee Chang, right?"

"Right."

"He's been found. Dead. Want to know where?"

"No, I want to guess, Nestor. Then you can surprise me with the answer when I get it wrong three or four times."

"You are tired," said Nestor.

"I am tired. I'm irritable. I'm sorry."

"He was found on the lawn in front of the apartment building where he lived," said Nestor. "You want to know who found him?"

"No," said Bill. "I prefer complete ignorance."

"I'll tell you anyway. Big, heavyset blond guy who the responding officer described as looking like he was low on some drug. Said he had just gotten dressed, walked out of some hospital, and got in a cab. Guy was talking crazy, said the dead guy had shot his testicles off."

"He did," said Bill, "but it was just one testicle."

"Thank the Lord," said Nestor.

"Guy's name is Lindqvist."

"You got it right."

"Who got the call?"

"Nobody yet. Kearney says call you, tell you you'll get overtime."

"I don't need overtime. I need a quiet night at home."

"I get a lot of those," said Nestor. "Believe me, it gets boring fast."

"Fine," said Bill. "I'll take the dog home and get over to the scene of the crime. Oh, shit."

"What?"

"This is being recorded, isn't it? New policy."

"My recording device is not working as it should," said Nestor. "It seldom does. They keep giving me new ones."

"I'm on my way," said Bill.

He flipped the phone closed and watched the dog till he was finished. Then he cleaned it up, dumped it in the trash can nearby, and headed for home.

Nestor Briggs was right. It was kicking in. The questions. The chase. He thought of calling Abe, but then he remembered that his partner had a talk to give.

Given the choice of making a speech and tracking down and facing a killer, it was no contest. The killer would win every time.

"Then He said to Adam, 'Tell them their names.' And when Adam had named them, He said, 'Did I not tell you that I know the secrets of heaven and earth, and all that you hide and all that you reveal?' "

Omar Mehem finished the reading and put the Koran aside. He looked at the clock on the white pegboard wall of the tiny WTUR studio that smelled liked damp wood. He had almost an hour to go on his weekly late night call-in show. He had somewhere to be, something to do. A sign of the success of his show was that the lights were almost always flashing on the panel in front of him. There couldn't have been many listeners at this hour, but those who were there were loyal and passionate Turks. He would miss them.

"Yes," he said, picking up the phone and looking at the boy in the engineering booth.

"Mr. Mehem, I heard your debate with the professor earlier today."

It was a woman. He recognized her voice. A frequent caller. He wondered what she looked like. He had never found the time to pursue his curiosity on the subject.

"And what did you think?" he asked, knowing full well what the woman would say.

"You were magnificent. You reduced him to dust."

"Thank you."

He wondered if she was young or old or in-between. He regretted not having explored her possibilities in the past. No possibility of that now.

"The next time you get him," she said, "tell him of the accomplishments of our country, our people, the move to prosperity and modernization. We have been waiting for forty years to join the European Union. We have abolished the death penalty, increased tourism."

"You mean Turkey, not the United States," he said.

She laughed. It was a full, throaty laugh. Ah, regrets. He

considered asking her why she referred to Turkey as "we." She was obviously an American. She had no accent.

"Based on current demographic trends, Turkey will become the European Union's most populous nation by 2035, and by 2018 Turkey will be a major contributor to the EU budget. Turkey is growing at four times the rate of any EU country."

Omar was bored. He had other things on his mind, but he said, "Turkey cannot and will not be ignored. Economically, socially, politically, Turkey is growing and the untrue taint of the past will be washed away as evidence continues to be found and revealed."

He was thinking of the Aziz papers.

Having executed four people to obtain the Aziz journal and profit from it, Omar Mehem now had to get the prize to his buyer after the show and collect the money as soon as the journal was authenticated tomorrow. The buyer was almost certainly among the five richest Turkish businessmen in the world. He was also a devout Muslim and a passionately loyal Turk. The three million dollars would mean little to him, certainly not enough to betray the man who was offering the prize that might well mean vindication for a generation of Turks.

"Are you an economist?" Omar asked the caller.

"A graduate student in economics at Northwestern," she said.

"A Cub fan?" he asked with his trademarked lightening-of-the-discussion sense of humor.

"No," she said, with that laugh again.

For a fleeting moment, he considered making the contact, but just for a fleeting moment.

The buyer would not pay until the authenticity of the papers had been verified. It was a reasonable condition, but

Omar was in an unreasonable situation. He was not complaining. He had no one to complain to and though he could feign a religious fervor even in the presence of an imam, Omar Mehem did not believe.

"You should play more Turkish music," the next caller, definitely an old man, said in Turkish.

"We will bear that in mind," Omar answered in Turkish. He could also speak Greek and enough Kurdish, Arabic, and Armenian to carry on a reasonable conversation.

He let the caller ramble on in Turkish. It helped fill the time.

"Ibrahim Tatlises," the caller said. "And the traditional music of our saz, our instruments, the baglama, the kanun, the kemence, the nev, the ud, the tanbur. My grandson, did you know, can play them all."

"He must be very talented," said Omar.

The clock moved slowly.

The risks were simple. The Jewish policeman might, in his questioning of people in the Turkish community, come across a picture of Omar. There were plenty of them on flyers when he was speaking, in Turkish newsletters and newspapers. Omar's favorite was the one of him in a suit, half turned to the left, looking back at the camera, his dark hair brushed back, showing glints of light, his almost flawless dark skin and subdued hawkish nose, his fine full mouth open slightly to show perfectly aligned white teeth, and his eyes, his dark eyes that seemed to vibrate even in still photographs.

"We would like to invite you to our annual dinner," said the next caller, a deep-voiced man.

Omar Mehem was in demand as a speaker, an apologist, an icon of the community. He could have, as Oliver Martin, crossed over to local, perhaps even national news shows and talk shows. He had the wit and the looks, but he also had a secret.

Admired among his Turkish fans for his refusal to go beyond his roots and outside of his community, the truth was that Omar would have embraced any camera that offered him a platform, an opportunity to smile, persuade, make sense, seek out sources of revenue. Omar could have used the money. He was not greedy, but he did live marginally, projecting himself as a man of means, but making very little from his radio show, his infrequent lectures, his lunch and dinner presentations for civic groups.

Total average annual income of Omar Mehem and Oliver Martin combined over the past four years was $38,000. If not for his secret, his prospects might have been boundless. Now, when he collected the money, he would need no prospects.

He had no choice but to push his luck till the representatives of the buyer paid him. The Jewish policeman he had deceived in the Anatolia would eventually find him. He had made the mistake of going back to kill the witnesses, the fat little restaurant owner and his equally fat little wife. The Jew policeman was a far better witness.

That had not been his only mistake. Yes, he had panicked when he hired the Mexican lout to kill Kemal.

Kemal had to be killed because he knew the story of George Macrapolis and had demanded $15,000. It was $15,000 George did not have, not yet. Kemal was not inclined to wait. Omar had corrected that, but there was too much to correct. It was far better to leave it behind.

"And your group is?" he asked the caller.

"Coalition of Turkish Businessmen," the caller said.

"Men?"

It was a joke, a jibe. The caller didn't get it.

"We have two women who are members," the caller said. "We would very much like to have you as a speaker at the dinner."

"Leave your number and I will have someone call you back," Omar said.

There was no one but Omar to call anyone back, and he had no intention of doing so in this or any other case.

Omar Mehem's secret was that he was neither a Turk nor a Muslim. He was George Macrapolis, born in Tampa, Florida, and raised by his grandparents in Thessaloniki, Greece, where he learned the craft of a confidence man. Now he was wanted in Massachusetts, Virginia, Arizona, and Wisconsin for a variety of felonies ranging from forgery to assault with a deadly weapon.

So George Macrapolis had to play out the game and take the risk of discovery. He admitted to himself that he found the game an interesting one. Living on the edge was, for him, its own reward.

Tonight the validation of the document would take place. The wealthy Turk's emissaries, two document experts, were already in the city at the Drake Hotel. George would deliver the documents for scrutiny in the morning. The experts, he understood, were prepared to pay cash once the validation took place.

That was tomorrow. Tonight he would lose himself in well-deserved lust with Sarina, whose real name was Jennifer Holsmunder, who by day was a married realtor in Orland Park and by night—actually only Thursdays, Fridays, and Saturdays—was a belly dancer at the Constantinople Restaurant. George frequently exploited his notoriety and gladly joined the tables of people who recognized him at the Constantinople. Often George's status had to be pointed out to a patron by one of the Constantinople's waiters who were rewarded by George's chiding of his varying hosts to increase their tips.

"I am a poet," the next caller said.

The voice was male, young, nervous.

"Poetry is a gateway to the heavens," said Omar, thinking that all poetry, and he had read and memorized quite a bit of it, was ego-building bullshit.

"I'd like to read one of my poems," the caller said.

"In English?"

"I have some in Turkish too."

"A short poem would be fine," said Omar.

"I'm nervous," the caller said.

"Those listening are like extended family. Please read."

Omar thought about the woman he was to meet as the young man droned on, first in English and then in Turkish.

Jennifer Holsmunder would be at his apartment at eleven that night. He would be there to let her in. She would stay for an hour, two at the most, which suited them both.

Jennifer had confided some remorse for deceiving her husband, but not enough remorse and guilt to keep her from coupling with the very virile and creative Omar Mehem. He had considered that his final coupling in Chicago would be not with Jennifer but with the lovely blond widow. He had decided, regretfully, that visiting the widow might be a bit too dangerous and Jennifer was readily available.

". . . and ever ready to give our lives," the caller concluded.

"Very good," said Omar. "I was moved and I'm sure our listeners were too."

"I was nervous."

"You sounded confident."

Omar wondered if he should have listened to the young man's reading. What had preceded this call to suicide?

While punching in the next caller, Omar was not in the world of poetry about martyrdom. He was in the world that he navigated with the help of lies great and small.

What Jennifer did not know was that the thirty-eight-year-old Omar was really the forty-nine-year-old George Macrapolis. She also did not know that he planned by afternoon of the following day to disappear forever and reemerge in London, England, as a wealthy Armenian determined to force the Turkish government to apologize to the Armenian people for past atrocities.

"And it must be done. It must be done now," said the final caller of the night.

The caller was a man, his voice teetering on the edge of recognizable madness. Omar had no idea of what had to be done and done now. Coherence was not one of the man's conversational tools.

"They are trying to extract our souls," the man said. "At secret underground laboratories. They are experimenting with ways to extract our souls and they are close to succeeding."

"The souls of Turks?" Omar asked.

"The souls of all of us."

"This is a Turkish show, a Turkish station," said Omar.

"I do not discriminate," said the man. "We're all in the same goddamn hole."

"Thank you," said Omar.

He pushed the button to end the call.

Omar Mehem watched the clock in the cramped cloister of the WTUR radio studio. One more call if it was quick. It would be, if all went well, the last call he would ever take.

"Omar Mehem," he said.

"The camel spoke," came the voice of a man.

George paused and said, "And what did he say?"

He felt a parable coming, an utterance of supposed wisdom from a fool who thought himself clever.

"He knew a secret."

"What was the camel's secret?" asked George, coaxing.

"A name."

George reached over to press the button to end the call.

"Would you deny me a passage from the Koran then?"

It was he, Omar, who always began and ended the show with a passage from the Koran.

"No," said George. "Please go ahead."

"As for the unbelievers," the man said, "their works are like a mirage in the desert. The thirsty traveler thinks it is water, but when he comes near he finds that it is nothing. He finds Allah there, who pays him back in full. Swift is Allah's reckoning."

"*Salam Alechem,*" said George.

"The name the camel spoke was George the Greek," said the man.

George's hand was shaking as he pushed the button ending the call. He was relieved that the caller had recited the passage because George's mouth was dry.

He could barely say his closing, *"Iyi geceler."*

13

"Your mother is going to have a baby."

Abe sat at the head of dining room table. He wore his blue suit and the tie Bess had given him two Hanukkahs ago, a purple tie, silk with thin red stripes.

Barry and Melissa had finished an early dinner of grilled cheese sandwiches, fresh sugared strawberries, and chocolate milk. They sat on Abe's right. Bess was on the left, hands folded on the table.

They had to leave for the men's club dinner soon, very soon. Abe would have preferred to postpone this discussion for a day, but the phone had rung twice since he had come home. Once it had been Maish reminding him that he was going to announce his departure from the congregation tonight. The second call had been from a crime scene detective telling him that Kemal the Camel had been stabbed six times, deep, by someone powerful and a. right-handed, and b. taller than the dead man. Time of death: no more than two hours before Lieberman and Officer Kazmaka had found the body.

When the phone had rung those two times since Abe got home, Abe and Bess both winced. They feared it might be Lisa bearing news to be tactlessly presented to her two children in spite of her earlier request for them to tell the children.

And so, Abe and Bess had chosen the moment.

Melissa was ten, her curly dark ringlets with which she had been born had turned to soft waves. Her eyes were the deep brown of her mother. Her concentration and serious look, which she now wore, was definitely the gift of her father. Abe frequently had to remind himself that his grandchildren were half Cresswell, which he considered a good thing.

"Will it be a boy or a girl?" Melissa asked.

Abe looked at Barry who showed no emotion.

"We don't know yet," said Abe. "When the news flashes on CNN, we'll pass it on to you."

"CNN wouldn't have news about my mother having a baby," Melissa said.

"But they might bear witness to my daughter having a baby," said Abe.

"You're not famous," said Melissa.

"No," admitted Abe, "but I am eccentric. It would be a human interest story."

"Will the baby be brown?" asked Barry.

His eyes met those of his grandfather. Bess started to reach out to touch her husband's hand and then thought better of it.

"If we're lucky," said Abe.

"Lucky?" asked Melissa.

"The baby could be green or orange," said Abe. "Your mother loves salad and she eats lots of carrots. People can turn orange from eating too many carrots."

"The baby can't be green or orange can it, Grandma?" asked Melissa.

"No," said Bess.

"Will she give the baby to you?" Barry asked.

"No," said Abe. "I don't think so."

"She gave us to you," said Barry.

"Just to raise," said Bess. "And love. You are a blessing."

"Your mother has changed," said Abe, believing what he was saying but not clarifying what he meant by "changed." "I have changed. Your grandmother has changed. Your sister has changed and you have changed. You are now a teenager."

Barry held back a smile. His grandfather had called him neither man nor boy.

"I will love him," said Melissa.

"Or her," said Bess. "We all will."

Barry was silent, looking down at his plate, playing with the remnant of crust from his grilled cheese sandwich. He never ate the crusts. Bess had been willing to cut off the crusts, but her grandson said he wanted them left on. Lisa had done exactly the same thing when she was his age.

"Will the baby be Jewish?" asked Melissa.

"Your mother is Jewish. Therefore your new brother will be Jewish just as you are," said Abe.

"We don't have any brown babies in the synagogue," said Melissa.

"That is about to change," said Abe.

"Mr. Tarkovsky is sort of brown," Melissa said.

"Like a hickory nut," Abe agreed. "He's from Morocco."

"Can Barry and I order pizza?"

"You just ate grilled cheese," said Bess.

"We'll get hungry," Melissa said.

"You test us, small child," said Abe. "Payment in pizza

currency as a reward for your ready acceptance of a new sibling."

"What?" Melissa asked.

"No pizza," said Barry, looking at his grandfather. "I feel sorry for the baby."

"Why?" asked Bess. "Your stepfather is a good man."

"It's not Marvin I'm worried about," said Barry.

Nothing more had to be said. Abe thought the crisis was over, at least for now. The next crisis at the temple dinner would be upon him in less than two hours. He still didn't know what he was going to talk about. He didn't know what Maish was going to say.

"Can you hear me?"

Jonas Lindqvist was lying in the hospital bed, eyes closed, occasionally moaning low.

Hanrahan repeated the question.

"Can you hear me?"

A nurse in white, her arms crossed, checked the IV attached to her patient's arm.

"Is he in pain?" asked Bill.

"Not being fitted with the same equipment that's been damaged, I can only imagine," the nurse said. "I'd say he is in pain."

Lindqvist's eyes opened. His mouth moved. He was pale, very pale, his lips dry.

"My wife," he said. "Lydia."

"You want me to call your wife?" asked the nurse.

"No," Lindqvist burst out, his head rising from the pillow. "No."

His head fell back on the pillow.

"Water," he said.

The nurse reached for the glass next to the bed. Lindqvist sipped and licked his lips.

"Why did you do it?" asked Hanrahan.

"It was a mistake," said Lindqvist. "I meant to use sugar, but I added salt. I wasn't thinking. I was tired."

The nurse shook her head, looked at her watch, and left the room.

"Why did you leave the hospital and go to Chang's?" asked Bill.

"Chang? The dead Chinese guy who shot off my . . . I thought I might kill him. I don't kill people, but I thought it might be a good idea. I got dressed, got a cab in front of the hospital, and went there. He was lying there dead."

"You didn't kill him?"

"I don't know what killed him," said Lindqvist, now trying to keep his eyes open. "Suicide? Remorse?"

"Did you hit him?"

"No. Why would I hit him? He was dead."

"Let's talk about the other two."

"The other . . . oh, the ones who punched me. They came to my room here with the Chinese guy who had the gun."

"I know. Who are they?"

"Sugar and salt do look alike," he said. "They don't smell alike or . . . they do have somewhat similar texture."

"The two who came here, the man and woman who beat you," said Bill. "You know who they are?"

"No, who?"

"You tell me."

"I've seen them before. On television. Their hands are lethal weapons. That's what they always say in the old movies. They're boxers. Maybe I saw them in the *Sun-Times* or on WGN. I have a mind that races."

"I can see that," said Bill with a sigh.

"It's a curse," said Jonas.

"The name Cuervo mean anything to you?"

"Cuervo. It's a rum, isn't it?"

Bill put his notebook away and said, "I'll come back later when the drugs wear off."

"It is my sincere hope," said Lindqvist, licking his dry lips, "that they never wear off."

"What about the gun?" Bill asked.

"The gun?"

"We found it under Chang's body."

"The Chinese guy was shot?"

"No," said Bill. "He was beaten."

"Like I was," said Jonas.

"He died," said Bill. "You were lucky."

"I suppose," said Jonas. "It hurts."

"I can imagine," said Bill.

"You can," said Jonas, "but I don't think you'll come close. The gun you found. Is it the one he shot me with?"

"We don't know yet."

"It is," said Jonas, blinking his eyes, his voice drifting off as he said, "I could have sworn it was sugar."

Bill left.

Jonas Lindqvist closed his eyes. He was numb, which was a good thing, but his mind refused to join the nirvana his body was temporarily relishing. He felt the necessity of baking a cake in his imagination, le Galette des Rois, to be served on January sixth, Epiphany, the Feast of Kings. The cake, celebrating the three kings who brought gifts to the infant Jesus, is baked with a bean inside. Whoever finds the bean in his cake is king for a day.

Unsalted butter, sugar—sugar, sugar, sugar, not salt, no

salt in this recipe—eggs, ground blanched almonds, puff pastry, and one dry bean.

He imagined himself, Lydia, the policeman who looked like a bear, the dead Chinese man who had shot him, and the husband and wife terrorists. They were sitting at a table at Le Sourire eating le Galette des Rois. Lydia got the bean. She was king. No, she had to be queen. She and the policeman who looked like a bear walked away from the table, arm in arm. Everyone applauded except the Chinese man who had shot off Jonas's testicle. He was dead.

The two men sat in the hotel room at a desk.

They had eaten in a restaurant, Le Sourire, known for its French cuisine and recommended by the hotel concierge. It had proved to be a very satisfactory recommendation for which they had agreed, without having to discuss it, that the concierge should be generously tipped when they checked out of the hotel some time the next day.

Ekrem Nasuh was forty-eight, balding, always immaculately dressed and carrying his girth puissantly. Yasar Hikmet, seventy-one, was lean, nearsighted, and given to wearing very expensive Hong Kong–made suits that never quite seemed to fit and which he flecked with ashes from the endless cigarettes he smoked in a stained ivory holder.

They had worked together many times before.

They had separate rooms.

Yasar Hikmet was given to snore with an odd, discordant whistle. Ekrem liked to keep the lights on and read tales of horror by Koontz and King.

Now they were working. It might take them a few minutes. It might take hours. The leather-bound package had just been given to them by an unctuous handsome man of no certain age who reminded them politely that the figure agreed upon was three million U.S. dollars.

Hikmet and Ekrem were to determine the authenticity of the package and the document it contained. They well understood the importance of their mission and its meaning to their patron.

It was Hikmet, because he was the elder in the duo, who untied and folded over the corners of the leather packet. Inside, as they had been told, was the notebook, the dimensions of a standard book and bearing the name Aziz and the scrawled inscription in thick, fading, black ink: 1913.

The two men leaned forward and began.

The Chinese guy they had taken the briefcase from had a pocket watch. They had forgotten that until they took the watch out of his pocket after he was dead.

Nobody, almost nobody, wears a pocket watch except the former heavyweight and sometimes cornerman, Paddles Patalnowitz. The watch had belonged to Paddles's father and his grandfather before that. Paddles would have given it to a son long ago, but he had no son. He had a daughter who had a daughter who was taking her sweet time having a boy baby.

Elsie and Jamie sat in a back booth in the Melody Lounge on Lunt and watched Paddles, sitting across from them, remove his pocket watch slowly, open the lid with a flick, squint at the dials, and click it shut.

"Now, what can I do you for?" he asked.

This was Paddles's North Side office. He owned the Melody, didn't much care if it did a hell of a lot of business, just so it was a quiet place to come, smell draft beer fumes, feel the familiar bumps and old knobs on the pine-top tables, talk to friends. The walls were lined with signed photographs of boxers, many of them with Paddles's arms around their neck. Some of them had been famous once—Sandy Saddler, Barney Ross, Carmen Basilio, Georgie "Sonny" Horne.

"We got trouble," said Elsie.

Paddles, who was almost ninety years old, was called Paddles because they had used the paddles on his chest the last time he had a heart attack. He had pulled through, was fine now, and didn't like being called Paddles, but it was better than the nickname he had before, Zotz. Ernie Crisco had called him that once. Didn't make any sense, but it had stuck till Paddles.

Paddles liked to come to the gym and watch. He told stories to anyone who would listen about how the fight game had been different in the forties and fifties when he had been a light-heavy, when he was a kid. He quit the game after two big losses, one to Joe Louis himself in one of the Brown Bomber's barnstorming trips. Bum of the month.

"We could use some advice," said Elsie.

The bartender, Heinz Hoff, was almost as old as Paddles. They had fought twice. Hoff, who had lost whatever significant mental capacity he had more than thirty years ago, had worked for Paddles for almost half a century, all of it inside the Melody. Heinz, who wore suspenders and now weighed close to three hundred pounds, was content. He brought fresh steins of beer for the Cuervos and a Diet Sprite for Paddles.

"You need money?" asked Paddles. "Can be done."

"No," said Jamie. "We need help. Like Else said, 'advice.'"

When Paddles had fought Joe Louis, Paddles had bet everything he had and could borrow from his parents, brother, sister, in-laws, and friends on the fight. Paddles, who was known as Slugging "The Zotz" Sidney at the time, knew he couldn't win. Paddles was, however, sure he could go the full six rounds with the champ without going down once and without dancing away. That's what he had bet on. The fight had been a stinker, a bore, but Paddles hung on, taking one hell of a beating, collected on his bet, and with the money bought three houses in Bridgeport—bought them outright. Houses were cheap in Bridgeport in the fifties. Paddles lived in one house, sold the two others at double what he had paid, and found three other houses he could buy. And that's the way it went.

"So, what's the problem, the discrepancy here?" asked Paddles.

They told him. Paddles listened, started to reach into his pocket for a cigar, remembered that they were forbidden and that he hadn't had one in almost ten years. He pulled his hand away from his pocket and reached instead for a peanut.

Fighters, handlers, managers, boxers, all listened to Paddles's story. Most of them had heard it at least three times. Why did they listen? Because Paddles was a soft touch for a loan or even a fifty dollar bill tucked into a sweaty pair of shorts.

This, however, wasn't your ordinary touch or request for wisdom.

"So what do we do?" asked Elsie.

"What do you do?" repeated Paddles. "You go back and find the big crazy guy, turn him into raw burger or diced pork is what you do. You come out of the ring in one piece and no one on your ass, I'll pull some favors, see what rubs in K.C. or Vegas for a while."

"Okay," said Elsie.

"I like you kids," Paddles said. "You got a good combination finish with that right cross."

He had said it to Jamie. Then he turned to Elsie.

"And you, sis," he said. "You got the blood running when you step in. You ain't scared of shit. I'm still alive when you take care of business and get back to Chicago, you know where to come. For now, be right here, tomorrow from maybe six till closing, which is whenever Heinz and me want closing to be, after you take care of that guy. Any other business?"

"No. Thanks," Elsie and Jamie said together.

"Amen," said Paddles, reaching for some peanuts.

Peanuts were on the forbidden list, but what the hell, thought Paddles, almost everything was and you only die once.

There were ten tables set up in the multipurpose room of Temple Mir Shavot. Each table had a white linen tablecloth. Each table was surrounded by seven chairs at which sat male members of the men's club and their male guests.

There were no women in the room except Bess Lieberman, president of the congregation. Rabbi Wass said a prayer before the meal and then excused himself to go to the building-fund meeting in his study. Bess remained at the table. She had a few announcements to make before she too left the room to join the building-fund meeting. Besides, she had to watch Abe to be sure he didn't clog his arteries.

The dinner, catered by Terrill and Maish, was served by three waiters hired for the evening. The headwaiter was the grandson of Herschel Rosen, who sat at an all *alter cocker* table with Sy Weintraub, Al Bloombach, and Howie Chen. The other two waiters were the grandson's friends. They were smart boys all, students at the University of Illinois in Chicago. But they were terrible waiters. And a few members of the men's club were not in a forgiving mood, nor were they by nature forgiving in character and the least forgiving of all was, as always, Noah Nathanson.

"What's so hard?" said Nathanson, whose *kepah* kept falling off his head of billowy white hair. "Everybody's having chicken. Everybody's having salad. You bring out the bread. You bring out the butter. You pour the water, bring ice tea. What's so hard?"

Herschel Rosen, at the next table, fumed in near silence. Those near him could hear small grunts, like the sound of an old train gathering steam, getting ready to break loose.

"They're kids. They're trying," said Mel Horowitz.

"Horowitz the Mediator has been heard from," said Nathanson. "He is half right. They are kids, but they are not trying."

He broke a soft warm roll in half and shook his head.

Nathanson was tolerated because he had a good heart. The heart had originally belonged to a woman born in Guatemala. It had been deftly sewn into the chest cavity of Noah Nathanson two years ago. He had been warned to remain calm. His friends were constantly betting on him to be calm. The result was that Noah spoke his mind more and more frequently, which might have been a good thing if he had anything constructive to say.

The waiters, in starched white jackets supplied by Bob Binsky's son's dry-cleaning and laundry service, continued to serve and pretend that they didn't hear Noah's ranting.

The only one capable of calming Noah was his wife, Janet, who was in the rabbi's study waiting for the arrival of Bess, Rabbi Wass, and Irving Trammel. Janet had replaced the deceased Ida Katzman on the building committee. Ida had died almost a year ago, leaving her considerable but far-from-mind-boggling fortune primarily to the temple. She had also left $250,000 to Abraham Lieberman. In her will, Ida, who had shriveled to near nonexistence at the age of ninety, said, "The money I leave to the synagogue, I leave because it is what we must do to keep our dwindling numbers in a condition of some security. The money I leave to Abraham Lieberman is what I wish to do because he is an honest man who tells the truth with concern for those around him."

Irving Trammel had persuaded Ida Katzman to alter the wording of her will so that it came out like this. In the original, she had said not "an honest man who tells the truth" but "a man who will not abide bullshit."

Filling Ida Katzman's tiny electric shoes was a challenge Janet Nathanson did not feel she could meet. Her only real qualifications were her heroic forty-five-year tolerance of her husband and the considerable success Noah had made of her father's ice cream store on Lawrence Avenue. Actually, the store had been only a moderate success, but it had made her more popular with her friends at Von Stueben High School. No, her father's success had come from a slow, gradual buying of property on both sides of the ice cream shop and down the street.

Noah had continued the purchase of property and land when Lawrence Avenue was in decline in the seventies. Then the value of the holdings rocketed.

Janet and Noah and their two daughters, now married to a music shop owner and a realtor, were comfortable. The courtship of Janet by the temple had been gradual and unplanned. As much as her husband was merely tolerated, Janet was genuinely liked.

All this and the chatter of voices at each table—the sound of a cough, a laugh, a single word—were not lost on Abe. He ate his chicken and looked at the table across from him where Maish sat. Maish did not meet his eyes or engage in the conversation at his table. He wore the look of determination that Abe had learned at an early age to walk away from. Tonight he could not walk away.

Abe liked the chicken. He would have sinned incessantly had he been allowed to eat the mashed potatoes that accompanied it, but Bess had put a hand on his arm when his fork descended toward Terrill's perfectly fluffed and gravy-covered potatoes.

When the chocolate cake came, he quickly took one bite before Bess could touch his arm. After the bite, he placed his fork on the plate and pushed the cake and plate toward the center of the table.

The mood of Abraham Lieberman was not good.

His mind was on mashed potatoes, chocolate cake, his brother, and four dead people. He should not be here. He should be out on the streets finding the white-toothed killer with perfect hair who had fooled him at the Anatolia Restaurant. Four dead in less than twenty-four hours.

Joe Greenblatt, president of the men's club, rose and tapped on a glass to get the attention of the room. Greenblatt, at the age of fifty-one, was one of the youngest people in the room. He was also running for alderman in this district at the far northern tip of the city, which included the temple in which they now sat.

Joe, now standing next to Abe, was a smiler and a sympathetic head-nodder. He had learned to put a hand on the shoulder of any person who asked for favors.

Joe was big, loud, full of jokes and funny stories. He dominated conversations and was generally ridiculed by the *alter cockers*, who dreaded the day he would be old enough to join them.

Joe moved to the rickety dark wooden podium that had been used for events like this for at least three decades. There was a microphone, but Joe didn't need it.

"Gentlemen, before we get to our speaker, our Congregation President has a few announcements."

Bess rose and joined the beaming Joe Greenblatt at the podium. Abe considered pulling the cake back for a quick bite or two, but as she spoke, Bess kept glancing at him.

He sat back in defeat.

"Two bar mitzvahs and one bat mitzvah next month," she said. "Mark and Lawrence Knobloch, twin grandsons of Asher Knobloch, and Shari Trammel, daughter of Irving and Susan Trammel. Mark your calendars."

Polite applause.

"In the last two months we have lost two members of our congregation," said Bess. "As most of you know, David Feinstein and Esther Glick were interred at our cemetery in Arlington Heights."

"*Aleviah shalom,*" said someone aloud.

"*Aleviah shalom,*" a few voices answered.

Maish looked ready to say something. Abe was sure Bess could handle him.

"Now," said Bess. "We need committee members for the work ahead. I know, there is always work ahead. There always will be. We will always need volunteers to work, really work, on committees. We need you. A list of committees is in the program in front of you. Check off the ones you want to serve on, sign your name on the bottom, and hand it to Joe Greenblatt before you leave. Thank you."

Applause was again led by the beaming Greenblatt as Bess stopped at the table for her purse and leaned over to Abe.

"Avrum," she whispered. "Resist temptation."

She kissed his cheek and left the room.

"Our speaker tonight," said Greenblatt, "is one of our own, Abraham Lieberman, a Chicago police detective. Husband to Bess, father to Lisa, grandfather of Melissa and Barry, who had a bar mitzvah two months ago. Our speaker has not confided in me the nature of what he will be saying tonight. He is a policeman. He knows how to keep secrets, but now to the brotherhood within these walls some of them may be revealed."

A few chuckles from the gathering, not the number Greenblatt would have liked, but it would suffice.

"Gentlemen, I give you Chicago Police Department Detective, our own Abraham Lieberman."

Abe had no notes. He had decided on two courses of action. The second would be to open the floor for questions and hope they were forthcoming. The first was about to go into a state of preventive action. Maish had begun to rise. Abe knew he had chosen this moment to announce his defection.

"I'd like to answer your questions about what I do and how I protect and serve you . . ."

Laughter. More, Greenblatt noted, than the chuckles he had received. It had something to do with Lieberman's deadpan delivery.

"But first my brother Maish and I will engage in a short debate that we hope you find of some interest. Maish, as almost all of you know, catered tonight's dinner."

Genuine applause. Maish nodded.

"I hope he isn't responsible for the waiters," Noah Nathanson of the new heart said loudly.

"We're all responsible for the waiters, Mr. Nathanson," said Abe. "And for each other. Lesson one we learn as policemen and as Jews."

More genuine applause, the best of the night so far. Joe Greenblatt turned his full attention to the brothers Lieberman.

Abe motioned his brother to the podium. Maish moved reluctantly to his brother's side. There was little doubt that the two were brothers, though Maish had no mustache and carried two years and more than fifty pounds more than Abe. The face of their father, forlorn and serious, was their joint legacy.

"Maish is considering a departure from our midst," said Abe.

Having lost the drama of the announcement, the only part of his plan that he had rehearsed, Maish moved to his second point and said emphatically, "I'm not considering it. I'm doing it."

"Why?" asked Abe.

"God has failed me."

"How?"

"He let my son be taken and when I called on Him for an answer, He didn't answer."

"Did you expect him to?"

"No."

"So God was condemned to failure?" asked Abe.

"He tests us. Like mice in a laboratory and we don't know what the experiment is."

"But you haven't lost your belief in God?" asked Abe.

"No. Would I be this angry if I thought David's death was a random thing?"

"Born from the chaos of mingled purposes," said Abe.

Maish looked at the ceiling and shook his head.

"You are the atheist," he said.

"I don't spend a lot of time thinking about it," said Abe.

"I'm satisfied being part of this community, part of something that extends my family, that invites me to get up here and make a fool of myself with my brother, and then tolerates it."

"You're evading the question," said Maish.

"I didn't hear one," said Abe.

"Are you or are you not an atheist?"

"My brother has become the Joseph McCarthy of religion," said Abe.

Laughter and then the voice of Noah Nathanson.

"I came here to hear about policemen. I could have learned more staying home and watching a couple of reruns of *Law and Order*."

Herschel Rosen, whose grandson in a white starched jacket was clearing the table, had had enough.

"Nathanson, shut the hell up for a change, why don't you?"

Noah Nathanson pounded his palms on the table and said, "I'll say what I want to say when I want to say it. America is still a free country as far as I know, so I will say what I want to say when I want to say it until the day I fall over dead."

His voice had risen. The brothers Lieberman were silent.

Herschel Rosen was about to respond.

Nathanson stood, his mouth open, his eyes open, his face red. His right hand went up to his chest and began to move about as if he were searching for the source of some hidden pain.

Then he grabbed for the table, caught the tablecloth in his left hand, and began to fall. As he went, he took the remnants of his chocolate cake and his half-full cup of coffee with him.

Before his head hit hard wood, Nathanson's white *kepah* glided across the floor like a Frisbee in slow motion. Before his head hit the floor, Noah Nathanson was dead. The heart of the Guatemalan woman had stopped beating.

There was no shortage of doctors in the room. Four were at the side of the fallen man in seconds.

Abe and Maish were ignored. They looked at each other. There was nothing more to say. Maish left the podium and made his way back to his table. Everyone looked toward the fallen Nathanson, everyone except Maish, who looked at his untouched slice of chocolate cake.

Abe took out his cell phone and turned it on. He had two messages. He punched in 911.

Yasar Hikmet lifted the sweat- and age-darkened cracking leather scrap that had been the wrapping of the journal.

He put his tongue to the surface of the scrap and then ran the tip of his tongue slowly over the roof of his mouth. Then he nodded, a nod that was almost not a nod, a nearly perceptible tilt of the head, a closing of the eyes for an instant. Ekrem Nasuh understood. The shrouding was genuine, a century old or more.

Laying the leather wrapping aside, the old man took a sip of water and lifted the journal itself. He opened the thin gray cloth cover and this time touched his tongue to a random page. It took him longer this time. He looked at the wall, seemed to be savoring the taste, and then repeated the tiny nod with which he had validated the age of the cover.

It was Ekrem Nasuh's turn. Hikmet handed the thin journal to him. The document was handwritten in Armenian.

Nasuh began to read aloud slowly: "January 3, 1913—General Andranik told us, when he led us into Bulgaria, that we were going to have a secure homeland but we would have to fight for it. I believed him. He was wrong. We are at war with the Ottoman Empire, at war with the Young Turks. We cannot win. May we but survive.

"Bombshell noise is everywhere, women and children crying. Men crying even louder. We are trapped deep inside this cave. I write by the light of candles, which have been brought in here by a storekeeper whose name I do not know. We are outside of Artashat in a cave. It is damp. They are afraid to come in here after us, afraid we will kill them in the darkness. They fire their guns into the darkness. We can't be seen. We are around two turns. Will they starve us out, seal us in?

"We are a Christian people. We are a Christian people since early in the fourth century. We were the first state to adopt Christianity as an official religion. Our apostles are Bartholomew and Thaddeus. We are of the Armenian Apostolic Church. They mean to take us from our church to slaughter us, to take our nation, to replace us with Muslims.

"They fire bullets into the cave into the blackness. We are safe if they do not come in. We are not soldiers but some were and we have a few weapons, not many but a few. We too can shoot but out of darkness not into it.

"My wife, my daughter, my two sons, are dead, shot by these animals who I cannot bring myself to forgive. They have earned the wrath of me if not God.

"We are the direct descendants of Noah who founded Nakhchevan, which is the oldest of Armenian cities. We live in the shadows of Mt. Ararat.

"I have heard from a man in here that more than two hundred Armenians—teachers, writers, community leaders in Constantinople—have been arrested and murdered.

"A bomb, a small bomb. I can hear the entrance of the cave rumbling, chunks of stone falling, crashing. Will they block our way? Will we starve in here in darkness?

"We have been plagued by them. They have murdered our

people. These Kurds who believe in madness. Those who massacre us are Kurds on the backs of horses. Not Turks but Kurds. These Kurds slaughter us like cattle. No—cattle are more precious to them.

"I stop for the day, maybe forever. It is time to put the candles out and sit in darkness quietly if we can. The Kurdish monster may decide to flee. The Turks do not interfere but it is the Kurdish hordes and the renegade criminals—Turks, Russians, Bulgarians, Greeks—who have caused our destruction. I have borne witness to this in town and village. I will answer all of this violence when I leave this cave as Jesus left his cave after he was resurrected. I will double the number of bullets I fire. If there are no bullets left I shall fight the Kurdish ravishers with my fingernails."

Ekrem Nasuh squinted, rubbed the bridge of his nose, and sat up. His back ached. He gently slid the journal in front of Yasar Hikmet.

The room they were in was Nasuh's. It had already begun to smell of strong Turkish tobacco, decades of the smell clung to the old man. It could not be washed off and it always left a trail, a residue behind him. Ekrem had long grown used to it. It was the smell of his country. It clung to him too.

"It has value," Ekrem said.

Yasar nodded.

"No doubt it was written long, long ago," Ekrem said slowly, enjoying the moment of revelation.

"I concur," said Yasar, absently taking a cigarette from the box in his pocket and inserting it in the ivory holder.

"But it is a forgery, an old forgery, but a forgery," said Ekrem with a sigh. "Historically interesting. Worth . . . ?"

"No more than twenty thousand dollars," said Yasar,

lighting his cigarette with the lighter he always carried with him, a lighter given to him by Pasha Gabin fifty years ago.

"Twenty thousand sounds right," said Ekrem. "We can't even consider authenticating it. Pity. It blames everything on the Kurds."

"It is probably filled with small errors," said Hikmet, inhaling, coughing, emitting a billow of smoke.

"The massacre in Constantinople," said Ekrem. "The journal entry is dated January 1913. The alleged massacre did not take place until April."

"Ergo," said Hikmet, "the entry was made after April of 1913."

"Ergo indeed," said Ekrem. "The mythical document of Aziz is a fraud."

"Do we offer this Omar ten thousand for the journal?" asked Yasar, now tranquil with his nicotine inhalation.

"Five," said Ekrem. "He has no choice. Besides I do not like nor trust him."

"Nor do I," said Hikmet. "Could he be trying to dupe us with this journal perhaps?"

Ekrem shook his head.

"I do not think so. He believes this is authentic."

"We can have him killed," said Yasar. "Perhaps we should. He alluded to what he had to do to obtain this artifact. He has killed."

"No, Yasar Hikmet," sighed Ekrem. "I suggest we simply make our offer and go home with or without the document."

"Home, yes," agreed Yasar. "Home."

Jamie bit his lower lip hard, not hard enough to break the skin, but hard.

"I just thought of something," he said.

They were back at the hospital. This time they had a plan. They were dressed in their best. Jamie was wearing a suit and tie, blue suit, red tie. It was the suit Elsie had picked out at Sears, the suit he wore to the dinner to honor Ernie Terrell three years ago. Terrell was supposed to mention up-and-coming contenders including Jamie. Jamie was to stand up to the crowd's applause. Terrell forgot the mention. Or maybe nobody told him. But Jamie still had the suit and he was wearing it now. Elsie was wearing a no-nonsense black dress and unsubdued makeup.

Jamie had said they might be recognized. They had, he reminded her, been there twelve hours ago. Elsie had said the day staff was home. No one on the night staff would recognize them. All they had to do was keep up the act, not be nervous. Jamie was to look busy, check his watch from time to time. He had places to go, people to save. He was a doctor.

They knew Lindqvist's name and his room number, providing they hadn't changed his room. Elsie and Jamie would soon know.

Jamie stopped.

"We forgot something, Else," he said.

They were in the reception area about a dozen feet from the desk.

"What did we forget?" Elsie asked, looking at the man behind the reception desk. He was old, very old. He looked like a bewildered bird with white skin and whiter hair. In his left ear was a hearing aid.

"Fingerprints," said Jamie.

A man and woman and three children were the only ones in the seats of the reception area. They were talking. Spanish. The children, two boys and a girl. The girl was the oldest. She couldn't have been more than seven or eight. She was herding her smaller brothers. Elsie had herded her three younger brothers. That was her job. She hated that job, didn't like her brothers.

"What about fingerprints?" Elsie asked.

"I think I left them on the gun," Jamie said.

"You handled the gun? We wiped it. You were supposed to just put your finger through the trigger and drop it next to the body."

"I forgot," he said. "I guess I panicked."

"I guess you did," Elsie said. "Never mind. We'll fix it if they get your prints. Besides, the Chinese guy wasn't shot."

"Things aren't going right for us today, Else. It has come to shit," he said.

"We'll clean it up. We've got the money, Jamie. Now act like a doctor. We can't stand here."

The bird-man behind the desk looked up with a tiny smile.

"Can I help you?" he said.

"I'm Doctor Johnson and this is Doctor Clark," Elsie said. "We're here for a consultation, a Mr. Lindqvist, Jonas Lindqvist. Had his testicle shot off."

"Yeah, he's back," said the old man.

"Back?" asked Elsie.

"Left his room, got himself dressed, got into a cab right outside, and then they brought him back. It was something."

"Is he still in 311?" asked Elsie.

"He's in 311," said the old man.

"Thank you," said Elsie.

Elsie and Jamie started toward the elevators.

"Wait a second," called the old man.

They could run, run right now. They could also run after they found out what the old man wanted. ID probably. ID they didn't have. They could run and he would never catch them. They could run and lose what might be their last chance of killing Lindqvist.

"You'll need badges," the old man said when they turned to face him.

He had two badges in his hand. He was holding them up.

Elsie took them and said, "Thanks."

The old man nodded and looked at Jamie, who forced a smile and said, "Thanks."

Fully badged and knowing the right room, Elsie and Jamie, dressed in their best, moved down the hall on the way to commit murder.

14

Abe Lieberman lay next to his wife in the dark. If he was unable to sleep, and he was reasonably sure he wouldn't, he had a half-finished biography of Alexander Hamilton to read, and there was a two A.M. show on the History Channel about the role of Madagascar in World War II.

"Janet's sister is staying with her tonight," said Bess, who, Abe decided, smelled very good.

"Good," said Abe.

"Noah Nathanson wasn't a popular man," Bess said.

Lieberman's eyes were closed in the hope of actually falling asleep and staying there for at least four hours.

"He was not," Abe agreed. "People called him Moe when he was a kid."

"Moe? You sure?"

"Moe."

"Moe is not a pleasant name."

"Not when applied to Noah Nathanson. It has the ring of slumpf and shuffle about it," said Abe.

"He never hurt anyone."

"His wife can put that on his tombstone. 'Here lies Noah Nathanson. He never hurt anyone. He just kvetched,'" said Abe.

"They'll be sitting shiva in their condo," said Bess.

"I'll drop in when I can."

The next day promised or threatened to be a busy one for Abe. He would first find Pinn Taibo who, he hoped, would lead him to the handsome man who had murdered four people. The man who had pretended to be Erhan Turkalu was a preening, confident son-of-a-bitch. He had fooled Abe. Abe took umbrage at this.

"Did I tell you you did a good job talking to Melissa and Barry about the baby and Lisa?" she asked.

"Thanks," he said.

"Roll this way, Avrum. Put an arm around me."

He did.

"Think you can get some sleep now?"

Abe thought he could not. Raspberries. Bess smelled of raspberries and felt like a ripening peach. The memory of the way she looked before she turned off the light, the first hint of arousal in his body made him reasonably sure that he could not sleep. Respect for the dead also made it wrong for him to respond to what his body wanted to do. Bess might refuse him. She seldom did, but while it felt right, he was reasonably sure it wasn't. Not tonight. Not so close to the death of Noah, sometimes known as Moe, Nathanson.

"Janet Nathanson's not the only woman widowed today," Lieberman said.

"Who else?"

He told her about Sahin's widow and son. She listened.

"You know what you just did?" Bess's voice came to him.

"What?"

"You talked about your work again. You never do that. Why today?"

"Attribute it to age, early dementia," he said.

"Not funny, Lieberman," she said.

"Sardonically amusing?" he asked.

"I'll give it that. You want to make love?" she asked.

"Yes, you?"

"I want to be close. It's a dark night and I'd like to keep you in bed where I can touch you instead of you wandering about the house with an old issue of the *Smithsonian*."

"There's an interesting article in the issue I'm reading. It's about lemurs."

"Fascinating," she said, reaching back with her left hand to touch his thigh.

Later Bess kissed him and said, "Shave in the morning. Good night."

Then she purred, as she always did after they had made love. She purred like a kitten.

Certain that he would be up in an hour, maybe two, Abe put an arm around his naked wife and closed his eyes.

He awoke less than four hours later grateful that he had not been attacked and killed by bad cholesterol during the night. Abe shuffled toward the bathroom and paused in front of the mirror on the door. By the light of the moon through the windows, the thin, naked man in front of him was not impressive. He imagined the good-looking killer examining himself in the morning mirror, preening, smiling, showing his white teeth, pleased by what he saw.

"I will," he told his mirror image, "get that son-of-a-bitch."

Mary-Catherine Sahin lay alone in the dark. She had stayed awake till just before one in the morning, waiting for him to call. No call had come.

She had loved Lemi. He had been sincerely thoughtful, kind, generous, a good husband, a good man, and a terrible lover.

Omar Mehem, on the other hand, had been thoughtful and kind and a wonderful lover. She had sensed that the thoughtfulness and kindness were restless captives inside of Omar's mask. Whatever her lover really was had never emerged when he was with her or inside of her.

He had come into her life through Lemi, who had invited him home one night for dinner. Lemi talked about nothing but getting the world to respect Turkey. He talked about someone named Aziz and said he was willing to pay to get something this Aziz had.

Omar had nodded agreeably, said he could, indeed, get this thing. All the while as he spoke, Omar had from time to time taken in Mary-Catherine. These had not been stolen glances but confident appraisal. She recognized it, knew what was happening. Lemi, wrapped tightly in his obsession, had noticed nothing.

The next day, the very next day, he had called. Max had been in nursery school. Lemi at his office. Omar had said that he wanted to see her.

"No games," he had said. "With you I want no games. If you want to hang up, I'll understand and I'll bother you no more."

"I'm not hanging up," she had said.

"When can I see you?"

"Now," she said.

"I'll be there in less than half an hour."

And that was how it had started.

One night, a few weeks later, Lemi had been called by Omar. Lemi had been polite, but far more distant than he had been the night Omar had come to dinner. Had he suspected? When the call was over, Lemi had said, "I don't trust that man."

The truth was that Mary-Catherine didn't either, but that had nothing to do with his being her lover. There was no going back. She didn't want to go back.

And then, just two nights ago, in bed after Omar had explored her in a variation she had never before experienced, he had commented on Lemi's continued interest in the Aziz business, commented in such a way that he gave the impression of feeling sorry for Lemi and his inability to put away his hobbyhorse.

"Tomorrow I'm going to give him something that he will treasure," Omar had said.

She had thought little about what he had said. It was a snippet of information shared casually by two lovers who had in common only her husband.

Now, in darkness, she wondered if that piece of information shared by Omar was connected to Lemi's death. It was improbable. It was possible.

If it was so, than Omar's interest in her might well have been only a means of keeping track of Lemi's search for the Aziz material. It was possible, however, that his interest in her was also sexual. Both reasons could be true. They were not mutually exclusive.

But he had not called. Lemi had died and Omar had not called. The longer she lay there in the darkness, the more she was certain that Omar was involved in her husband's murder.

In the morning, she would call the Jew. She had his name on a card downstairs, in the Rolodex near the phone. On the card had been only his name, rank, and a phone number. She needed no more.

The doorbell was ringing beyond the closed bedroom door, down the stairs. She had not heard it at first. She looked at the clock next to the bed. Its glowing red digital numbers told her it was almost two.

The doorbell was ringing. It would wake Max. She would bring Max into her room and bed to comfort him and herself.

The doorbell rang. She put on her pink silk robe, the one Lemi had given her for her birthday. No, it wasn't her birthday. He had simply chosen a day to give her a present.

The doorbell rang. She hurried down the stairs. The last time she had hurried down these stairs at night it had been the Jewish detective coming to tell her that Lemi had died.

The doorbell rang.

"Who is it?" she called, putting her eye to the small hole in the door.

The outdoor light above the entrance was lit. She could see clearly. The person on the other side of the door was distorted by the glass in the peephole. Even with that there was no doubting who it was. She opened the door and let George Macrapolis, Oliver Martin, Omar Mehem in.

Five thousand dollars. They had offered him five thousand dollars. That would come out to one thousand and two hundred and fifty dollars for each person he had killed in the last two days. He could make far more money as a hit man. He couldn't buy a decent used car for five thousand dollars.

But George Macrapolis was not a hit man and he did not need a car. He needed money to get away from Chicago, to start again in comfort. No, at this point the goal would simply be to get away.

The old Turk and the fat Turk had met with him in the lobby of their hotel at one in the morning. George hoped, expected, that they would have a check. He could and would trust them with a check he could deposit in a Bank of America account he could access from London. Cash might be more certain, but it would be very awkward to carry cases filled with millions of dollars.

He had given the package to the two men, hurried home to meet and bed Jennifer, the belly dancer. When he finished with her she had kissed him and quickly left after George had lied, "I'll see you soon."

George had drunk coffee, watched television, looked out the window at the street below, wondered who the person was who had called him on his show. He wondered if the caller planned to blackmail or kill him or if he simply wanted to drive him mad with fear.

If it was money the caller was after, George hoped that he would have money enough in a few hours when the Turks paid him. If it were his life the person sought, George would be gone in a few hours and a man with a different name and identity, compete with driver's license and bank account, would emerge in London.

In his new identity with a massive bank account, George would need no Social Security card, for he did not plan to enter into a health plan, get a job, or vote.

If he could make it through a few more hours, all would be well. A sound? The sticky sound of rubber-soled shoes on the floor outside his apartment?

George had a gun—a model 410S Smith & Wesson pistol. He had never used it. He preferred a knife, the silence of a knife, the face-to-face satisfaction of being almost nose to nose with the person he was going to kill. It was sick, he knew. Sick, but too compelling and certain to resist. Maybe something was wrong inside his head, something that had been there since before his birth. He didn't care. He was what he was. Understanding why, if that were even possible, would change nothing.

Another sound outside the door?

The door was double dead-bolted and firmly chained.

George got his gun. He knew very little about the gun except that one pulled the trigger and it fired. The gun had the added feature of being small and light enough to fit into his pocket.

George went to the door, put his ear against it, and then imagined the person on the other side with a gun in his hand, his ear to the door. When he heard George at the door, had his footsteps betrayed him?—would he simply fire through the thick wood? A bullet racing through his ear and into his brain, carrying with it microscopic shards of wood?

George stepped back from the door quickly.

The phone was ringing. He moved across the room to it. It was the fat Turk who asked him to come to the lobby of the hotel in one hour. George said he would be there.

George was dressed, his best suit. He had already packed all that he needed in his brown leather duffel bag. He would get the money and drive out of town. A check of the airlines, trains, buses, would yield nothing to the police or the person who might be stalking Omar Mehem or Oliver Martin. He was George Macrapolis, a fully documented, passported Greek.

After a double-check of the apartment and no tinge of regret for the items he was leaving behind, George picked up his duffel with his left hand. In his right hand, he clutched the pistol. He had to leave now.

He put down the bag, carefully, noiselessly undid the chains and, with minimum sound, unlocked the dead bolts.

He moved to the right of the door, back against the wall, and threw open the door.

No time to think. Would he step out and find himself face-to-face with a man with a gun? George stepped into the door frame. There was no one there.

He picked up the duffel again, stepped out into the hall looking both ways, closed the door, pocketed the gun but kept his hand on it, and headed toward the stairs.

He didn't know if he was being followed. He didn't think so, but all thoughts about the real or imagined pursuer vanished when he had gotten to the hotel and the fat man had said, "The document is a fake, written a year or so after the events the writer describes. Of this there is no doubt."

The lobby was empty, the lights low. They sat in an alcove, the Turks next to each other on a sofa, George across from them in a wooden armed chair with a paisley print cushion.

He had looked at the old man, who was smoking a particularly foul-smelling cigarette in a stained ivory holder.

"It is worth no more than five thousand dollars," said the fat Turk. "It is of interest as a century-old attempt to alter history."

"It's real," George had insisted.

"Would to Allah that it were," said the old Turk with a nod of his head.

"Any attempt to present it as authentic would be doomed to failure," said the fat Turk. "So . . ."

"It is real," George insisted.

"Then take it and may Allah forgive you in your attempts to profit from a falsity," said the fat Turk.

"The Prophet," the old man said, "has said, 'riches come

not from abundance of worldly goods, but from a contented mind.' "

"Does this apply to the man for whom you work?" George said, trying to control his anger, his disappointment.

"To us all," said the old man.

"We have been informed that four Turkish-Americans have died in the last day," said the fat Turk.

"I don't know anything about that," said George.

The fat man grunted, shifted his weight.

"Did you think we mean to harm you?" asked the fat man. "Or cheat you?"

"No," said George, puzzled.

"Then the person lurking in the shadows of the drapery to our right has probably followed you," said the fat Turk. "I suggest you not acknowledge your awareness of his presence."

The old Turk nodded. George resisted the urge to turn his head and look. Was the fat Turk lying? Why? To get George to run?

"If you shoot him," said the old man, "please do it away from this hotel. We would prefer not to be connected with misfortune."

"And if he were to shoot me," said George, "you would want that done far away too. Does he work for you?"

"No," said the fat Turk. "There is no reason for us to have you killed, is there?"

"No," said George, "but you might want your five thousand dollars back."

The fat Turk smiled.

"Mr. Mehem," he said leaning forward, "I spend ten thousand dollars in a random week on custom-made clothes. As the Americans say, at five thousand dollars, you are a cheap date."

"I think we no longer want this," the old man said, handing George the journal.

"But you said you would pay five thousand dollars for it," said George.

"No," said the fat man. "We said it was worth five thousand dollars. But it is covered in the unseen blood of four people, is it not?"

"No."

"We have nothing more to say," said the fat man. "You may go."

George considered killing them. There really was nothing to gain from that and the person hiding behind the drapes, if there was such a person, would see him. Though there were no members of the hotel staff in sight, even a swift professional killing might be heard.

The fat man was shaking his head no.

"Do not consider it," the fat man said. "Under this table, I hold in my hand a gun whose report will scarcely break the silence."

George unzipped the duffel bag next to him, put the journal inside, and zipped the bag closed.

"*Gül gül,* goodbye," said the old man.

George was being dismissed.

"*Hayir*, no," said George, "I . . ."

"You are in no position to threaten, challenge, or be rude," said the fat Turk calmly. "You have murdered four people, four Turkish people, and that might well offend not only the friends and relatives of the dead, but people who would mourn over the death of any Turkish member of the faith."

They knew. How could they be so certain? How did the man who called his show know? George could no longer resist. He stood and turned to face the darkness in the corner of the vast lobby. His eyes scanned the drapery. His hand gripped the gun in his pocket. Something moved.

"Not here," said the fat Turk firmly.

George picked up his duffel bag and hurried across the lobby without looking back.

Someone was following him, probably going to kill and rob him.

George did not want a shoot-out. George knew he was unlikely to win unless the stalker was palsy-afflicted and half-blind.

A valet had parked his car. He waited for the young man's return. George had planned to come out of the hotel a rich man. He had planned to tip the slow-moving valet so generously that the young man would talk about it to the moment of his death. But now that reality had spat on his dream, he gave the valet two dollars and drove off.

Was he followed? He didn't know, but he took no chances. He watched his rearview mirror as he drove onto Lake Shore Drive and headed north.

A new plan came to him. Maybe it had always been there as a backup he didn't want to use. He knew she had more than one hundred thousand dollars in checking and savings accounts in the bank. She had told him one night when they had talked about her leaving her husband, starting over. George knew she was lying about leaving Sahin, maybe lying both to him and herself. It didn't matter. George had no intention of starting a new life with her, as surprisingly good as she had been in bed.

Lemi Sahin had a two-million-dollar life-insurance policy. George was not greedy or stupid enough to risk trying to get his hands on the two million. It would be weeks, possibly months, before she got the insurance money. The cash and savings could be obtained in minutes when the bank opened in the morning.

The only problem would be getting her to get the money and give it to him. Time to think, plan, watch the rearview mirror.

Traffic was light. To his right less than a hundred yards away was the lake. He couldn't see it. He saw endless blackness.

He tilted the mirror to examine his face. He looked good, not his best, but good enough. When he passed Devon on Sheridan Road, he stopped at a BP station, took his duffel into the rest room, shaved, brushed his teeth, combed his hair, straightened his tie, and filled his tank with regular unleaded. He was ready.

He made one more stop on the way to where he was going. There was no reason the police would be watching, but he checked carefully before he got out of the car and went inside. It took him no more than two minutes and then he was back in his car and heading north.

When he got to Lincolnwood, he parked, as he always had when he came here, about four blocks away on a side street. The sun was about to rise. The houses took shape. Duffel bag in hand, he walked quickly in street-lamp yellow and early-morning brume to the door and pressed the button. It took her a long time to open the door.

The man who was following George sat watching. He had arrived here fifteen minutes before George. It had been clear to the man where George was heading so he had stopped following and drove ahead to find a parking spot from which he could see the front of the house.

He had watched Ekrem Nasuh hand something to George, watched George look toward the shadows in which the man was hiding, watched George pick up his bag, and hurry away.

He could have confronted George on the street, talked to him, made him beg for mercy, but that would be too noisy. Certainly firing a gun would alert someone in this quiet neighborhood. And it was always possible that a car would come past or someone might decide to walk his complaining dog.

No, the best thing to do was go into the house.

The complications were great. He might have to shoot the widow, the adulterous widow, the beautiful widow. He did not want to do that. And then there was the child. He could not kill the child, the son of Lemi Sahin.

The child would live. The widow would live if it were possible, but George Macrapolis was certain to be slain. The only question was, how long should he take before entering the house?

15

It beckoned to him, the large cheese blintz in the refrigerator. Abe had not dreamed of it, but it came to mind and to his alert taste buds the moment he woke up at 3:37 A.M. He had hoped to make it to four A.M. but he was reasonably satisfied with three-and-a-half hours of undisturbed sleep.

Now he sat, barefooted, in his pajamas at the small kitchen table, the door to the dining room closed, knife and fork at the ready. Terrill's microwaved ode to cholesterol in front of him. The blintz was not fat-free. Jerome Terrill did not skimp on cream cheese, eggs, or sugar. It was what a cheese blintz should be, tempting, tasty, and potentially lethal, like almost all worthwhile Jewish food.

The ability to weigh down the table with the cuisine of Eastern European Jewish dishes was based on the belief that no dish worth consumption could be made without massive helpings of schmaltz, the fat of chickens.

Abe's mother had been a firm believer that no one should

leave the table without indigestion. Her favored dishes were gehockten layber, chopped liver, made with schmaltz; gribenes, pieces of chicken skin deep-fried in schmaltz; and kishke, the gut of a cow turned inside out, scalded, scraped, one end sewn, and the length filled with an ever-varying mix of flour, schmaltz, onions, eggs, salt, pepper, and whatever looked interesting.

Abe made the first incision and the smell released was beyond tempting. The house phone on the wall near the door rang before Abe could finish cutting that first small piece.

Abe got to it before the second ring, hoping that the deep-sleeping Bess hadn't been awakened.

"Hello," said Abe, walking back to the table, phone to his ear.

"Abe, I knew you'd answer."

There was a tone of weary certainty in her voice. The last time they had met in person Lisa had said she would start calling him Dad instead of Abe, but after more than thirty-five years it was difficult to stop. In truth, it didn't seem natural to either father or daughter.

"You are prescient."

"No," Lisa said. "I'm a Lieberman who has inherited the family curse from her father. I'm an insomniac."

She had said it not as a sad statement of fact nor as a declaration of resignation. It was an assignment of blame.

"I know," said Abe, holding the phone to his ear and trying to cut off a piece of the blintz with his fork.

"Did you talk to them?" asked Lisa.

"About the baby? Yes," he said.

"And?"

"And they wanted to know if the baby would be brown and if he or she would come here and live with us."

The still steaming piece of blintz was raggedly cut but neatly skewered.

"And what did you tell them?"

"The baby would almost certainly be brown and would not be living with us."

The piece of blintz was hot, too hot. He had, as was often the case, overheated it in the microwave. He put his fork back on the plate.

"What do you think?" she asked.

"I'll have a third grandchild," he said. "I will give that grandchild the attention and affection and occasional nuggets of questionable knowledge that I give to his siblings."

"You said 'his.' You want it to be a boy."

"I said 'his' because it is more animate and personal than 'its' and less awkward than saying 'his or her.' You said 'it.' "

"We're going to argue about nothing again," said Lisa.

"No, I'm just being a barefoot, insomniac curmudgeon in need of coffee, sustenance, and a shave."

"I talked to them, Barry and Melissa, last night," Lisa said.

"I know."

"They were, I don't know, distant."

"Two thousand miles distant," said Abe. "Wait, check, I take that back. Let's put it another way. They have nothing against having a new brother, be he black, white, purple, or fudge ripple."

"It's me," Lisa said. "They think I've abandoned them."

Well, you have, thought Abe, who was not about to say this aloud. Besides, they had been over this five or six times since Lisa had decided that she was not up to raising her children. Her children, in turn, were not up to completely forgiving her and Abe couldn't help wondering how his daughter would deal with the new baby after the first rush of ecstasy was replaced by the slow pace of reality. Would he and Bess be raising yet another grandchild?

"Marvin's happy about the baby?" asked Abe.

Marvin Alexander, M.D., was Lisa's second husband. He was a highly visible and much published Los Angeles–based pathologist. Having done his internship and residency in Israel, Marvin could speak fluent Hebrew and knew more about Israeli history than any member of Temple Mir Shavot, with the possible exception of Rabbi Wass. With all that, Marvin was neither Jew nor Christian. He was a practicing atheist.

"Ecstatic," said Lisa flatly.

He tried for the piece of blintz again.

"Abe, I'm feeling a lot of stress here."

So, thought Abe, what else was new? Wherever his daughter went, stress was sure to follow and seek her out.

"I'm sorry," said Abe, finally getting that first taste of blintz. It was even better for having been delayed.

"I'm thinking of coming home for a while. Marvin thinks it would be a good idea."

"Your job?"

Lisa was a biochemist in the same hospital where her husband had daily sessions with the dead. Abe had no idea of what his daughter actually did. When he imagined her at work, he saw her in a white lab coat huddled over a very large glittering metallic microscope with a line of petri dishes on the table where she was working.

"It will be here when I get back," she said. "Am I welcome?"

"Always," said Abe.

"No," she said. "Not always, not when we fight."

"Not when we fight," Abe agreed, thinking that a sincere dollop of sour cream would enhance the near perfection of the blintz before him.

"Why do we fight, Abe?"

It was too early in the morning for this conversation and Abe knew what the outcome would be if he entered it further.

" 'You have always been compelled to seek out my imperfections with your wit.' "

"Shakespeare," she said. "That's from Shakespeare, isn't it?"

"I confess."

"Shakespeare, not Lieberman," she said.

"Shakespeare is far more eloquent than Lieberman," said Abe, rising and moving to the refrigerator.

"You don't want to talk now, do you?" she asked.

He did not, but he said, "To paraphrase Tigger and not Shakespeare, talking is what Liebermans do best. So, when are you coming?"

"In about two weeks. I'll call Mom later."

Mom, not Bess. Abe, not Dad or Pop or Abba.

The silence was long. Lisa sighed and said, "Are you all right?"

"Fine," he said.

"That's good. I'll call Mom later."

She hung up and so did Abe after he put the container of sour cream on the table along with a large spoon for scooping it.

Then the kitchen door opened. Barry and Melissa came in, looking as if they had traveled a a dozen miles in bare feet.

"We couldn't sleep," said Barry.

Melissa shook her head. Abe couldn't tell if she was agreeing or disagreeing with her brother.

"The Lieberman curse," Abe said.

"We're hungry," said Melissa.

"We've got six cereals drenched in chocolate and sugar," Abe said.

"What are you eating?" Barry asked.

"This? A lonely beckoning cheese blintz."

"Smells good," said Melissa.

"It's full of cholesterol," said Barry. "You're not supposed to be eating cholesterol or you'll have a heart attack like Uncle Maish."

"Somehow, the prospect of enjoying this repast has been diminished," Abe said.

"Why do you talk so funny?" asked Melissa.

Abe's grandchildren got themselves plates and forks and joined him at the table.

"I only do it at home and at the wrong times," said Abe. "Normally, I talk like everyone else. You want some of this blintz?"

It was question that needed no answer. The question wasn't even necessary. He cut the large blintz into three more-or-less even pieces and doled the pieces out. They reached for the sour cream before he could offer it.

"You have any other questions, Grandpa?" asked Melissa.

"One," said Abe, attacking the blintz before his wife could come in and either shame it from him or force him to divide his meager piece and give half to her. "How did the killer know where the Turkish doctor would be and when he would be there?"

"That from an old movie?" asked Barry, cheeks full.

"No," said Abe.

"I know the answer," Melissa said, holding up her hand.

"And what is it?" asked Abe.

"He knew because someone told him," she said.

Abe was nodding in agreement.

"I was thinking the same thing," he said.

The lights were out in Jonas Lindqvist's room. All the lights. Elsie and Jamie stood waiting for their eyes to adjust to the darkness. Neither spoke. There was no need to. They moved toward where they remembered the bed to be. They were beginning to see things Jamie preferred not to see. He would do what he had to do but he didn't like it, didn't like it one bit.

Before the last two days, Jamie had found meaning in the feeling of a solid punch when it landed. It was better than making a three-pointer or hitting a solid single to right field. Jamie hadn't played much basketball or baseball, but he could imagine.

Jamie had felt no satisfaction in pummeling the big blond guy, the guy in the bed in front of him, and he had felt the rattling of nausea when he landed solidly on the chest of the Chinese guy. He had killed that guy with a punch. He was about to do it again to the big blond in the bed. Jamie feared that after tonight he would forever hesitate before throwing the big jab or a right cross. That would be the end of his career. All that he had done in the last day had been to keep his and Elsie's ring hopes alive. What had happened, instead, was that a rug from Elsie's aunt had been thrown over his career.

They could make out the bed now, the shape of the man they had come to kill.

"No, no, no sheep in the soufflé," Lindqvist muttered in his sleep. "No, please, no."

Jamie hesitated. The man was sleeping but was he also talking to Jamie? Subconscious, unconscious talking?

The plan was that Elsie would cover the man's mouth and Jamie would throw two, three, four rights to his chest and stomach. *Woompf, woompf, woompf.* Then they would leave him there, a puzzle for the hospital, a puzzle for the police.

As they stepped to the side of the bed, Jamie realized that

he wouldn't be able to hit the big man hard enough if he was lying down. He had no angle. He could climb up on the bed, spread-eagle the man, but even that wouldn't be enough.

"We've got to sit him up," Jamie whispered.

Elsie understood. She nodded. Jamie couldn't see the nod. They would have to hope Lindqvist stayed asleep, but they knew he would probably wake up. It depended on how doped-up the hospital was keeping him.

"Let's do it," said Elsie.

"No," said Jamie, looking at the man in the bed. "Let's just get out of here."

"Let's just stay."

The last came not from Elsie but from a voice in the corner of the room near the door. The lights came on, twinkling, pinging, and they saw the man standing in front of a chair in the corner.

The man was big, broad, not as tall as Lindqvist but more solid. He had a gun in his right hand.

Lindqvist mumbled something, blinked his eyes, groaned in pain, and bit his lower lip.

"On the floor," said Hanrahan.

Elsie and Jamie stood still in their confusion. Everything was going wrong.

"On the floor," Hanrahan repeated, a little louder.

Lindqvist moaned, sat up at the side of the bed, stood, and went to his knees.

"Not you," Bill said to him.

Lindqvist nodded his head and painfully returned to the bed where he sat blinking his eyes.

For Hanrahan, putting the perp face-down and then searching and cuffing him was routine.

For Jamie, going face-down on the floor was humiliation.

Prone position. Simulation of a knockout, the worst kind, face-down. He was sure Elsie felt the same. Well, almost the same. Not so deep down, Jamie knew he was about to lose it—his career, his wife, his freedom, his dignity.

"They're the ones," said Lindqvist, gritting his teeth in pain and pointing at Elsie and Jamie. "I need a pain pill."

"Get down," Hanrahan demanded firmly.

"No," said Jamie. "I can't."

Some of the haze cleared for Jonas Lindqvist and he took in the scene.

Bill was facing a dilemma. Could he shoot Cuervo? Should he? The man didn't seem to have a weapon. There were regulations, piles and piles of them, and Bill was certain more than one of them dealt with not shooting an unarmed man even if he were Charles Manson smiling and looking for a knife. There was probably a regulation somewhere about firing a weapon in a hospital.

"Else," said Jamie. "Get up."

She was on her knees. Jamie reached down to help her up. She stood, looked at him and then at Hanrahan and the gun in his hand. Jamie, Elsie behind him, took a step toward the door.

"Stop," said Hanrahan. "I don't want to shoot, but I will do it."

He was lying. Until things had turned around, until Abe and Iris had turned him around, William Hanrahan was a card-carrying, certified alcoholic with enough citations for dereliction, delinquency, and negligence to close out a career and lose a badge. Bill Hanrahan had been given another chance. The paper file and cyberspace report that listed all of his mistakes also listed his successes including bravery under fire.

But what was happening in this hospital room threatened

the star he wore. He couldn't shoot them. He couldn't let them go. They were unarmed. They had killed a man. They were here to kill another.

"Wait," Lindqvist said. "For God's sake, stop them. They tried to kill me. Twice."

Elsie and Jamie had been moving slowly, watching the big cop with the gun in his hand, unsure of whether or not he was going to shoot, unsure of what they would do when and if they got out of this room.

Hanrahan moved, not fast but quick enough to beat Elsie and Jamie to the door and to block their exit with his body.

They were playing different games. The cop was playing right guard protecting a door. The boxers were moving in on a heavyweight, determined to go through him.

"Move," said Jamie, fists clenched.

"I told you once to get your face on the floor. Now do it."

"Never gonna happen," said Jamie.

Then Hanrahan understood.

"Okay," he said. "Just turn around, hands behind the back, both of you."

Lindqvist had plopped on his back, arm across his eyes, and said, "*Det sprider sig sa han som sket i fläkten.* It's spreading, said he who shat in the fan."

Hanrahan wasn't as fast as Jamie Cuervo, but he was first. He also knew that if the two boxers didn't lose their heads completely, they wouldn't be going for Bill's head or face. They wouldn't want to collide bone-to-bone and break their knuckles.

So before Jamie could throw the setup jab, Bill turned to the side and brought his revolver down hard to the side of the boxer's head. Jamie staggered back, head bleeding. Elsie threw a solid right to Bill's left kidney. It hurt like holy hell. He winced. She hit him again, this time with a hard left to the belly. It closed his eyes, but didn't keep him from swinging at her. He felt the gun make contact, heard her grunt.

Eyes open now, he looked at Elsie whose mouth was open, who screamed, who had a red-blotched cheek. Her jaw was broken. Jamie, blood streaming into his left eye, was on him with a howl and a hell-with-my-hands jab at Hanrahan's face. He connected. Hanrahan slumping against the door thought he heard bones breaking. He wasn't sure if they were his or Jamie Cuervo's.

Bill's knees were giving out. Jamie would be all over him, take his gun, shoot him, leave Iris a widow, Jane Mei with no father. Bill decided to shoot Jamie, who stood over him now, his face red with blood, right arm cocked.

Then a noise, a *thunk,* and Jamie backed away, holding his head with both hands.

Behind him stood Jonas Lindqvist with a metal water pitcher in hand.

"When I have a fever I talk Swedish," said Jonas. "I talk Swedish and I hit people who want to kill me. It's an old Swedish custom."

Bill pushed away from the wall, cuffed the moaning Elsie and dazed Jamie, and whispered to him, "TKO in the first."

Lindqvist, one hand on his crotch, the other holding the pitcher, shuffled to the bed, sat, grimaced, and pushed the button on the cable next to the bed.

Jonas said, "I need a pain pill. I very much need a pain pill. And they need medical attention. And I would very much appreciate it if you put them somewhere where they would stop trying to kill me."

Mr. Woo was awakened by a light tap on his bedroom door. He had been dreaming of the Yalu River, its mud-yellow water rising almost to flood level. This was a curious dream since he had never seen the river and the river held no special meaning for him. The dream was neither pleasant nor a nightmare. It simply was.

Another rap at the door, but no louder than the first.

"Come in," he said.

There was a light on in the room, a small shaded lamp that glowed a comforting yellow, a yellow not like the muddy river of his dream but very much like a slowly dying candle. Mr. Woo felt a kinship with his evoked candle. Mr. Woo estimated his age at eighty-three, but he wasn't certain.

"Telephone," said the man who entered the room.

Woo was sitting up. He slept sitting up, four silk encased pillows behind his head and back. He reached for his glasses slowly, calmly, found them and put them on. There were few, very few, people who had his phone number and those few had been told that they could call at any time providing they had something truly urgent to say.

Woo looked up at the messenger who left the room, closing the door behind him as Woo picked up the phone.

"Speak," he said.

"It's me."

There was no mistaking the voice. American, cocky, making a dollar on either side of the law. Woo had no doubt that Detective Donald Spotswoode was an excellent policeman. He also had no doubt that as long as Spotswoode believed the information he passed on did not compromise his duty, he would continue to supply it.

"Ten minutes ago, in Woodrow Wilson Hospital, Hanrahan arrested an Elsie and Jamie Cuervo in connection with the murder of Robert E. Lee Chang. Seems the Cuervos were at the hospital to kill a patient. I don't know why. I do know Hanrahan inflicted some real damage. Woman's jaw is broken. Man's head is fractured."

"Where do these Cuervos live?"

Spotswoode told him and went silent.

"And how much time would one have who chose to go to that apartment before the police arrive?"

"Depends," said Spotswoode. "My guess is Hanrahan will go there on his own. Take him a while. The Cuervos landed a few punches before he took them down."

"Was the Jewish detective there?" asked Woo.

"No, he's working another case."

"I appreciate your prompt call."

"You're welcome," said Spotswoode.

They both hung up.

Woo pushed button number seven on his phone followed by the pound sign. Then he listened to the seven tones that automatically dialed the number. Two rings. When the man answered, Woo told him precisely where to go and what to do.

"Go yourself. Do not send one of your people," said Woo. "Find my money. Bring it to me."

Woo went back to sleep to dream of the Yalu River.

While he slept, the man he had just spoken to over the phone quickly dressed in neatly pressed black slacks and a recently ironed blue pullover shirt. He put on his holster and gun, donned a black sports jacket and seventeen minutes later was at the door to the Cuervos' apartment. Getting in was no problem. The door lock was bulky, primitive, and useless. One of his seven all-purpose keys easily fit the lock.

After putting on white surgical gloves, he entered noiselessly and noted that the light in the kitchen space was on. It would be sufficient. He had a flashlight in his pocket if it were not.

He searched quickly, efficiently. Under the bed he found a bloody rug and an empty briefcase. He placed the briefcase on the table and unrolled the rug in the middle of the floor on the chance that the money was wrapped inside it. It wasn't.

Closet, drawers, refrigerator, bed, toilet, ceiling panels, floors. Nothing. He wasn't discouraged. He opened the window and looked both up and down. Back inside the apartment, he tapped the walls and found no hollow sound. He unscrewed the plates over the vents and found nothing beyond them. He didn't bother to put the screws back on.

Pantry. It was full of cans and boxes of health food. Huge clear plastic bowls with snap-on lids stood atop one another. Then he looked at the high shelf at the boxes of cereal, a dozen of them, giant-size. Enough cereal to withstand a siege for weeks if whoever was after them tried to starve them out. He pulled down a box of Cheerios. It was not rattling with tiny lifeboat circles of whole wheat. It felt solid, firm, heavy.

He placed the box on the table, opened it, and removed a stack of bills wrapped in brown paper bands. He repeated this till twelve empty cereal boxes were strewn on the table and floor and he had the entire $150,000 in front of him. He placed reasonably neat packages of two-thousand-dollar packets of hundred dollar bills into the briefcase. It was a tight fit.

At the door, he put the briefcase full of cash on the ground and removed his rubber gloves. Then he looked around at the mess he had created, and was satisfied. He picked up the briefcase.

It was then that the door to the small apartment opened. The man with the briefcase took his gun from the holster under his jacket. Then he saw that the man entering the apartment had a gun just as large.

16

Pinn Taibo opened the door. Both he and Abe Lieberman were surprised. Pinn was surprised to see the policeman at his door. Abe was surprised to see Pinn in ironed tan slacks, a white shirt, and a tie.

"I hope this is a convenient time for a chat," said Abe.

It was a little after eight in the morning.

"What the fuck are you—?" said Pinn.

"I'll take that as a yes. Let's go inside and you can offer me a cup of coffee or tea and a cruller."

"A what?"

The apartment was on the third floor of a three-story thirties's six-flat brick building on Thorndale just off Ridge.

"Invite me in," said Abe.

"I'm gonna be late for a job interview," Pinn said.

"With who?"

"None of your fuckin' business."

"I'll give you a tardy excuse note," said Abe. "I do it all the time. Now we go in or I arrest you and we talk in the comfort of an interrogation room."

"Arrest me for what?"

"I'd like to make it for having an unpleasant disposition," said Abe, "but since that's not against the law, let's go for income tax evasion."

"You are crazy, man."

"There are those who have said that," said Abe. "But that didn't stop me from arresting them."

Pinn shook his head and said, "Hey, I'm tryin' to take a dangerous man—me—off the street and get him into a straight job and . . . oh, shit, come in."

The alcove smelled of fresh lemony soap. Pinn led the way to the living room. The room was neat. The furniture red and blue and modern. On the wall was a painting—a big painting of a man in a peasant's sombrero. The man was squatting as he handed something to a small child whose hand was out.

"You like that?" asked Pinn.

"The painting? Yes."

"My grandfather painted it. That's supposed to be my father and me back in Dominica. What do you want?"

"The man who hired you to kill the Camel in Lincoln Park yesterday," said Abe.

"I wasn't hired to—"

"¿Quién es?" asked a woman, entering the room through an open door to the kitchen.

"Abuela, no es importante," said Pinn.

The woman who Pinn called grandmother couldn't have been more than sixty years old. She was lean, had dark long hair tied in the back, and was wearing a uniform. The uniform was one Abe recognized. She worked at a Burger King.

She looked at her grandson and then at the visitor.

"My name is Abraham Lieberman. I came by to ask your grandson for a favor."

"You are a Jew," the woman said.

Her accent was distinct, but not thick.

"That I am."

"We are Catholics," she said. "We give money to that rabbi on television to get Russian Jews to Israel. You are the chosen people."

"And an odd choice it is," said Abe.

Pinn checked his watch.

"I've got to get to that interview," said Pinn.

"I will leave you to your talk," said the woman. "Don't be late, Pinto."

When she left the room, Abe asked, "Who hired you to kill the Camel?"

"If I was hired, and I'm not saying I was, why should I tell you?"

"Because I can talk to El Perro and convince him to refrain from killing you," said Abe. "You brought Herve, a Tentaculo, into this. El Perro has taken offense."

"Oh, man," Pinn groaned, turning to look out the window.

Across the tops of lower single-family homes, Lieberman could see Senn High School. Abe wondered, not for the first time, if the gym still looked the same as it had forty-four years ago when he, Maish, and the rest of the Marshall Commandos had devastated Senn. Marshall had won 98–32. Abe could still taste, feel the pass he made to Ordell Wayne, who had laid the ball up and in for the first two points of the game.

"So?" asked Pinn.

"Sorry, I was thinking about basketball," said Abe.

"Basketball? You are *uno loco hombre.*"

"Your brother home?"

"José went to school already."

"Neither of us has a lot of time," said Abe. "So, you talk and I leave and you get to your job interview on time."

"I didn't know the guy, the one who paid us to waste the old freak in the park. I mean we're not friends, anything like that. I see him *de vez en cuando,* you know."

"Where?"

"At the radio station. I clean up there, other places at night. I'm looking to move up though, which is why I want to get to that job interview."

"What radio station?"

"Little back-of-the-ass place, WTUR. They do shows in goofy-sounding languages. The guy who wanted me to get rid of the old guy in the park is a DJ or something."

"He have a name?"

"Everybody's got a name. Omar something. Don't remember the last name. Got a picture of him though."

"What kind of picture?"

"On a flyer I got somewhere in my room."

"Can I trouble you to get it for me?"

Pinn stood for a few seconds looking down at Abe.

"I could crush you with one hand, you know that?"

"No, you could not," said Abe. "You just threatened the life of a police officer. You take a step toward me instead of toward your bedroom and I'll reluctantly shoot you somewhere that will result in your walking with a limp for the rest of your life."

"You would, wouldn't you?"

"I would."

"Shooting a man isn't easy," said Pinn.

"I know. I've never gotten completely comfortable with it, but I've done it anyway. Now, that poster."

"You win," Pinn said.

He turned, walked quickly to the lemon-smelling alcove, and disappeared. Abe walked closer to the painting of the man and boy, neither of whom was smiling. For them it was a sad connection.

Pinn returned and handed a green sheet of paper folded in half. Abe unfolded the sheet. All the words, except for an address on Chicago Avenue, were in a foreign language that didn't matter to Abe. He was interested in the picture of the man on the front of the poster.

"Him," said Pinn.

The copy of the photograph wasn't great, but it was good enough. The man on the sheet was the same man Abe had talked to in the Anatolia Restaurant, the man who had said he was Turkalu, the man who had murdered four Turkish-Americans.

"Good luck with the interview," said Abe, moving to the door.

"Thanks," said Pinn.

Finding the name and address of the murderer had been easy. Abe called the radio station, got the day manager who was also the morning DJ. Two minutes later he had what he needed.

Less than an hour later Abe Lieberman was in the apartment rented by Omar Mehem, aka Oliver Martin.

Omar or Oliver was not home. The building supervisor, a grumbling man with a limp and a nick on his cheek from a bad morning's shave, let Abe in and then departed.

It took Abe less than five minutes to find the bottom drawer in the dresser that contained photographs. They were all photographs of women, women standing, sitting, lying down, eating. All the women were smiling except one. She was a blonde, a very pretty blonde in slacks and a very revealing white blouse. The woman was lost in thought. The woman was the widow of Lemi Sahin.

The man in the Cuervo apartment with the gun in one hand and the briefcase in the other was Parker Liao, leader of the Twin Dragons gang. Parker was lean, handsome, definitely brooding, and not yet thirty years old.

The man who had just entered the apartment was not lean, handsome, nor brooding, and he was fifty-three years old. Bill Hanrahan was leader of no one.

The two men recognized each other in the shadowed light from the kitchen and the haze of morning light through the shaded windows. They both knew what the other was doing here.

"That it?" asked Hanrahan, nodding at the briefcase.

Mr. Woo did not control the Twin Dragons, the gang of thirty-eight Chinese-American men and boys, but he did ask their leader for favors from time to time. Mr. Woo, who oversaw the criminal enterprises of Chinatown, had no gang, only four bodyguards, one of whom had some expertise in martial arts. The bodyguard's martial arts skills were primarily for show. Mr. Woo thought martial arts were a nice, harmless form of exercise. He had learned, however, that no kick, leap, or turn matched a bullet fired from the gun of one who practiced diligently. Besides, if Mr. Woo needed to display evidence of his control, he had only to make a few phone calls and he could have seventy men from both the United States and Canada standing before him in one day.

"This is it," said Parker Liao.

He held up the briefcase.

He was smiling.

"So, for fifty-five thousand dollars, we can immediately generate two hundred thousand dollars."

Mary-Catherine Sahin didn't believe him. Not for a second.

In fact, she wondered why she had ever believed him about anything. The man she knew as Omar Mehem sat across from her in the living room. He was talking. She was nodding. She wasn't really listening.

Mary-Catherine held the cup of coffee in both hands and pursed her lips as if concentrating and considering his every word. Across from her, Omar leaned forward and kept talking. He had downed his cup of coffee in three hot nervous gulps.

"So, I just take the money from the bank and bring it to this professor at the University of Chicago. He needs money. His wife is ill. He gives me the document—the document your husband wanted so badly."

Mary-Catherine was glad that the low inlaid coffee table stood between her and Omar. It would be awkward for him now to get up, come around the table, and sit next to her. She would have time to rise and go for more coffee if he tried it. In truth, she wasn't sure of what she would do if he did come around the table, did put an arm around her, did touch her cheek.

"Then I take the package to these two old Turkish representatives of a very wealthy man, and they give me cash, yes, cash, immediately."

There was something frantic in his delivery, not his usual calm, sensitive, adoring, flowing voice. And he was almost whispering, a conspiratorial whisper though there was no one in the house but her and Max, who was asleep. Omar wasn't sitting straight up, as confidently as he had in the past. She forced herself not to look over his shoulder at the stairway that led up to her stepson's room.

". . . we meet somewhere. You decide. Belize. São Paulo, Bermuda. The grieving widow deserves, needs, time away on her own. We meet and start a life together in my family villa in Turkey."

"And this has to be done this morning?"

"The moment the bank opens," he said. "In two hours. I have to get to Arlington Heights to pick up the package and then downtown to deliver it by noon. The Turks leave for the airport at noon."

"Didn't you say before that the man was a University of Chicago professor?" she asked.

"Yes."

"And he lives in Arlington Heights?"

On a day of normal weekend traffic, she knew the trip to or from the University would take at least two hours. Most University of Chicago faculty lived in Hyde Park, minutes from their classrooms.

"Yes.

"Do you have a passport?" he asked, trying to change the subject.

"Yes."

"Then you can pack, make the necessary calls, and we can be on a plane early tonight."

"What about Max?" she asked.

"Max? Oh, yes, Max. If you want him to come with us, I welcome it. I will be like a father to him. In fact, I insist that he come."

"What if I don't want him to be with us?"

"Then he won't be."

That was enough. His lies were weak. His desire to please odious. It meant only one thing. If she were fool enough to give him the money, he would disappear with it through a bathroom window or around a corner or worse, he might kill her and Max. She could feel and see that he was capable of doing just that, but she couldn't stop herself, couldn't control her anger.

"Who are you afraid of?" she asked.

"Me, afraid? Nothing. I just don't want us to miss this opportunity."

"You killed Lemi, didn't you?"

"No," he said firmly. "But I think I know who did."

"Who?"

"A man called the Camel," George said. "Perhaps Lemi Sahin mentioned him?"

"No."

"If you want revenge, which is your due, I will end his life."

"You murder so easily?"

"No," he said. "By Allah, by my life, I have never killed another person, but what does it mean to take a life? Most who mourn and most who are about to die are hypocrites. They say they believe in an afterlife, but instead of rejoicing, they mourn and cry and tear their clothes. All religions are cowardly, people afraid to face reality, grasping at silly myths, trying to believe in nonsense."

He wasn't talking to her. He was remembering, seeing something distant.

"Those mourners, those martyrs, those believers, spend their time on earth building a book of good deeds, pious utterings, interpretations of God, which justify their actions. Be it Jesus, Allah, Buddha, a thousand gods, or the God of the

Hebrews to whom they pray, it is always because they are cowards who convince themselves that they will be rewarded with some kind of eternal life."

He shook himself out of his reverie and began to rub his palms together.

"My father once told me that," he said. "I have never killed, but for this, for you . . ."

"No," said Mary-Catherine.

"No?"

"I don't want him killed. And I am not giving you any money. And I want you out of my house now."

"I don't understand," said George, standing, coming around the table.

Mary-Catherine rose, considered throwing the coffee in his face and running for the stairs to somehow protect Max, but the coffee was no longer hot and the stairs were too far away.

"You're afraid of me?" he asked, shaking his head. "Of me." He put his hand on his chest. "I love you."

"Define 'love,'" she said, trying to keep the table between them.

"Define . . . it's what I feel for you, what I've never felt before. It's wanting to be with you, to hear your voice, touch your hand, find you next to me naked and ready just before dawn."

"I can't imagine the horror of waking up next to you for the rest of my life," she said.

The kitchen would be better than the stairs. There were knives in the kitchen.

"You want me," he said with a smile, standing straight now. "I know it."

"Not anymore," she said.

He ran around the table as the doorbell rang. His knee hit

the table, a vase of garden flowers and his own now-overturned coffee cup clattered to the floor. He hesitated.

"I'm answering the door," she said. "Try to stop me and I'll scream. Whoever is out there will hear it."

The bell kept ringing.

"I'm not going to try to stop you," he said. "I just want whoever it is to go and leave us in peace. I've got a lot to explain to you."

"No," she said.

The doorbell kept ringing. George looked toward the door and held up both of his hands, palms out.

"Then," he said, "I'll just go. Maybe a little later you'll be more calm, more willing to talk."

She crossed behind the sofa facing the wood-burning fireplace and went to the front door. The bell rang one more time before she opened it.

In front of her was a man—a man in worn blue jeans, a gray sweatshirt, and a black knit watch cap that hid his face. In his hand was a gun, a very big gun. He stepped past her, looked around, and saw George Macrapolis standing in the living room, regarding him with surprise.

Mary-Catherine realized that it would do no good to order a masked man with a gun to leave her house. She stood, frozen, expecting to die.

The masked intruder moved toward George who stood in fright, trying to understand, even be ready if he was going to die. How would he become "ready"? He had no idea. He needed time to think, dammit.

"I need time to think," he called out.

The masked man fired. A single shot. The bullet spat out, not loud, something like one of the sounds Mary-Catherine's computer made.

The masked man moved forward and fired again. George went down to his knees, looked at Mary-Catherine, and weakly cried out, *"Mporeite na me bohahsete para kalalw."*

A bullet tore into his neck. Another punched him in the stomach. He had become a human target and the masked man was very good at hitting it. Still, George did not die, not until the masked man stood over him. George was on his knees, now unable to speak. He did not plead. He wondered. The masked man put the gun to the top of George's head and rapidly fired two shots. George was definitely dead now.

Mary-Catherine Sahin could have run screaming. The door was still open. Yes, he could follow, try to shoot her on the street. Then she thought of Max, imagined the boy being awakened by the noise. What would happen if he appeared at the top of the stairs, rubbing his eyes? Would this masked man shoot him?

She started slowly toward the stairs as the masked killer slowly turned around. Then she ran. There were fourteen steps. She knew that. After the steps, there was Max's room. She would go in, lock the door, use the phone on the table near the little boy's bed. There were extensions in every room including the two bathrooms and the laundry room.

She got a little more than halfway up the stairs when a voice, not a bullet, pierced her.

"Did you know what he did?" the man asked.

She stopped.

"No, I swear. Not till tonight. Even tonight I'm not sure. I swear."

She kept her back turned to him.

"He murdered four people, four Turks," the man said. "One of them was your husband."

"I'm sorry," she said, but she wasn't sure what she was sorry about. The murders Omar had committed? Sleeping with him, the man who had killed her husband? The people Omar had killed? Her part in any of this?

She heard a stirring in Max's room.

She didn't respond. She stood there, afraid of losing control, tumbling backwards on the steps.

"Please," she said.

No answer came. She waited a few, perhaps fifteen, seconds more before she turned her head and looked down. The man in the mask was gone, the front door open. She could see into the living room, see the bloody body of the man she knew as Omar. She didn't stir. She was oddly unfrightened and unmoved. She was happy to be alive.

She tried to remember a prayer she had learned, a prayer she hadn't said in more than twenty years.

"Hail Mary, full of grace, the Lord is with you. Blessed are you among women and blessed is the fruit of your womb, Jesus. Holy Mary, Mother of God, pray for us sinners, now and at the hour of our death. Amen."

"Hand me the briefcase and just walk by me," said Bill Hanrahan.

"This is a favor for a friend," said Liao. "I can't give it to you."

"I know your friend, don't I?"

"It's possible," said Parker.

"Tough decision," said Hanrahan with a sigh.

It had been a very long night—a very, very long night. In the afternoon, providing Iris and the baby were still doing well, Bill was scheduled to take them home. He would hide his bruises, ignore the pain of the punches the Cuervos had landed. Meanwhile, he would have to file a report on what had happened in the hospital with only the fogbound Jonas Lindqvist to back him up.

Adding the shooting of a young Chinese man to the report would be one whiskey and beer chaser too many.

"If I know your friend," said Bill, "I don't think he would want you to shoot me."

Bill had no illusions about Woo. Woo would probably be happy to see the cop who had stolen away his intended bride dead. The problem was that there was no chance Iris could ever forgive him if she believed there was even a slight possibility of his having had anything to do with her husband's death.

"No," said Parker, "but it would be better to shoot you and walk out with this"—he held up the briefcase—"than to have to give it to you."

Abe would have known what to do, Bill thought. Bill was reasonably certain Abe would have shot Parker Liao. No hesitation. He would have shot. He would have understood Bill's predicament, but acted and taken responsibility. But Abe wasn't there and Bill had been through a lot that long night. He wasn't up for more blood and a hell of a lot of thinking.

He stepped into the room and away from the door to let Parker Liao pass.

"Blood on the rug," said Parker.

Bill nodded. Parker couldn't see the nod. Bill was in shadows.

"The money is going back to whom it belongs," said Parker, angling toward the door.

"Glad to hear that," said Bill. "On a better day with some rest I might begin to wonder how it came to belong to him in the first place."

Parker Liao maintained the distance between himself and the policeman, put down the briefcase, opened the door, picked up the case, and was gone.

Bill flipped on the lights and looked around. It was one hell of a mess. He began by going over to look at the unfurled rug.

Abe Lieberman parked as close as he could to the front of Lemi Sahin's house. There were three squad cars, all with flashing lights. Two of the cars were at the curb. The third was double-parked. An ambulance sat in front of the double-parked car. There were no gawkers. It was too early and the neighbors, as curious as they might be, were not about to get involved. They certainly knew by now that the physician who owned the house had been murdered. They would wonder, as Lieberman did, what had now happened inside the house.

Abe moved quickly, showed his star at the door, and stepped into the house. The room Abe was shown into was a mess. The body on the floor was badly treated by bullet holes, but there was no doubt that the dead man was the one who had claimed to be Erhan Turkalu, owner of the Anatolia Restaurant, the one Abe now knew was Omar Mehem, aka Oliver Martin.

A lone man stood in the room about five feet from the body.

"Chippendale," said Abe to Detective Frank Chapin.

No one knew, not even Chapin, how he got the nickname Chippendale. He was an ordinary-looking man in his late forties who always needed a shave. Others had said he looked like the actor Dan Hedaya, who often played cops in movies. Abe didn't see the resemblance.

"Rabbi Abe," said Chapin. "This one yours?"

"I think so," said Abe.

"Connection to the death of the man of the house?" asked Chapin.

"Looks that way."

"You got here before crime scene. You on his ass?"

"That I was."

"You want it?"

Abe nodded, looking at the dead man.

"Lady of the house is upstairs with her son," said Chapin.

"Stepson," said Abe.

"I stand corrected," said Chapin, plunging gloved hands into his pockets. "Lots of bullets for forensics to play with."

"She say anything?" asked Abe.

"Not much. She seemed pulled together, but I had the sense that she could break like a dry twig if someone asked her the wrong or right questions. Dead guy was visiting, condolence call, friend of her husband she says."

Condolence call at nine in the morning. Both detectives thought it. Neither said it.

"Doorbell rings. She goes. Lets in this guy with a mask, big guy, navy or black knit ski mask. He pushes past her. The guy shoots this one, turns, and walks out. End of tale so far."

"I'll go up and talk to her," said Abe.

"Be my guest," said Chapin.

As he started up the stairs, a forensics duo walked through the front door carrying their investigation kits. Abe didn't know them.

He got to the top of the stairs, considered which closed door to knock on, and picked the one directly in front of him.

"Yes," came the woman's voice.

"May I come in?" Abe asked. "I have to talk to you."

"I'll come out," she said.

Abe stood listening to the low bustle and chatter of Chapin and the forensics team. The floor was a light inlaid wood, well polished, definitely expensive.

The door opened and Mary-Catherine Sahin came out.

"It's you," she said, sounding relieved.

She looked slightly pale, slightly thinner than she had the last time he had talked to her. Her blond hair was in place and neatly combed and her face was tastefully made-up. Judging by the smell and lack of even slight wrinkles, she had also just changed clothes.

"Max's sleeping again. He has no idea what went on. I wouldn't want him to wake up and see . . . could you ask them to be a little quiet downstairs?"

"As soon as we're finished talking," said Abe. "I'll be quick. I guess you've already thought about what your answers to my questions were going to be."

"The truth," she said.

"Sometimes the truth can be painful and unkind," said Abe. "It may give the truth-teller an ego boost and it may be unnecessarily painful to the person who's being told or about whom it's told."

She gave him an odd look.

"You're telling me I might want to lie?"

"Absolutely not," said Abe. "I was just quoting something that jumped into my mind. Can't remember if it was from *Sesame Street* or a Bill Moyers interview."

"You are a strange policeman," she said.

"So I've been told. Did you shoot Omar Mehem?"

"No, I did not. It was . . . I told the other policeman . . . it was a big man with a ski mask pulled down."

She demonstrated with a make-believe mask.

"And you didn't recognize him?"

"I'm certain I've never seen him before."

"What was your relationship with Omar Mehem?"

"He was an acquaintance of my husband, a business and social acquaintance."

"And he came here for a social call before nine in the morning?"

"A condolence call," she said. "He works till late in the evening. This was really the only time he could make it."

"How did he know you would be up?"

"He called first," she said.

"Phone records," said Abe.

"No, wait," she said, putting one hand around her waist and the other to her forehead. "That's right. He didn't call. He just came to the door. I had the lights on. I haven't been able to get much sleep since . . . he just came to the door. Oh, yes, he came with his suitcase. It's downstairs somewhere. He said he had come so late because he had to catch a plane. He didn't say where he was going."

"Okay," said Abe. "What did you talk about?"

"My husband," she said. "His work. The things he believed in, wanted to do."

"You loved him?"

"What?"

"Your husband," said Abe.

"Very much," she said.

Her lower lip was now trembling.

The important thing was that Abe believed her.

"And the boy?" he asked.

"Max is the everything I cling to now," she said. "Do you have any children?"

"A daughter and two grandchildren," said Abe.

She touched his right hand and then pulled her hand back.

There had been nothing seductive in the touch, just a second of understanding and, maybe, hope.

"That's enough," said Abe. "You might want to stick to the answers you just gave me."

"It won't end here?" she asked.

"No," he said. "It begins here, but you've been very cooperative and I'm sure you will be when we catch the killer. Anything else you want to say?"

"No—yes, after he was shot one or two times, he—I'll never forget—he called out something to me. A cry for help, I think. It wasn't in English."

"Turkish," said Abe.

"I have heard a lot of Turkish in this house and I've learned a little," she said. "What he said wasn't in Turkish."

17

Bill couldn't stand to be at the hospital another minute. He told Iris he was going home to get a few hours of sleep, and he'll be back to take her and the baby home at noon, the time she was scheduled to be released. Before he left the hospital, they had agreed on a name for the dog.

They had furnished the bedroom across from theirs for the baby. All the furniture had been purchased at a big discount from one of Abe's friends who owned a seventy-year-old children's furniture shop on Irving Park Road.

Bill kicked off his shoes when he went into the house. The dog was waiting.

"We've got a name for you," Bill said, sitting heavily onto his favorite armchair.

The dog came over to listen to the news. There was something about the human's voice that told the dog to listen.

"Gideon," said Bill, looking at the dog. "You're Gideon. I'll say the name till you learn it, if you want to learn it. You're under no obligation, Gideon. When I get up I'll officially baptize you with bottled water."

The dog came closer to the man who had said something important to him. He wasn't sure what it was. Maybe he would find out.

The chair had a high back, just right for Bill to lean his head against. Bill slept, dog resting on its side on the floor, eyes closed. The dog dreamt of alleys, garbage cans overturned to find food, attacks by dogs, cats, rats, and other animals of the night, and sometimes men. He snarled in his sleep. He would not let them attack this house.

An hour later, Bill's cell phone played a song. Abe's grandson Barry had programmed in "When Irish Eyes Are Smiling." It woke both him and the dog.

"Yes," said Bill.

The dog was on its feet now. It yawned and listened.

"Right," Bill said. "I'll be there."

The phone began to play its song again before he had time to pocket it. This time the caller was Abe Lieberman.

"How's it going, Father Murphy?"

"It goes," said Bill. "I'll tell you about it after I see Kearney in a little while."

"Then you'll be back on the streets and ready to pursue your metier?"

"If I come out of Kearney's office with my weapon in my holster and my star in my wallet. You in need of some help, Rabbi?"

"Your presence would be welcome. I'm working five related murders."

"A new record," said Bill with a yawn. The dog yawned too. "Clear that five and the closed homicide rate on the board plummets and Kearney gets rosy. Got to go, Rabbi."

Lieutenant Alan Kearney didn't pace the floor. He didn't smoke cigars and he didn't drink. He was only forty-one years old, still had his dark Irish good looks clouded by a brooding air.

Kearney had almost given up on women. He was, considering the scandal four years earlier, lucky to be where he was and who he was. Before his former partner, Bernie Shepard, had held the city at bay for more than a day and denounced Kearney as the man who had seduced Shepard's wife, Kearney had been on track to marry the daughter of a very rich and influential man. Kearney had also been on track to move up to District Commander with a clear view of the road to the top. But Shepard's rant from the rooftop where he was later shot had put an end to that.

Kearney's bitterness had turned to regret. Regret had turned to resignation. Resignation had turned into indifference, indifference to everything but the job.

He was looking out the window at nothing in particular, not wanting to get involved in any calls before he talked to Bill Hanrahan.

The knock at his door came after a few minutes during which Kearney decided that every passerby he saw on Clark Street looked to him like a predator or victim. There were no in-betweens. No one was out of the box.

"Come in," he said.

Bill Hanrahan came in and Kearney motioned for him to sit down. Kearney continued to stand as he leaned over to look at the notes on the pad on the desk.

"How are the wife and baby?" he asked.

"Fine. Coming home today."

"Great. You managed to get in a little trouble at the hospital."

"I did," said Bill.

"You tell it and make it brief."

Bill told the story of the Cuervos, Robert E. Lee Chang's death, and Jonas Lindqvist. He left out the part about Parker Liao and the money he had taken.

"Yeah," said Kearney. "Can Lindqvist testify if we need him?"

"I think he can."

"Think?"

"He's—I don't know—kind of a flake. Could be because he's taking a lot of pain medicine."

"Pain medicine didn't keep him from leaving the hospital and finding a dead man," said Kearney.

"No, it did not. He's a chef."

Bill had no idea why he had added that piece of information. It seemed right to him and to Kearney who nodded.

"The Cuervos claim that they were just there to visit and you assaulted them."

"They were going to kill me. They'd punched Chang to death and they were going to do the same to Lindqvist."

"Because of the money they stole from Chang?"

"Lindqvist can identify them," said Bill.

"What about the money. Where is it?"

"I don't know."

"We get the Cuervos for Chang's murder and I don't think we'll be hearing about police brutality," said Kearney. "Their lawyer's willing to forget the assault for a plea bargain. The State's Attorney's office is willing to deal to protect your ass and the department's and close the case."

Bill nodded in relief.

"Go home. Spend the day with your wife and baby. Tomorrow you're back on the job finding the bad guys."

Bill said nothing. He left the office.

Lieberman was at his desk against the wall on Bill's right. He headed for it. Four other detectives were at their desks talking to perps, witnesses, suspects who were sitting next to them or on the phone to their mothers, wives, husbands, children, and bookies. Ron Starkey was doing the crossword puzzle.

"Verdict?" asked Abe.

"Kearney's covering for me."

"Good news. How about a breakfast at the T&L?"

"Thought you'd never ask, Rabbi."

The man who had shot George Macrapolis sat in his dining room looking up at a photograph of his grandfather. The photograph was old, large, oval, in a dark wood frame.

His grandfather was in profile.

The dining room was small, no windows, but he and his family spent more time in here than in any other room. There were six dark wooden chairs around a not-very-large round wooden table covered with a lace cloth. On the table in front of each seat was a solid red rectangular place mat. On the place mat next to the man was a still-steaming cup of coffee.

"You all right?" his wife called from the kitchen.

"Fine," he said.

He kept looking at the photograph of his grandfather. He didn't really think there were any answers in the fading picture, no da Vinci secrets that could be revealed to whoever understood what to look for. It wasn't answers he sought, just solace.

He had killed. Without remorse. Brutally. He had heard Omar Mehem call out for help. The cry had been in neither English nor Turkish. It had been in Greek. The man knew enough of the Greek language to know this. The conclusion was clear: Omar was not a Turk or even an Armenian. He was a threat to the new Turkey's hope for recognition in Europe, but even a small threat was a blow Turkey's enemies could point to.

But that was not why he had killed Omar. He had killed him because he had murdered Lemi Sahin and Kemal and, yes, Turkalu and his wife.

Time moved slowly. He drank more coffee, talked to his wife about his daughter, said he would very much like spaghetti and meatballs for dinner. After a while, she left.

He expected to hear the door chime and did. He knew who would be there when he opened the door.

He moved quickly from the table, out of the room, and to the front door in the alcove.

He opened the door. Standing before him were Abraham Lieberman and Bill Hanrahan.

The man invited them in.

An hour earlier Bill and Abe had sat in their booth at the T&L. Not many customers. A few *alter cockers* were at their table near the window, arguing loudly about whether or not Israel should build walls around the country.

"We named the dog," Bill said after taking a sip of hot coffee.

"What?" asked Abe.

"Gideon. A 'mighty warrior' from the Bible," said Bill.

"Good name," said Abe. "You know about the murder last night? The one I caught in Lincolnwood?"

"A little," said Bill.

Abe filled him in. It took five minutes and covered all five murders. He ended with, "So, I go in alone. You watch the door."

"Shall be done," said Bill. "When?"

"When we finish here," said Abe.

"I've got to go to confession and then take Iris and the baby home."

"We'll make it quick, Father Murphy."

"Thanks, Rabbi."

They were about to get up when Maish sidled up to the booth, set down a tray of rugelach, pushed his white apron down, and slid in next to his brother.

"A new torture?" asked Abe, leaning over to smell the treat. "Cholesterol torture? See if I can withstand temptation?"

"No, eat, you too," Maish said, nodding at Bill who went for a poppy-seed-filled rugelach.

Abe picked one up, peach, and said, "This is a trick."

"It's a celebration," said Maish.

"Of what?"

"I'm not leaving the congregation," said Maish.

"And that we're celebrating?"

"No," said Maish.

"Then what's the celebration for?"

"My brother is the new president of the Mir Shavot Men's Club. I can't leave."

"I decline the nomination and declare the election void," said Abe calmly.

"You can't. There was no election. The board appointed you. Bess abstained."

"Congratulations, Rabbi," said Bill, reaching for another rugelach.

"When the hell did this happen?" asked Abe.

"Early morning meeting. We were a smash at the dinner."

"I didn't get to say anything," said Abe.

"You had gravitas, *mein klene brutter.*"

Maish had made his announcement loud enough for the *alter cockers* to hear. There were three of them. They got up and stood next to the booth, offering their congratulations, condolences, and advice.

"You're responsible for the Sukkot committee," said Herschel Rosen.

"And the book talks," said Sy Weintraub. "I think you should get Jonathan Kellerman."

"They're going to hock you a *chinik,* Abraham," warned Al Bloombach. "But since we're talking, I think my son Larry the lawyer would be a good dinner speaker for next year."

"Larry the lawyer?" said Rosen. "Your son has a goddamn speech impediment for God's sake."

"He's a good speaker," defended Bloombach. "You want to strike down the Citizens with Disabilities Act?"

"Court has ended," said Abe. "I will retire to my chambers and ponder the issues you've set before me."

Abe motioned for his brother to move and let him out.

Maish moved, smiling.

"I'm glad I could bring a smile to your face," said Abe.

"Listen, we take our pleasures where we can get them," said Maish.

The three *alter cockers* gave the detectives room to get through. Abe reached back and grabbed a handful of rugelach. He could feel the sugared honey against his palms. If he were to be sacrificed for the cause, he would exact the tribute.

"If you get up again," said the Indian or Pakistani doctor named Prajeet, "I'll not be responsible."

"I won't get up," said Jonas Lindqvist.

Jonas had no intention of getting up until they decided to dress him and carry him out. He liked it just where he was.

"You've said your thoughts are racing, that you are full of energy?" asked Dr. Prajeet, whose age Jonas estimated at twelve or thirteen.

"Yes."

Dr. Prajeet looked down at the top paper of the clipboard in his dark hands.

"You are taking Adderall tablets?"

"The little orange ones, yes. Weight-loss pills," said Jonas.

"They are amphetamines," said the doctor. "They make your mind race, make it difficult for you to be still, give you a sense of euphoria. Who prescribed them?"

"A friend who uses them all the time to keep his weight down. We cook all day, taste the food. I do a lot of pastry and I'm big boned," said Jonas.

"You must stop taking them," said the doctor.

That was when Lydia came in the room. She was wearing a short skirt, a tight white blouse, and too much lipstick. Jonas had learned how to deal with her need to come on to almost any male who might be interested. As far as he knew, she had never gone further than flirtation. Now, with him minus a testicle, things would probably get worse between them. She had a birthday coming up. She hated birthdays, the passage of time. She would be forty-one years old. Jonas could see she was sizing up the young Indian doctor. She smiled at him and said softly, almost a Marilyn Monroe purr, "How is my husband doing?"

"Recuperating slowly, but recuperating," said the doctor clinically.

"Will he be able to engage in sex again?" she asked.

"Yes, I think so, when he is healed."

He turned back to the bed, ignoring Lydia, and said to Jonas, "We will monitor your medication and you will rid yourself of the remainder of those pills."

"I have no more pills," Jonas said. "I'm going nuts on my own."

"Good. We have a clinical psychologist on staff. I'll have her come and see you."

He bid his farewell to Jonas and nodded at Lydia, who breathed heavily and turned to her husband.

"You find them?" he asked.

She moved to the bed and brought a plastic container from her pocket. She handed it to Jonas. He opened it and took one pill. He was determined to cut back. Deep down he knew he would fail. He would fail because no matter how horrible the effects of the pills was, the lack of them promised to be even worse. On the other side of those pills was depression, possible thoughts of suicide.

"How's Peter?" he asked

"He's coming to see you. He'll be here tomorrow," she said in her normal voice.

"Great. It's been very strange here."

"I'm sorry," she said, taking his hand.

"It's been . . . I don't know, stimulating."

"Doctor said you'd be all right for sex," she said.

"I heard. You want a man with only one testicle?"

"Sounds intriguing," she said.

On another floor in the hospital, Iris had just awakened. She'd been walked, with some pain, to a room with other mothers of newborns. They were given last-minute instructions about taking care of the baby. Iris already knew all of this, but she listened patiently.

Twenty minutes later she was walked back to her room. There was a large box on the bed. The box was wrapped in green paper with repeating images of the same small dragon.

The card attached was in Chinese. It read, "For Iris Chen and the Baby Jane Mei." There was no name. When the nurse left the room, Iris opened the box. It was filled with money, stacks of bills. When she counted it later she would find there was a total of $150,000 in the box. She also found a second card inside. This one read, "The money is legal and not ill-gotten."

She considered what she would tell Bill when he arrived to take her and the baby home. It took her no more than two minutes to make the decision.

Abe Lieberman stood in the open doorway. Behind him stood a man Turhan Kazmaka had never seen before, a solid man wearing a rumpled suit and a sad face in need of a shave.

Turhan was clean-shaved, in pressed uniform.

"Come in," Kazmaka said.

"Detective Hanrahan prefers to wait in the hall," said Lieberman.

Kazmaka understood. What Lieberman wanted to say was best said without a witness. In addition, the presence of Detective Hanrahan would make flight very difficult, not that Turhan would ever consider fleeing his wife and his responsibilities.

"This way," Turhan said, leading Abe to the dining room. "My wife is at the store. I'll get us coffee. Please sit."

Abe unbuttoned his jacket, his holstered gun showing.

"That won't be necessary," said Turhan, looking at the gun.

"I know," said Abe.

"Some Turkish coffee cake?"

"No, thanks," said Abe. "I just downed a half dozen rugelach. That's half a dozen over my quota."

"I'll be right back," said Turhan. "I think the coffee is ready."

When he left the room, Abe looked up at the photograph

of the man on the wall. There was a resemblance, not striking, between the man in the photograph and Kazmaka the policeman. There were differences too. The man in the photograph had a more angular face, something slightly off in the tone of his cheek and an ear that drooped slightly at the top.

Abe was looking at the photograph when Kazmaka returned with two demitasse cups of almost-black coffee.

"That's my grandfather," said Kazmaka, putting down the cups.

"There's something—" Abe began.

"Airbrushed. My grandfather had scars from the old country."

Lieberman nodded, picked up his coffee, and sipped it carefully. It was hot, strong, and sweet.

"Honey and cinnamon," explained Kazmaka, taking a sip.

"Man got killed more than four hours ago in Lincolnwood," said Lieberman.

"Umm," said Kazmaka.

"Man's name was Omar Mehem," said Abe. "Sometimes called Oliver Martin."

"And seldom called by his real name, George Macrapolis," said Kazmaka.

"Greek?"

"Greek," Kazmaka confirmed. "But had he lived, the country where he would be least welcome would be Greece. He is wanted there for various crimes ranging from theft to murder."

"You did your research," said Abe.

The coffee had the kick of a double espresso. Abe became an instant convert to it.

"Internet, phone calls, documents," said Kazmaka.

"Documents in his apartment and Kemal's," said Abe.

It wasn't a question. Turhan Kazmaka didn't reply, but after a beat, he began, "I—"

"Hold it," said Abe. "For now let's keep this hypothetical."

"Hypothetical?"

"This Macrapolis murdered four people," said Abe. "That's why you volunteered to work with me, that and something else."

"Not just four people were murdered. They were Turkish people," Kazmaka amended.

"And this Macrapolis looked like he was going to get away with it and disappear. Had his bag packed and was visiting a lady who might be inclined to help him. Sound possible?"

"Very," said Kazmaka, whose fists were tight under the table, nails digging into his palms.

"Kemal knew about Macrapolis's background, knew he wasn't a Turk," Abe went on. "When he found out from you just before we met him in the park that Dr. Sahin had been murdered, I'm guessing he got on the phone to some people he thought might be responsible for Sahin's murder. One of his suspects was Macrapolis. Whether it was the first call or the last, our fugitive Greek fell in the trap, agreed to meet with Kemal, but he had no intention of keeping that appointment. Instead he got in touch with Pinn Taibo who he had done some business with before. He figured it would be cheaper and easier to pay Taibo a few hundred to kill Kemal than to do it himself. All this make sense to you?"

"It's all possible," said Kazmaka.

"Pinn failed to kill Kemal, so Macrapolis did it himself. Right?"

"Yes."

"But not before you got to Kemal's apartment and he told you Macrapolis was the killer of Turkalu and his wife and Dr. Sahin."

Kazmaka didn't speak. He ground his nails deeper into his palms. Lieberman went on, "You didn't find out about Macrapolis from the Internet and phone calls. You found it out from Kemal before you and I got to Kemal's apartment. You said you hadn't been there before. In the hallway of his building, you said, 'Wait till you see the Camel's apartment,' plus there were no names on the doorbells. You went right up to the second floor and to the right door."

"He murdered Kemal. Stabbed him seven times. I've known Kemal my whole life. When others weren't around I called him Uncle."

"Macrapolis had to be stopped," said Abe. "And there wasn't enough evidence to hold or charge the respected and popular man known as Omar Mehem. Kemal gave you his file on Omar Mehem, didn't he?"

"He did. It was clear that the man known as Omar had something that belongs to my family—a memento, a valuable memento—a diary that my grandfather brought with him when he fled from Turkey when he was a boy. It was stolen from my father a dozen years ago. The Greek got hold of it, I don't know how, wanted to sell it to a couple of wealthy Turks. I saw him, followed him, watched while they handed the wrapped diary back to Omar. They didn't want it."

"Why?"

"I don't know," said Kazmaka. "I tried to follow him from the hotel, but he lost me for about half an hour. It didn't matter. I knew where he was going. More coffee?"

"No, thanks. Did he have the diary on him when he was killed?" asked Abe.

"No. He must have stopped somewhere to hide it," said Kazmaka. "He knew someone was following him."

"He said something before he died," said Abe.

"In Greek. He asked for help. He asked the widow of Dr. Sahin who he had killed. He asked her for help."

"Your grandfather's name was . . ."

"Aziz," said Kazmaka, looking up at the photograph.

"That's why you volunteered to work with me," said Abe.

"Yes," said Kazmaka.

"Thanks for the coffee," said Abe, standing up. "I'm making you late for duty. Want me to call to your commander?"

"No, I can handle it. What's next?"

"Next?"

"Aren't you going to—"

"Arrest you? You haven't confessed to anything, and I have no evidence to present other than my guesses. My guess is that the weapon used on Macrapolis is gone forever. Your guess?"

"The same," said Kazmaka.

"I wonder if whoever killed Macrapolis had ever killed anyone before," said Abe.

"I don't think he had," said Kazmaka.

Both men were standing now.

"You might want to consider another career than being a cop," said Abe.

"I'll think about it," said Kazmaka, ushering Abe to the front door.

"Think hard about it, Turhan. Think very hard," said Abe, going out the front door where Bill Hanrahan stood waiting.

On the way down the stairs, Abe said, "You ever have Turkish coffee?"

"Don't remember," said Bill.

"Good stuff. Turkish coffee's my new drug of choice. Legal, tastes good, potentially lethal, and socially acceptable."

"I'll drink to that, Rabbi. I'll drink to that, but my drink's going to be a Diet Dr Pepper."

18

That night Abe Lieberman walked through the door of his home on Birchwood with a plastic shopping bag in his hand. He kicked off his shoes.

Barry and Melissa were watching *Veronica Mars* on television. They looked up.

"I bear gifts for all," said Abe.

The children got up and looked at the plastic bag.

Abe took out identical boxes of chocolate bars, twenty-four bars in each box. The chocolates were from Israel, clearly marked parve, kosher for Pesach. Passover was a week away.

"Can we eat it now?" asked Melissa.

"After dinner you can have a few, providing you share with me."

"Did you—" Barry began, the ritual nighttime question.

"No, I shot no one today, killed no one today, inflicted no bodily harm on any violator of the law of our city and country. Go wash up."

His grandchildren moved past him and up the stairs.

Abe turned off the television set thinking that TiVo would be a wise investment. He could record whatever he wanted, thirties' and forties' movies on Turner Classic Movies, and watch them on the long nights of his insomnia.

He moved across the room and into the dining room where the table was set for Shabbat dinner. It was Friday night. Abe had truly forgotten the Sabbath. The table reminded him. Fresh tablecloth, twin brass candlesticks that had been in Bess's family for generations, a challah resting on a familiar blue bread plate, and a bottle of wine with the silver-plated kiddush cup next to it at the head of the table where Abe would sit.

As he entered the dining room, the kitchen door opened. Bess had a bowl of sweet potatoes in one hand, a bowl of salad in the other.

"I heard you come in," she said, placing the bowls on the table. "Wash up. I'll get the chicken on the table."

"You're looking very lovely tonight, Mata Hari," he said.

She brushed back a stray wisp of hair from her forehead. Abe savored that familiar gesture.

"Mata Hari," she said. "No one says that anymore, Avrum."

"Then I shall simply call you 'traitor,'" he said, reaching into the plastic bag and pulling out six white roses held together by a rubber band.

"They're beautiful," Bess said. "I'll put them on the table."

"Nope," he said. "They're yours. They belong in the bedroom, on the dresser or on the table on your side of the bed."

"All right," she said, moving forward to kiss him. "I'm sorry."

"For?"

"The men's club presidency. That's why you called me a traitor, isn't it?"

"It is," he said.

"I'll help you. So will Joe Greenblatt."

"I'm comforted in my affliction."

"By Mata Hari," said Bess.

"Could be worse," he said. "Garbo was Mata Hari. Lisa called you?"

"Yes," said Bess.

"And?"

"Another grandchild will be a blessing," she said.

"A blessing with strings attached."

"Probably," she said. "We'll welcome her visit and endure."

"The kids?"

"Barry says he's fine with it, so does Melissa, but . . ."

"Yes, 'but,'" said Abe. "They've earned that 'but.'"

It took him five minutes to take off his jacket, put his gun and holster into the drawer of the table next to his side of the bed and lock it in with the key he wore around his neck, change his shirt, wash his face and hands.

Back at the table, Barry, Melissa, and Bess were seated.

Candles were in the candlesticks and Bess had a match in her hand ready to begin.

Abe took his place. Bess lit the candles and she and Melissa covered their eyes with their hands as they ushered in Shabbat with the blessing that began, *"Barukh atah Adonai E'loehinu, melekh ha'olam . . ."*

Abe uttered a silent prayer that he would have a quiet weekend with his family. The weekend was all he asked for now. It wasn't much to ask, but he wouldn't be surprised if it didn't happen.

When they had arrived at home, Iris, Bill, and Jane Mei were met by Gideon, who cautiously approached. The people had taken in the dog, fed it, protected it, gave it attention. His connection to them was protective. He needed them and would protect them. The new one, the little one, smelled like both of the big humans. The little human was, therefore, to be protected.

That night when the baby was asleep in her crib and the dog was lying in front of the nursery door, Iris opened the box she had received in the hospital. Bill looked at the money.

"One hundred and fifty thousand dollars," Bill said.

"How did you know?" asked Iris.

"It came from Woo, didn't it?" he said.

Iris lay back in the bed in her robe. Bill considered himself a very lucky man, a lucky man with problems. He had been to confession with Father Sam Parker at St. Bart's. After confession, he had told Sam that he wanted to be sure that Iris wanted to convert, to be absolutely certain.

"I won't do anything till I'm sure," Sam said.

They shook hands and Bill had gone home to see his wife and daughter and face a new problem that lay in a box on his bed.

"Yes, it came from Mr. Woo," said Iris.

"Then we give it back," said Bill. "I know where this money came from."

"The note reads," said Iris calmly, "that it was obtained quite legally."

Bill raised his eyes to heaven, sat on the bed, and said, "Mr. Woo's definition of legality is far broader than mine."

"The money was given to me and the baby," said Iris. "Look at the card. It isn't addressed to you. You are free of any responsibility for accepting it."

"Doesn't work that way, love," he said.

She reached over to touch him. He took her hand and kissed the palm.

"How much money do we have in the bank?" she asked.

"Savings? You tell me."

"Twenty-seven thousand dollars, the money given by my father and family when we got married. Checking, we have two thousand and four hundred dollars. Do you think we will have more or less in the bank when you retire?"

"Probably less, but I'll have my annuity," he said.

"And how will we be able to pay for Jane Mei's education?"

"Her education? She's two days old."

"But she'll not always be," said Iris, looking at the money.

"When I married you," he said, looking at her, "I thought you were sympathetic and beautiful. I didn't know you were smarter than I am. It's a revelation in our marriage that I'm still getting used to."

She pushed the box of cash to the side and moved next to him. She held back the pain. Later, she would take a pain pill.

"There will be more surprises," she said.

"I'm sure."

"We keep the money?" she asked.

"You keep the money," he said. "I go back to confession tomorrow."

That night Turhan Kazmaka considered his options.

He sat at the table. His wife, his parents, and his daughter knew where to find him when he was home. He was seldom in the living room watching television or reading or talking. He and his wife used the bedroom only for sleep and making love. He sat in the dining room, drank coffee, ate, read, talked to his family under the photograph of his grandfather on the wall.

There were few options. He was certain that he would quit the force. It was the price he had to pay for what he had done. It was a fair price. It was a hard price. The alternatives were even harder.

He had no intention of taking his own life, certainly not over having executed a monster. Turhan Kazmaka was a very young man. With a little help from his father and encouragement from his wife, who could return to her job as a social worker, he could go to law school, become a lawyer, carry a briefcase instead of a gun.

His wife, he was certain, would welcome the decision, encourage it, not question for fear he would change his mind. She had never wanted him to be a policeman. That he knew though she had never given voice to it. His father and mother would rejoice in his pursuit of a professional and far more safe life.

It was late. His wife had gone to bed. The children were asleep. He sat, still in his uniform, coffee in front of him, the comforting scent of honey and cinnamon filling the small room.

Perhaps he should be haunted by what he had done, but he wasn't. Maybe that would come later, but he didn't think so.

That night Mary-Catherine tucked Max under the covers and handed him Oliver, his stuffed panda. She had installed a new burglar alarm system and triple locks on all the doors. But she knew that would not be enough to keep the demons out. She would sell the house, move away. Friends of her husband would help her, especially since she planned to raise Max within the Turkish culture and tradition.

"Loo-loo, sleep," the boy said, closing his eyes.

She started to get up from bed.

"No, Loo-loo sleep here," Max said, eyes still closed.

It was a soft request and not an order. Mary-Catherine welcomed it. She lay down next to him, touched his cheek, and tried not to hear the sounds of night in the darkness beyond the door.

That night Clark Jackson used his key to get into the Anatolia Restaurant.

The smell of death, grease, and oil clung to the kitchen and wafted into the restaurant. Clark turned on the lights, looked around. Not bad. No customers since the murder. Front door locked. Sign saying, CLOSED UNTIL FURTHER NOTICE.

Clark didn't know when he would be getting paid next or who would be paying him if anybody would. One good cleanup, maybe the last. He owed it to Turkalu and his wife. They had been good people. Good people died. Clark knew that, knew it too well.

He placed his small CD player on one of the tables and turned on his Best of Big Band album. He didn't dance, sway, or hum to it. It was just there to block out thought, run into and flow through him like a memory he could catch if he wanted to.

He decided to start in the kitchen. If he could get that back in shape, get rid of the smell of death and the sight of blood, he would feel a small redemption.

Everything you invest in life has a payback. The trick was to invest as little as possible, but Clark knew that was a trick he couldn't carry off. He had tried hiding in his mother's house when he came back from Vietnam. It had worked for all of no days. First it was only his mother who started to treat him like a leper. Then it was his sister and cousins and aunts and uncles and his mother's friends. His own friends had come to nervously make contact with the war-shaken veteran and then they disappeared.

He filled the bucket he had retrieved from the closet with hot water and cleaning detergent. Then he lined up four sponges, a full roll of paper towels, the sponge mop, a heavy bristle brush that his mother had bought during World War II, and the blue detergent spray.

With the kitchen door open, Clark could hear the Count Basie Band and Joe Williams singing "Every Day I Have the Blues." About ten minutes into his scrubbing, Clark decided that he would definitely do it right. He would move the refrigerator, clean behind it regardless of what horrors he might encounter. He had only cleaned back there once before and that had left much to be desired.

He was surprised to find that the refrigerator did not stick when he put his back and arms into moving it. He was even more surprised to look down and see a paper bag, not an old encrusted one dappled by time and a thousand meals, but a fresh one. And there was something inside it.

Clark wiped his hands on his jeans, opened the bag, and found a book wrapped in an old piece of cracking leather. The book had the number 1915 printed on it. It could have been a date. It looked old enough. He ran his fingers along the pages of what now looked like to him like a diary, not unlike the one he had kept when he was in Nam. Only this one was in a language that bore no resemblance to English or any language he recognized.

It had fallen or been hidden back there not long ago. Maybe it was Turkalu's or his wife's. No. They weren't old enough to have written anything back in 1915.

It didn't matter. He decided to treat these words of the dead the way he had treated the dead words in his own journal.

He threw the book and paper bag in the blue heavy-duty Hefty trash bag he was gradually filling. He would take it all to the Dumpster in the back when he finished.

Clark straightened out and stretched. His back was beginning to bother him. He would take a long hot bath when he got home, drape a small wet towel over the bad shoulder. He'd keep the water hot, listen to the big bands, read some more of *The Count of Monte Cristo* if he could concentrate.

Meanwhile, Clark kept working to the voice of Sarah Vaughan backed by the Billy Eckstine band.

Paddles Patalnowitz checked his pocket watch, wound it carefully, and tried to straighten up in his booth at the Melody Lounge.

"They ain't coming," said Heinz, the bartender, sitting across from him.

There were no customers. Neither man cared.

"They ain't coming," Paddles agreed.

"Too bad?" asked Heinz.

"That a question? That 'too bad'?"

"Yeah," said Heinz.

"It's too bad," said Paddles, reaching for his Diet Sprite, eyes on the little wooden bowl of peanuts and pretzels.

"So, you want to go home?"

"Give 'em another half hour maybe," said Paddles. "I got the time."

"Yeah," agreed Heinz. "You got the time. Want some old music, somethin'?"

"No," said Paddles. "I got enough old music in my head."

19

Beirut, Lebanon, 1915

Aziz Akan, deaf in one ear, blind in one eye, twenty-one years old, and in possession of a journal he had taken from a dead man in a cave in Armenia, sat with his back against the ancient stone blocks of a jetty.

The stub of his finger had stopped throbbing and blood had ceased to worm its way through the series of pieces of cloth he had wrapped around the joint. The ring he wore on the finger was held painfully tight because of the swelling. When he got to where he was going, he would sell the ring and begin a new life.

Aziz had read the journal over and over many times since he began his trek. It wasn't a long journal, but it was an interesting one, one he determined was a useless rambling compilation of boring detail, allusions to events not spelled out, lamentations. The journal was worth little or nothing.

His knowledge of language had gotten him a berth on a Polish freighter bound for the United States. The captain could only speak Polish and some English. The first mate could speak English and some Greek. Aziz would talk to the first mate who would issue orders to the crew for Aziz to translate into Turkish, Kurdish, Bulgarian, Russian, and Armenian. The cargo, he was told, was none of his or the other crew members' business. Aziz agreed. His pay would be a below-deck cabin shared with the crew and enough food to eat. He was warned to be prepared to protect himself from those among whom he slept and with whom he ate. In return for doing his share of labor and serving as interpreter, he would have the opportunity, with no help from the Polish captain, to jump overboard and swim for the shore when the boat left New York.

He knew the captain was lying, that he would try to keep Aziz on board after the ship left New York. He would jump off the ship before it docked. It was too good an opportunity for Aziz to turn down. When he was safely on land, he would no longer be Aziz Akan. He would become Ahmet Kazmaka, the name on the forged passport he had obtained from Gani Bey in Ankara. Ahmet meant thanking Allah, and Kazmaka was the town where his mother had been born. Thus, he would be thanking Allah for having been born.

But first he had to wait five days for the ship to leave. Nothing to do. He purchased a blank journal not unlike the one he had stolen, bought a pen holder and a box of nibs in addition to three bottles of ink. The days were cool. The sun was bright. He wrote from dawn to nightfall, eating whatever could be bought from dock peddlers for as little as he could spend.

By the time he had finished the journal and the fifth day had passed, Aziz Akan had no more money. He threw away the journal he had stolen and climbed the plank to the ship with nothing in his pockets, the ring on his finger, and his leather-wrapped book and the forged passport under his shirt. The leather wrapping would protect his created treasure when he had to leap into the water.

He smiled.

He was going to America.